# The Conquest of Night

## JUSTIN JAMES

This book is a work of fiction. Any resemblance or similarities to actual persons, living or dead, or actual events are purely coincidental.

Published by Webmad
1-200 N. Service Road #211
Oakville, Ontario
Canada L6M 2Y1
First Digital Edition August 2012
First Paperback Edition September 2012
Copyright © 2012, © 2025 by Justin James - v1.4c
All rights reserved, including the right of reproduction in whole or in part in any form worldwide.
For bulk purchasing discounts
contact Webmad (905) 582-4357 or info@webmad.ca

Made in the United States of America
ISBN 978-0-9881006-0-2

To my father,
for sparking my creativity and encouraging my writing.

# The Conquest of Night

# of Night

JUSTIN JAMES

# ⚜ Prologue ⚜

A cold wind swept across the city of Verden as the moon retreated behind the clouds. Hidden beneath a blanket of darkness, the infiltrators resumed their crouched sprint, hastening past the exposed ground and into the shadows of the imposing stone walls. Galen raised a fist, bringing his team to a stop. Teeth clenching with nerves, he apprehensively watched the sentries above the gate. So far, they had escaped notice.

Galen took stock of the soldiers pressed against the wall with him. At his right hand, Galfas, bravest and most loyal of all. Behind him, Clawfist the Brutal. The veteran brothers, Thorn and Tal. They were a dependable lot, which gave him the courage to lead on. His brow furrowed as his eyes passed over the runt of the litter, Nidle. Huffing and puffing at the rear, the scrawny boy lifted a thumb to indicate that he was ready to go on.

*Blast that boy. If the Baron hadn't insisted, I would never have brought the pup along,* he thought, scowling. At least he had no obligation to keep him alive.

The grim, determined faces of his men stared back at him, awaiting his command. On his signal, they would brave death and carve a path through the slumbering city, up to the ebony keep. They'd catch the lazy king and his kid brother unawares and end this war before it started. There would be peace—if everything went according to plan.

"When you're ready," grunted Galfas.

Clearing his mind, Galen drew his sword. With one last breath of frosty air to harden his courage, he stalked to the gate. Rounding the corner, he came face to face with two guards huddling against the cold. They clutched long spears against their coats.

One raised his head. "What's your bus—"

His inquiry was interrupted by Galen's sword. The second defender hastily aimed his spear at Galen's chest, but he was slow and unpracticed. Galen easily parried the silver tip and lunged forward with earned speed, silencing the guard before he could scream out.

One of Galen's black-clad soldiers raced past, flying up the steps to the winch. Staring off into the still night, the guardsman didn't hear Thorn's approach above the howling wind. The man's hewn body fell backward off the rampart as Thorn rounded on the second, an inattentive, portly man who sat reading a book by lantern light. Before the reader could rise, Thorn's heavy ax split through his book and into his forehead.

Then the night was eerily still once more.

Galen cleared his throat as Thorn rejoined the pack at the bottom of the stairs. "The keep is up ahead. Let's go."

With that, the second and third teams rose from the rocky outcrops before the gate, and fifty darkly dressed men wound their way through the twisting streets up to the keep, avoiding the main road. Minutes into the incursion, a civilian spotted them and shouted in frantic alarm to alert the watch. Irritated, Clawfist smashed his mace against the man's head. Once more, the only sound in the streets of Verden was the clanking of metal boots on cobblestones.

Beneath the black gate, twelve guards barred the way into the castle's courtyard. Hair disheveled and dressed in a mix of armor and civilian clothing, they looked hastily roused from sleep. Still, they raised their weapons defiantly, ready to make a stand against the black-plated swarm.

Galen slowed to a jog, and the others followed suit. The narrow straight fit no more than ten men abreast, which helped the odds for the outnumbered defenders. He wasn't concerned. His team had been preparing for this moment for months. They could easily handle a few local police officers whose only combat experience was in arresting petty thieves. He signaled to engage.

Swords clashed, but the skirmish didn't last long. His seasoned fighters crushed the defense, ripping through their armor with powerful strokes. Gore littered the streets, bodies of the watch messily strewn across the stones. There was no time to clean up after themselves. The warriors pressed on.

Galen risked a glance over his shoulder and noticed that one of his men lay dead with the guards. Two more had nicks and grazes, which he defined as anything short of a missing limb. Blood stained their armor. He couldn't tell how deep their cuts were, but he figured if they hadn't spoken up by now, they would be fine to finish the job.

Crossing through the abandoned courtyard, Galen's team reached the keep. Thorn kicked open the doors, and the soldiers surged inside like a flood of inky water. A shocked-looking serving boy in gray rags threw himself to the side to avoid being mowed down by Tal's shield, then recovered his senses and took off down the corridor to the right. Another corridor branched to the left, along with two heavy wooden doors directly ahead. Wasting no time in the annex, Galen motioned for teams two and three to split off, then chased after the servant.

The glory of the day's hunt belonged to him. Others could deal with the garrison. He would tail the serving boy, who was surely scampering off to the throne room to tell the king of their arrival.

The warning would come too late.

They chased up spiraling stairs to the top floor. With no turns or offshoots, the carpeted hall was easy to follow to its end, where two green doors stood. A bird of some kind adorned the wood. A hawk or an eagle, perhaps. Its painted wings would give no protection against very real swords. If there had been any question of where the servant was leading them, the gold trim along the edges hinted at the importance of the chamber within. Taking a second to make sure at least half of his team was with him, Galen readjusted his grip on his sword and stepped forward to kick open the door.

The doors swung inward, and two brawny guards leaped out. Galen instinctively dove to the side as their spears slashed through the empty air his head had been a second before. Galfas and Thorn charged in immediately, collapsing on the ambushers in a storm of iron. Tal and three others spilled into the room after them, encircling the defenders and driving them away from the doors by wielding their shields as battering rams. The guards desperately hacked and slashed at the Night soldiers, but every blow was stopped by their impenetrable bulwark. The rest of Galen's men surged into the room and surrounded the pair in an instant. Their lives ended swiftly and dishonorably, each stabbed in the back.

Galen turned his eyes to the throne. His smile faded as he registered that on the golden chair sat neither the king nor his prince brother, but the lowly serving boy. Smirking, the servant reclined with one leg draped over the side of the throne and waved to the soldiers in black.

"Search the room!" Galen shouted, seething. He felt the veins on his forehead throbbing with rage. How could his prize have eluded him? "Look for a secret escape! They can't have gotten far." Rounding on the servant with his sword, he snarled, "You! Where did they go?"

The servant shared a cold, reptilian smile and calmy replied, "The King and the Prince? They're long gone, I'm afraid. Don't look so sad; Talon told me to pass something along to you! Let's see here…" The servant reached into his robe. As Galen advanced toward him, sword at the ready, the servant deftly pulled a knife from his robe and flung it.

The blade lodged deep into Galen's neck. Gurgled threats fizzed from his mouth as he stumbled forward. His wild slash missed the servant, who vaulted off the side of the throne as Galen fell on his face. The servant sprinted for the back of the room. He didn't get far before a pikeman impaled him through the heart. As he slumped to the floor in a heap, the servant won one final victory, flashing a triumphant grin at the would-be conquerors.

Galen let out a howl of pain. His head swam as color drained from his skin. "How did they escape?" Sputtering up blood, he numbly felt for the handle of the servant's knife and removed it from his neck. Green poison coated its tip. *Seipher's Venom.* He knew his fate was sealed. His eyes passed over the throne room as his head hit the floor. *He escaped this time, but the Night will overthrow the boy-king yet,* he thought, as death claimed him into an endless sleep.

# ⚜ **Chapter 1** ⚜

Digging his chin into his coat against the biting cold, Jackson Taeric trudged through eleven inches of dense winter snow blanketing the forest path back to his house. Even for December, the day was bitter.

The cold was only half of it. He'd moved with his family to the small town of Hartengle two years ago and hated every minute since. Today had been an exemplary picture of his routine. Walk to school. Sit in eight hours of teenage daycare. Learn nothing. A quick lunch—cold leftovers—then survive the resident hoodlums and ne'er-do-wells.

Why he seemed to be their favorite target to pick on, he wasn't sure. He suspected it was because he was new and had no friends to stick up for him. Otherwise, he thought of himself as a relatively normal tenth grader. Average height, maybe a little lean after his growth spurt last summer, walnut eyes and dirty blond hair. He liked reading and video games. Hated gym class. Didn't really know what he wanted to do with his life, but hey, what kid does?

Whatever their reasons, he knew he needed to keep his wits about him. That's why he had spent the last hour of history class planning his escape. Sure, he'd listened to the balding teacher drone on about tribal wars and diseases for the first ten minutes. That felt courteous. But what did those guys have to do with his life now? They died a hundred years before the internet. Theirs were simpler times before things like cyberbullying or existential dread. He couldn't help that his interest always shriveled up and died, followed by his comprehension of the federally required curriculum, followed by all hope of getting anything other than an 'F' on the test. He could, however, reduce his odds of getting jumped after school. That's why as soon as the final bell rang, he was on his feet and halfway out the door.

*The bell doesn't dismiss you—I dismiss you!* Something like that had been yelled after him, but Jackson had already ducked into the stairwell and was flying through the halls. As he'd reached the exit, he risked a glance behind him and saw the pack of thugs emerging from woodshop. Ducking his head, hoping he hadn't been seen, he'd stepped out into the gray afternoon. A walk through the park had brought him to this forest trail. Here, among the trees, he hoped he would be safe for the day. Surely, he had walked far enough already.

A slow, mocking voice dashed his hopes.

"Would you look who it is, Frank! Hey, little buddy! Haven't seen you in a while. C'mon, Frank, let's go give our lonely little friend a big hug?"

Jackson swore quietly to himself, then turned around to see King of the Morons, Gabe Drogo, sauntering toward him. Gabe's loyal lackeys, Frank Dregs and Dingo Froggat, followed obediently at his heels, grinning like foxes. All three were cut from the same cloth, from their bulky builds to their inexplicable taste for knockoff jewelry. They were starters for the football team, which seemed to be the one thing standing between them and expulsion for abysmal grades and frequent *unofficial* reprimands. If they struggled to express themselves emotionally, they had no problem doing so physically.

"What, got nobody here to hold your hand?" Gabe frowned in faux-sympathy.

Jackson cringed, not for the first time regretting his decision to be a hero in his first week of school. He'd stuck up for a scraggly kid named Joey—red hair, thick glasses, and awkward as anything—and the two had become fast friends. Unfortunately, two weeks later, Joey's father had taken a job in the city. And just like that, his one friend was gone. Worse, the fact that he had no one by his side had become a well of insults that never ran dry. It sucked, because most were true, and the truth hurt most.

Eyeing his opponents warily, he retreated a step. He might have taken his chances against Gabe alone, but the addition of his two cronies stacked the odds. He searched for an escape route instead.

It was too late.

As Jackson looked off into the trees, Frank dropped his bag and ran, circling around to trap him in a bear hug from behind.

"Trying to run from us? Huh?" Gabe cracked a hand across Jackson's cheek, leaving a stinging pain. Vacant brown eyes searched his victim's face for fear. Absentmindedly, he scratched his stubbly chin. "I'm trying to have a civil talk with you, and you just run away?" Gabe balled a fist and hit Jackson in the stomach, knocking the breath out of him and making him double over, gasping for air. By then the other two boys had rallied around their ringleader and were egging him on, praising him for his aggression. Their brutish taunts were as painful as Gabe's punch.

"Ha! You really showed him!"

"Don't let him off easy!"

Gabe grinned like a wolf. "Look, he's getting angry! Come on, then. Let him go, Frank. Little boy wants a scrap? Then let's have ourselves a scrap!" Unprovoked, as if injected by a powerful stimulant, Gabe started hopping around like a crazed kangaroo. Thumping his chest for added effect, he snarled and taunted, "Come at me, wimp!"

Jackson risked a glance behind him. Frank and Dingo stood barring his trail home. Realizing that he would need to break past them, an idea began to form in his head.

Steeling himself, he stepped to feint a jab at Gabe's ribs. Predictably, Gabe dropped his hands to guard his flank and backed off a step. Pivoting one-eighty, Jackson drove his fist into Frank's surprised face, connecting with a satisfying *pop*. With a roar of pain that would make any lion green with envy, Frank stumbled sideways and fell into the snow.

Seizing his fleeting opportunity, Jackson darted past Dingo and into the forest. It took a moment for the trio to register what had transpired, by which point he was already ten feet ahead of them, flying down the trail to his house.

"He's getting away!" Gabe yelled.

Frank stirred slowly, nursing his face with a fistful of snow. Dingo stooped to help him, and Gabe gave them both a shove. "After him!"

The path turned and weaved through the trees as Jackson tore down it. He lost sight of them for a moment, but he knew he couldn't slow down. The careless crash of his pursuers, like three elephants harrumphing through the snow and trumpeting their advance, warned that he would be in for a world of pain if they caught up. Begrudgingly, he realized the athletes would overtake him if he stayed on the straight path. Risking the forest, he darted into the thickest thicket.

A biting wind picked up against him, throwing snow from both the forest floor and the gloomy sky into his face. At first he groaned at his luck, but soon he saw that the dusting was obscuring both his shallow tracks and his visibility. Passing under the barren arms of a white birch, he entered an odd section of the forest he'd never explored before. Roots twisted and slithered out of the frozen ground like dried-up snakes. Careful not to trip over them, he ran until he found a lone evergreen. On the far side, he dropped to his knees and crawled beneath the low-hanging branches of pines. Trying to slow his breathing, he shut his eyes and listened.

They weren't far behind. Footsteps crunched in the snow. Branches snapped. They drew closer until their labored breaths filled the air just two or three trees away.

Resisting the urge to look, Jackson sunk lower against the ground, pressing his nose into the snow to make himself as small as possible. Sweating with nerves, he tried to hold his breath, though he feared that Gabe could hear the blood pounding in his ears.

Suddenly, Gabe broke the stillness of the forest with a roar of anger. "I'll find you! And when I do, I'll beat the tar out of you!"

Apparently satisfied with his threat, Gabe led his two lackeys back toward the school, presumably hoping they'd have time to terrorize another victim.

Once he was sure they were gone, Jackson breathed a sigh of relief and crawled out from under the tree. He was safe for now. Time to go home.

His feet froze as he realized what that meant. With the immediate danger passed, his mind was free to recall the events of the night before. His lip quivered in frustration as he balled his fists.

He had come home late after serving detention for dozing off in class. After a hard belting, his father kicked him out of the house, which was a generous term for the wooden shack with boarded-up windows and holes in the roof as old as him. His father had told him to stay away for the night. So he did. A long, restless night in the cold. Seeking protection against the wind, he had snuck into the neighbor's kennel, originally built for their family dog but eventually taken over by stray animals. A feisty raccoon had insisted on sharing the cramped box. After decorating his arms with claw marks, the critter had eventually let him get some sleep. By the morning light, the raccoon was long gone, replaced by an impossibly flatulent beagle. An unpleasant evening, but unfortunately, not that unusual.

An intolerable blend of alcohol, poor decisions, and rage, his father had been his living nightmare ever since his mother had left on the night of his tenth birthday. She had gone without a word. Many nights, he dreamed of her return and woke up with tears on his cheeks when he realized she never would. Less often now.

He wasn't that close with his mother. At least, that's how he remembered their relationship. But she had always been a buffer between him and his father. Always calm, level-headed, and looking out for him, she was his rock. He had loved her for this, so her sudden and unexpected departure was, unquestionably, the worst day of his life. Things hadn't changed much since then. He usually came home to find his father drunk or in a foul mood, nursing a hangover. The one new variable was Sonja, his stepmother, who moved in soon after. Another factor that made his life at home miserable.

With a cry of frustration, Jackson slammed his bag down and sat against a tree. Coming home late again was a bad idea, but what choice did he have? He had no friends he could visit. He had no money, no means of building shelter. Plain out of luck.

Taking a deep breath to settle himself against the hopelessness of it all, he stood and dusted the snow off his backpack. With no destination in mind, he set off away from Gabe and the school, choosing to wander through the trees.

The snow started coming down harder. Like a veil of whitish gray draped over his eyes, the sky fell, and visibility was reduced to near nothingness. The cold wind nipped at his face, stinging his cheek where Gabe had struck him. He raised a hand against the snowy barrage, but still he could see only a few steps ahead. Totally disoriented, he dropped his head and watched his worn boots take step after aimless step.

Minutes passed by. His surroundings became a blur as he blindly stumbled through the forest, and he lost track of time, deeply immersed in thought. Only when he realized that he had absentmindedly wandered into a small glade did he snap to. Lifting his head, he found himself standing in the center of a perfect circle, surrounded by densely packed trees.

*Where am I?*

It dawned on him that he had not paid the slightest attention to where he was walking. Already the eddying snow had covered his tracks, leaving him clueless as to which way he had come. The trees, too, seemed to have shifted around him, sealing up the gap he had entered through.

Something tapped his shoulder from behind. With a frightened yell, he leaped a foot in the air, then spun around and hastily retreated a step. A tall, wizened man with a curly white beard tumbling down to his hip stared at him with an expectant smile. His shoulders had a forward bend, but still the old-timer had height to spare, towering a head above Jackson. If not for the deep wrinkles, ranking on a scale from bulldog to aged leather, he might have had a stately, maybe even handsome face. A pointed red-and-yellow hat sat atop his head, lolling to one side, and his oversized tunic matched. In his left hand was a square mirror that reflected Jackson's puzzled stare back at him.

In sum, the old-timer looked like a mix of Merlin the wizard and the lankiest clown to ever step out of a clown car.

Jackson put all the strength he could into his voice, but his startled words came out as a weak stammer: "What… who are you?"

# ✦ Chapter 2 ✦

Merlin the Clown, as Jackson decided he ought to be called, let out a jolly chuckle. Especially weird, considering the geezer had snuck up on him in the middle of a forest. "It matters not who I am. I am but a simple man of the woods... and the worlds," he added as an afterthought. "As for who you are, that I know only in part, my boy. For I see you as you are, and as you might someday become, Jackson Taeric. The choices ahead of you, however, shall reveal who you truly are. Yours is the potential to save a world and the lives of all who inhabit it. To become a hero of the people.

"But be warned! The wrong choice would bring this world to ruin. For given to each man is free will—the power to make decisions that change the world for better or worse. Strangely, most do not realize their potential, and so do not act; rather, they let others decide as their own choices expire, standing idly by while life plays out before them. So, Jackson: will your destiny be your own? Or will you stand aside, merely watching life instead of truly living it?"

Jackson searched for words, but none seemed right for this bizarre situation. "How do you know my name?" he asked at last, shaking from the cold.

The old codger let out a sigh, then his knowing smile returned. "I see I'll have to explain it slower. I am Voldroun the Gatekeeper, appointed to watch over the gateways that connect all created worlds. Though I see all things, like you, it was not given to me to glimpse the future. We can guess at tomorrow, but we will only discover it as it unfolds."

Jackson blinked, certain he had misheard Merlin—Voldroun, rather. "Sorry, did you say *worlds*?" Batty old coot.

Voldroun looked puzzled, but his gentle smile came back before long. "Forgive me. The paradox of knowledge. You lack sight into the other realms, of course, but I forget how well their existence is hidden to you," he shook his head with a huff. "Few know of the gateways. You have stumbled upon this path ignorantly, unaware of the power in this glade. Still, I will offer you a choice," he said with a wink.

Baffled, Jackson started another question.

Voldroun raised a hand to stop him. "I'll explain. To oversimplify, your world exists parallel to another. Both are linked here through this glade. Other parallels exist, each with their own gateways. I understand that this is much for you to comprehend, so I won't bore you with ramblings of an old man. Instead, I'll present you with a simple choice. All right?"

Skeptical but curious, Jackson eventually nodded his understanding.

Satisfied, Voldroun tapped his mirror. Once he did, Jackson saw himself duplicated in the glass— two versions of him, side by side. The left version wore the same clothes he had on now. Standing in front of the familiar wooden shack he called his home, the image gave a timid wave.

The second version nodded at him, a confident grin on his face and a sword in each hand. He wore battle armor on his chest and a red bandana on his head. Behind him, a green banner featuring an eagle proudly flew in the wind.

Suddenly, both Jacksons in the mirror morphed into doors—the left into a black door and the right, a green one. Voldroun tapped the mirror again and they leaped from the glass, transforming before his eyes into two life-sized doors, side-by-side in the snow, unmistakably real. Jackson stared in wonder, taking in the mystery.

"The black door leads home. You'll continue the life you have known, and none of this will have ever happened. Nor will it again. The green door will bring you to Brillund, one of the two continents in the parallel world I spoke of and birthplace of the Eternai. You could change the fate of their world if you so choose. Be warned, however, that I shall not again permit you to cross through the gateways. In the land of the Eternai you shall remain—unless you find the portal. There is but one beyond my control connecting these worlds. Yet should you discover it, you could travel freely between the worlds. Now, I've said enough. Choose!"

Jackson looked at the black door. A deluge of images entered his mind. More of the same. A miserable routine. It didn't take too long to contemplate the pieces of his life. *Broken family. No friends. Awful school. What was he leaving behind?*

He turned his focus to the green door, and just one image took shape in his mind. Bizarre and unexplainable, the magical door evoked a single thought: how his mother had left without a word on the eve of his tenth birthday. Never to be seen again. That's what she had chosen.

Before he was aware of what he was doing, his hand pushed open the green door. He stared into a dark, swirling void that seemed to be growing from the door, opening like a yawning maw. Tentatively, he stepped across the threshold. The world around him faded from view until there was only blackness.

Voldroun's satisfied laugh met him in the darkness, echoing through his head. "Well chosen, Jackson. I wish you wisdom on the decisions you will soon make. Remember, I'll be watching…"

# ⚜ **Chapter 3** ⚜

J ackson awoke in the light with a start. His conversation with Voldroun was still fresh in mind. If at first he was inclined to believe it had all been a crazy dream, he threw out that notion as soon as he took in his surroundings.

Looking around, it might have appeared he was still in the same clearing, were it not transformed. The trees now seemed less dense, but the real shock was the long, verdant grass beneath his fingers, still wet with morning dew. The sun landed brightly upon him, filtering through boughs packed with green leaves. There was not a trace of snow to be seen, nor of the peculiar Gatekeeper.

As Jackson found his feet, dazed and disoriented, a young man burst from the trees. As the man glanced over his shoulder, watching for pursuers, he failed to notice Jackson and ran straight into him.

The impact staggered Jackson, but he stayed on his feet. Up close, he saw the stranger was about his age and only slightly taller. His walnut eyes were wide with alertness, and his hair was a matted tangle like a sparrow's nest. Alarmingly, he had a sword at his side and a chest of chainmail armor.

"Whoa! Who are—"

The stranger cut him off, grabbing his arm and starting toward the other side of the clearing. Without a word, he tore a path through the twists and turns of the deep woods, dragging Jackson through dense brush and thorny brambles. As they ran, the boy constantly threw nervous glances over his shoulder, no more than a few seconds apart. His jaw was tight with worry. Nevertheless, they emerged from the woods to an open space without incident. Once they reached the shade of a rocky overhang, the boy let go of him and doubled over, gasping for air.

Catching his own breath, Jackson felt his head spin with questions. *Who are you? Why are we running? Do they make that breastplate in a men's medium?* But before he could voice any of them, the boy launched into his own interrogation.

"I'm guessing you've got no clue what was going on just now, didja? Not likely if you're frolicking about the forest at a time like this. Right, so tell me: where are you from? One of them hill hamlets?"

Jackson stared at him blankly. They exchanged a few slow blinks. Eventually, he remembered he had the ability to speak. "I have absolutely no idea what you're talking about. I'm from Hartengle, if that helps?"

Now it was the other boy's turn to appear perplexed. "Hartengle? I ain't never heard of it, and I've been just about everywhere." A frown of suspicion creased his face. "You're not Night, are yeh?"

"A knight? No, I've never ridden a horse, and I don't have any nobility in my family," Jackson said uncertainly.

The boy stared with an open mouth. "You jest. Do yeh really not know the Night? How's that possible, unless

19

you've been living in this damp forest for all yer life? There are only two kingdoms, and I'd imagine their names aren't all that hard to memorize—even for you hill-ham folk…"

Jackson had no reply. Both he and the boy regarded the other as if he had just hatched from an egg. Then, all at once, he remembered the conversation in the clearing, and a wave of understanding washed over him. *Could this be what Voldroun meant by 'another world'?* Realizing just how far away he was from home, a second wave hit him—nausea.

*No, I can't really call that home,* he thought. Scrunching up his nose and tightening his fists, he looked up to the sky and tried to keep down the rising bile of his bitter emotions.

The other boy sighed. "Look, I can tell you're a bit confused… or loopier than a lasso," he added the possibility as an afterthought. "So for now, I'll bring you back to base. Ah! I almost forgot to introduce myself. The name's Canon. I'm a *Cavar*, one of the prince's elite guard."

"I'm Jackson. And, thanks. I guess I am a little lost," he admitted. Canon was on the more eccentric side, but it was kind of him to offer help. Despite only knowing the guy for fifteen minutes, Jackson decided he liked him. Maybe they'd even become fast friends. "So, who's this prince? And what were we running from?"

Canon froze, dumbfounded. "Come on. You don't know the prince?" Jackson shook his head, causing Canon to throw up his hands in exasperation. "Hill-ham folk. I swear. You people are a special bunch," he sighed. "Right, listen up. Your prince is Falcon. I know; you didn't vote for him in one of your council meetings. And that's okay. Monarchies don't need your permission. Now where was I… Talon's the king, but just between us two chickens, I like Falcon better. Talon inherited the throne when his father, King Gavin, passed a few months before the Night attacked. Gavin? Good man.

But Talon? Well, it's like I said: monarchies don't need your permission."

"You sure it's safe to be so… opinionated about the king?" Jackson asked nervously.

"Sure. I did say between us chickens."

"Fair point. Just checking," Jackson shrugged. Not like anyone could hear them. "What's so bad about Talon?"

"Bah," Canon snorted. "See, I've got this backward notion that a true leader serves his people. Our new king just helps himself. As long as the crown's on his head, he couldn't care less what happens to the rest of us. Not Falcon, though. The prince watches out for us all, from the poorest widow to his most loyal generals. People matter to him. He's qualified in every way to be a great king—every way except the order of his birth. Still, he's content with his lot as prince. Never wanted anything more than what was already his."

"Sounds rare," Jackson reflected. He couldn't name many in power from his world who fit that description. "And the thing that was chasing us?"

"Night. As in the opposite of *day*. Not a horseback-riding nobleman. Actually, come to think of it, I'd suppose some Night ride horses, and there could be nobility among them… In which case… hmm…"

"We're running from the night?" Jackson repeated, interrupting Canon's spiral. He looked up at the sky and let out a confused laugh. The sun was still high. It couldn't be much after noon. "I mean, I used to sleep with a nightlight, too, so… no judgement or anything. Just, well, I think we can relax for a few hours."

"Not *nightfall*, you fool—the *Night!* Soldiers from the Nightlands, the very same we're at war with. They attacked us without warning, killing and enslaving hundreds, thousands of our people. Because of the Night, our age of peace and prosperity is lost, and a time of fear darkens our days… A bit dramatic, you might be thinking, but I say that and more is well-warranted as soon as someone begins stabbing your neighbors unprovoked," Canon explained bluntly. "Anyway, to make a short story longer, I was out doing reconnaissance when one of them sighted me. Him and his blokes chased me into the forest. Not that I was scared, mind… just, I'd rather not fight four people at once. Bad for my knees, and all."

Jackson thought of his last run-in with Gabe's crew and was quick to agree. "Yeah, I hear you."

"Good enough," Canon nodded to himself. "Right. Let's get going."

With that, they trudged a path along the edge of the forest, leaving behind the clearing that had brought Jackson to this world. Though Voldroun's gateway grew further away, the mystery remained. This world was a strange place, yet also strangely familiar. He hadn't given it any thought at first, but even the fact he and Canon were able to understand one another was remarkable. There was a kind of magic in the air here. Despite his slowness to grasp the gravity of what had happened in the forest, he felt a new sense of weight on his soul. One that told him that he mattered, and that he had an important purpose ahead of him. Although the thought was foreign and perhaps even scary to dwell on, it made him feel alive in a way he had never felt before.

A gentle breeze at their backs made their steps a little lighter and the long walk a little shorter. As the sun climbed down from its apex, Canon pointed ahead to a small, lone mountain and announced that they had arrived.

The declaration was premature. It took them another half-hour to make their way to the far side. When at last they reached the encampment, the sudden bustle of activity was almost overwhelming.

It was like the largest renaissance fair Jackson could imagine. To his right, combat drills played out in an elaborate battle ballet. Boys younger than him sparred one-on-one with wooden sticks and light armor. One suffered a thrust to the gut and, raging, grabbed the 'blade' of his opponent's 'sword' and clubbed him over the head with his own. This did not escape the notice of an attentive drillmaster, who called them all to a halt and administered proportional discipline.

Close by, older boys around Jackson's age exchanged blows and blocks with swords and shields in a more orderly drill. There were others, still, trainees of all shapes and sizes sweating under the late sun, sparring, drilling, and exercising. The weapons they practiced were just as wide-ranging, but most commonly axes, spears, swords, and bows. Hundreds, maybe thousands of recruits were clashing arms, composing a metallic symphony of crisp clinks and ringing steel.

Canon led Jackson straight to the campground at the heart of the base. Identical tents were arranged in neat rows of fourteen, evenly divided by a broad path. In the distance, on the far side of the camp, an army of cooks worked over the fire pits, burning a pleasant smoky aroma into the air as they prepared the evening's supper. In the center of camp, a rectangular blue tent stood above all others.

Proud standards flanked the entrance of the tent, boasting a white hawk with wings spread and talons poised to strike—a terror for any unsuspecting field mouse to see. The forest-green background matched the pennon atop the tent and the ribbons that decorated the lances of four imposing knights standing outside. Easy to overlook, a shorter banner depicting a black bird on an orange background was planted a few feet off to the right. That one matched Canon's badge.

"Well, that's an unexpected twist," Canon muttered to himself, sounding rather unhappy. He gave a tight nod to the closest sentinel, who gave no response.

"All good?" Jackson asked.

Canon forced a smile. "His Majesty, King Talon, has decided to join us. Ready to meet the royals?"

# ✤ Chapter 4 ✤

After one of the stationed guards announced their arrival to those inside, Canon pushed through the tent's canvas flaps. Surprised that he wasn't being detained or pressed for security clearance, Jackson tried not to look suspicious and followed him inside.

The tent evidently served as their command center. There were no beds or storage for personal effects. Instead, the sparsely decorated room contained only a green carpet that matched the standards outside, a few lanterns as extra sources of light, a broad table in the center with a map and markers, and a smaller desk at the far side. Two men stood hunched over the latter desk, poring over some kind of schematic. A third man, tall and broad shouldered, stood just to the side of the entrance. His cold and piercing gray eyes studied Jackson warily. Though he had a tinge of silver in his black hair, Jackson held no delusions that the guardian had become dull with age.

When the two at the desk looked up to greet them, Jackson was surprised to see that the younger looked about his and Canon's age. The other, in part due to a prominent, almost cruel hawk nose, looked a few years older. Perhaps in his twenties. Both had leaf-green eyes and light brown hair. The younger wore his messy and long, but the elder kept his high and tight. They were obviously brothers, but their differing personalities became apparent as soon as they spoke.

The younger addressed them first. "Welcome back, Canon. Found a new friend?" he grinned at his Cavar, who gave a snort of laughter in return.

The elder brother studied Jackson with a sour frown. "And who might you be?"

"This'un's Jackson," Canon said on his behalf. "Our paths crossed in the woods on me way back from scouting. Strange bloke, but nice enough. Can you believe he says he's never heard of the Night?"

The brothers exchanged a glance. The younger's eyes lit up, but the elder snarled in annoyance.

"Good enough," the younger smiled easily. "I guess I'm technically *the prince*, but my name's Falcon. Please, feel free to use it."

"King Talon," the elder said stiffly. He waited with an expectant look on his face, as if Jackson should fall to one knee, or at least bow.

Choosing to do neither, Jackson offered a small nod of acknowledgement, then turned his attention to the prince.

Falcon shrugged. "Well, now that we've all made our introductions, I believe it would be valuable for you to meet Vandexin. Canon can guide you down to his hollow. He's a seer, and a skilled one at that. I suspect he'd be best to bring you up to speed on our situation. Perhaps he'll have more to explain—if I've perceived correctly where you have come from." Falcon considered him thoughtfully.

Talon threw back his head and laughed. Apparently, he didn't share his brother's coded speculations. "Give up your fantasies, Falcon. Those legends are no more than nonsense dreamt up by simpletons, limited by the understanding of their day. This boy is average—typical pond scum from a run-down hamlet somewhere in the hills. That is all. If he were from anywhere civilized, he'd have the decency to bathe before approaching royalty."

Falcon rolled his eyes but gave no objection. Leaving the matter, he turned to Jackson and said, "You had best be on your way. Oh, and Canon, will you deliver a message to Ezikael? Cancel training for this evening. All instructors. I'd like to share new plans with everyone. Thanks, Canon."

The prince's Cavar lifted a thumb to acknowledge the order, then led Jackson out of the tent.

"Seer's hollow is at the foot of the mountain. I'll drop you off before I go find Zeke. I should get back to you before Vandexin's done with you, but if not, just go for a walk about. Worst case, you'll find me by the food," Canon said as they walked toward the mountain.

Jackson wondered about this Vandexin. He was a seer who, Falcon seemed to have hinted, had the ability to tell that he was from another world. Could Vandexin be like Voldroun—another Gatekeeper? It seemed unlikely, but then again, no more unlikely than all of this being but a dream.

*Maybe Gabe had punched him all the way to la-la land?*

His thoughts drifted off as he raised his head to see a crack in the base of the mountain. The crevice was a few feet wide and barely taller than him. He peered into the cranny, but darkness was all he could see inside. When he turned, he saw Canon beaming just a few inches away from his face.

"Lovely little hovel, eh? Cozy. Oh, don't get fretful on me now. It's nicer once you're inside. If Vandexin would

27

consider a bit of decoration—a rug or some throw pillows, maybe—I'd imagine it could almost be pleasant." He paused to consider the aesthetic possibilities. "C'mon then, in you go," he gave Jackson a gentle shove toward the cavity.

Trying not to wonder if he was entering his own tomb, Jackson cautiously slid into the crack. He took one last look over his shoulder at Canon, who flashed a reassuring smile before abandoning him for his own errand. Praying that the rock wall wouldn't suddenly shift and crush every bone in his body, Jackson worked his way deeper inside. As the darkness grew around him, he relied on his other senses to guide him. His hands went before him, tracing the contours of the coarse rock and twice saving him from hitting his head. Deeper in, the air turned stale and musty. Every few seconds, a quiet *plop* resonated from unseen water dripping into a shallow puddle. One cold drop landed on his nose.

Finally, the crack widened into a small tunnel, where Jackson walked face-first into a dark purple curtain. Pushing the cloth aside, he stepped into a surprisingly well-lit room. A greater surprise than the abundant lanterns were the dozen fluffy pink throw pillows scattered around the tiny room. The mural, a childish drawing of a curly tree growing in green grass under a smiling sun and blue sky, was a fitting capstone to the peculiar space. Sadly, it appeared this 'window' was as much sunlight as Vandexin got.

A pale old man stood in the middle of the room next to a birdbath carved from smooth stone. A single footlocker contained all he owned, save for his ratty green robes. His hunched back and thin, gray hair did little to inspire further confidence in his health.

Presently, the seer's eyes were focused on the mural as he swirled his staff in the air, as if trying to summon rain for the tree. Between this ineffective rain dance, the vacant expression on his face, and the drool escaping his ajar mouth, Jackson feared he had intruded on the wrong hermit's cave.

"Hmm? Hmm! Sonny, my boy! Didn't see you come in. Put the flowers by the door. Please, please! Take a seat," Vandexin encouraged, waving to one of the throw pillows by the fountain.

Figuring it was too late to turn back, Jackson entered and settled onto the pink pillow. The space was bigger than he'd first thought. Cozy, even. Canon was spot-on about the décor. Shifting uncomfortably to find a position on the cave floor that his back could bear, he needlessly asked, "Sir? Are you Vandexin?"

"Yes, yes of course! Unless you see another old coot squatting in my cave," Vandexin let loose what could only be described as a creepy hermit laugh.

Jackson didn't know how to respond to that. He also wasn't so certain this man wasn't exactly that—an old coot. Fortunately, before the silence turned mutually awkward, the seer began circling Jackson with focused eyes, using his staff as a cane.

"So, you come with questions. Splendid! I come with answers. But what is most pressing on your mind? Confusion about this foreign world? Perhaps you wish to know about the Night? Tell me, Jackson."

Jackson's heart skipped a beat at his name. He stared at Vandexin, and Vandexin stared back. He almost believed that this old codger really was a seer, but then he reasoned the better explanation was that someone had simply reported his coming in advance.

"Is this really another world?" Jackson asked.

With a knowing smile, Vandexin asked him to stand. Once Jackson was on his feet, the seer pulled a small pouch from his robes and walked in a slow circle around the fountain. Jackson crept closer to the birdbath, leery of what might jump out. The seer opened the pouch and reached inside but suddenly seemed to recall that he had been asked a question.

"Indeed, Jackson. Reality is much stranger than the world you've known. Grander, wonderfully and frighteningly so. Our worlds are linked, though the connections are so well hidden that each appears to be alone. Perhaps it's just as well. If one knew of the other, I fear it is in our nature to swiftly arrive at conflict. Whether the fault be ours or theirs, the outcome would be a suffering people in a conquered land. An unfortunate irony, one should say, given the circumstances here. In this and more, the world you have known and the world you will discover share much in common."

Jackson felt his initial preconceptions about the man fall away, replaced by deep curiosity. "Can you tell me more? About these worlds?"

Vandexin smiled like a proud tutor. "We won't dwell on the other world—I imagine you know well enough about that one. But this world! Similar, but truly different. You are familiar with comfort. Peace and protection, yes, where roads are safe to walk and safety is assumed. Take heed! These lands have many dangers, and doubly so in the wilds. Beasts, highwaymen, and this war between the Night and our people, not least of all. Dark times that you may wonder whether this world has ever seen light, yet it was not always this way. For now, though, nobler days seem like relics of a lost past.

"In time, you will learn that there are strange truths about this world that words cannot prepare you for. Only by seeing will you truly believe. One such mystery is our portal. There is but one crossing that can be used to walk between the worlds at will. Few know of its existence, even fewer, its location. This secret is now yours to share and protect: the portal lies within the Citadel of Night."

Though unsure what that really meant, Jackson gave a small nod. His question nonetheless revealed him to be in the shallows of understanding: "Who are the Night?"

"Now that's the question, isn't it?" mused Vandexin. "I suppose they are the other half—other side, if you prefer. Rivals, counterparts, adversaries… enemies, I should say. As for us, we are the Eternai—*Eternals*. We rule this side of the Maelstrom—the great divide between East Sea and the West. For the most part, we look and sound as you'd call normal. The Night, however, are said to have the Touch of Night—a blessing or a curse, both are often said. Their appearance matches their name—sinister and gray. Their ways are not our ways, and of that more can be said. Even the creatures that roam their lands and the fruits of their vines are to us foreign and strange. Look for yourself and see!"

Reaching into his pouch, Vandexin scooped out a handful of blue powder and let the fine dust run through his fingers, adding a sickly tinge to his dirt-stained nails. He then pinched a more precise measure and held it under Jackson's nose. Flickering firelight glinted off the tiny crystals, giving them an almost spectral shimmer.

"This, Jackson, is Areithium. You shall see its use momentarily," Vandexin liberated a torch from the wall and lowered the flame into the bowl, igniting the moss and wood kindling. Setting the torch aside, he threw powder into the fire, causing blue flames to shoot up to the cave ceiling. Just as quickly, the fire returned to its original size. Wispy blue tendrils now mixed in amid the white smoke.

"Peer into the flames, Jackson, and you will see the Night," invited Vandexin.

Leaning in, Jackson stared at the dancing fire until its light was etched into his eyelids even as he blinked. Then, in the smoke above the flames, the form of a man materialized.

Rotating in place, the ghostly, gray figurine stood only a foot tall, but the details of his face were far sharper than shifting smoke should have allowed. Dark purple triangles of war paint shadowed his eyes, fitting the spectral gloom of his dark robes and ashen skin. A tall, black mohawk completed the intimidating look. The image made Jackson think of a brawl-hardy bouncer at the world's meanest biker bar. Fittingly, the man did not smile.

"I present to you: a Night soldier. Yes, they are as he appears; it is no figment of the flames. Almost all are gray skinned—which certainly helps to distinguish friend from foe in the heat of battle," the seer said with a wry smile that felt out of place.

His head swam with questions, but Jackson couldn't marshal his wild thoughts into words. He regretted that this first encounter could be his last chance to learn about this world's secrets. Finally, he resigned himself to the reality that he'd think of a hundred things to ask as soon as he left the cave and would just have to live with it. His last question was a curiosity from one who had never faced the fires of war. "Which side do you think is going to win?"

The question seemed to surprise Vandexin. First he looked amused. Then his brow furrowed in contemplation. Scratching his beard, he studied Jackson thoughtfully before answering. "I do not know; it has not been revealed to me. But this I do know: the choices you make along your journey will make all the difference, for one side or the other." Before Jackson could respond, Vandexin motioned toward the exit. "There is little more for us to discuss. A great destiny awaits you, Jackson Taeric. Good or bad, I do not know—I hope that the weight of the world does not feel too heavy on your shoulders. Farewell, Jackson! Farewell and be true! And if I may offer one parting word of advice: I suggest you choose the sword. No offense, but I doubt you would be any more use wielding a heavy battle-axe than a tree branch," Vandexin chuckled to himself.

Perplexed and again at a loss for words, Jackson gave a polite nod and showed himself out.

*That was strange,* he thought as he slipped through the curtain. He caught one last glimpse of a pink throw pillow as the purple cloth fell back into place and shook his head. *What have I gotten myself into?*

He didn't know the half of it at the time. But as he departed, Vandexin sat with a frown, staring at the fire. The boy had given him much to consider.

# ✦ Chapter 5 ✦

The light of day blinded Jackson as he stepped out of the cave. As his eyes adjusted to the sun, he noticed Canon sitting on a log a few feet away. The Cavar brightened as he spotted his new friend.

"Jackson! Had a nice chinwag with Vandexin, I take it? He sure is something... now what that is, I couldn't say. A mysterious wiseman? A total loon? I reckon so. Well, enough of caves and cavemen! It's healthy to touch grass and see the sun. Good thing you can do both on the way there!"

"Where are we going?" Jackson asked, feeling he had missed something.

"Falcon asked me to get you set up and feeling right at home, so I'll show you ropes and put you straight to work. No sense having you loafing about, falling out of shape while gorging on our good cheese and wine, is there? Hard work, earning your keep, a real sense of communal responsibility... these things are good for you—like leafy greens. And that's just the start; we'll make a fighter of you yet. But first things first, just to keep you from wandering off behind enemy lines into an occupied forest," Canon stared at him meaningfully, "I'd like to show you a map. You ought to know something about the land you live in. Now, as your ranking officer, I'll invite you to hold your questions for the next two minutes."

"Really?" Jackson rolled his eyes, too comfortable with his new friend to take the command seriously. "You're pulling rank for that?"

"You're an inquisitive one," Canon pointed. "I need a minute to get my thoughts straight. I ain't used to thinking, thinking—all this thinking—but there's a lot going on. If you aren't using your noggin, you might find yourself fooled—bamboozled, even."

Certain he did not know Canon's meaning, Jackson shrugged and motioned for him to lead. They made their way back to the campground in silence, where Canon led him to a dark green tent. From the outside, it looked no bigger than average, though the material seemed higher quality. Touching the plasticky fabric as he entered, he guessed it to be water-proof. Fitting for officers' quarters—functional comfort that kept up appearances of camaraderie.

The interior was sparse but not quite austere. Four cots were arranged in two pairs of bunk beds on either side of the tent. Like a coatrack of war, a vertical shelf with hooks and ties stood beside the entrance, holding up weapons and armor. Opposite the entrance, a map was laid out on a small desk, pinned down by a short knife. As Jackson followed Canon to the table, he noticed the tip was planted into a city labeled 'Kanrio'.

"See here," Canon gestured to the map needlessly, as Jackson was already studying the hand-drawn lines. He felt something like amazement, a mix of admiration and pity, as he realized someone had spent painstaking weeks in the field to create this. They didn't have the luxury of satellite GPS.

"This here," Canon tapped a black squiggle north of the knife, "is our current position. The foot of the mountain. There's a dense forest on our left flank. An enemy scouting party is lurking the other side of it. Then, a day south, you've got Kanrio. Not a pretty city—industrial might be the kindest term—but that's their forwardmost base," he tapped the hilt of the knife protruding from the map.

Jackson nodded to indicate he was following along. Satisfied, Canon continued his explanation, making extensive use of his hands to illustrate.

"In just a few days, we'll march south to take Kanrio. If everything goes to plan, we'll push them back, city by city, until we run them into the sea. They caught us sleeping and disorganized, but the Eternai are a free and proud people. We're not the surrendering type. And now that we've rallied our armies and made a habit of harrying supply lines, we're ready and raring to fight back. We'll liberate the farms and freedom fighters of Kanrio, but there will be no rest as long as even one of our people is under subjugation. The Night took three great cities; three cities we shall take back. Next is Orsadia, then our capital of Verden," he said, pointing them out on the map. His finger ended on the tip of the southern peninsula.

"But I repeat my disclaimer: that's *if everything goes to plan.* There's just as fair a chance the Night rebuffs our attack and captures our four remaining cities beyond the mountain. We might have a home-field advantage—helping hands from citizens in the conquered cities rising up to join us—but we can't count out the terrible weapons of our enemy. Dark, horrible creatures bred for killing. Real nightmare fuel. Who knows how many will fall... but thinking like that won't win the war, now will it? I'm sure everything will go to plan. So... yeah. That's about all. Now if I were a gambler, I might bet on Talon sending us over the sea to take the Citadel of Night afterwards, but I'd be content with my own soil back."

"Always good to have a plan," mused Jackson. He wondered what conversations the other side was having right about now. They surely had a plan, too.

"Good to start with one, anyway," shrugged Canon. "Righto, that's enough philosophy for one day. Time to hit stuff! Remember when we arrived, there were all those blokes bashin' each other with axes and swords and the like? Well, you're going to be one of them! We've got the finest weapons training money can't buy."

Jackson couldn't help but grin at Canon's cartoonish smile. Though he wasn't exactly stoked to begin training—he had always been exceedingly average in gym class—Canon's excitement bubbled over in a way that made him think it'd be more fun than expected. He cracked a joke at his enthusiasm, and the two enjoyed easy banter as they made their way to the center of the training ground, where they came to a tall pavilion shaded under a blue canopy.

Labored grunts and the ringing of steel spilled out of the open-sided tent. Sparks and sweat flew at the clashing of metal. Knowing that he would soon be part of these drills, Jackson felt a nervous knot forming in his stomach.

Oblivious of, or perhaps in response to his unease, Canon tilted his head toward a pair of ax-wielders who were producing a particularly strained series of "battle noises" and mimed a swing. Jackson cocked an eyebrow in return; he did not see himself going toe-to-toe with these boy-giants. One looked like he had to custom-order clothes from an online Tall-and-Wide store; the other seemed to have eaten a fridge-shaped linebacker.

Shrugging, Canon led the way to the lone desk in the tent. The table looked embarrassingly tiny for the grizzled but sturdy man who used it, sitting perfectly upright in his backless stool. The man was writing on a piece of parchment, but his script was entirely illegible to Jackson. Clearing his throat, Canon saluted and brokered the introduction. "Reporting in with new trainee Jackson of the Hill-Hams, Sir Reynald."

"That's *Instructor Reynald* or *Drill Sergeant* to you!" Reynald snapped at Jackson, standing up and slamming his palms on his tiny desk. Leaning forward, he narrowed his eyes at the unshaped clay before him. "Look at yourself, boy. Slouching—of all things! Straighten that back!" he hammered his desk again, then settled into a deep scowl. "Fresh meat. Always soft. Fleshy. By the time I'm done with you, you'll have more gristle than a chuck steak from the oldest cow on your grand-pappy's farm. Come closer! And get that wayward tuft of hair under control! I don't know how you yokels do it up in them hills, but we have rules here, son. I'll tell you right now: I'll tolerate no slouching, no backtalk, and absolutely no sassafras in my army. DO I MAKE MYSELF CLEAR?"

"Um, yessir, sir! Very clear, sir!" stammered Jackson, freaked out by how uncomfortably close the drill instructor's face had come to his.

"OOOH, I TOLD YOU—YOU'LL ADRESS ME AS *DRILL SERGEANT,* OR YOU'LL BE SCRUBBING LATRINES FOR THE REST OF YOUR SORRY LIFE!" Veins bulging, the unhinged instructor kicked over his table and pointed a warning finger at Jackson.

Recoiling back, Jackson spewed a stream of nervous babble, sweating under the hot gust of the drill instructor's snorted breath. Reynald exchanged a look with Canon. The two suddenly lost all composure and busted out in laughter.

"That was great, sir. You really had him. *Ooh! Oooh!*" cackled Canon, wiping a tear from his eye. "Oh, good health! My sides…"

"The highlight of my day. Thanks for that. I've been working on these blasted reports for Talon all afternoon," Reynald shook his head, still chuckling. "Sorry about that, Jackson. Just a bit of fun we like to have with new recruits. I'm Tapir Reynald, but call me Sir, Sergeant, or Instructor Reynald on training grounds. I'll be personally overseeing your progress. To start, I'll equip you with the tools and skills you'll need in battle. Oh, that reminders me—Canon, since I can't be in two places at once, would you mind taking inventory of our armory and filling out this excruciatingly detailed form for Talon? My thanks," Reynald handed him a booklet and swiftly steered Jackson toward the exit.

Canon huffed in disbelief. "Might as well have asked me to number each blade of grass from here to Verden!" he moaned, leafing through the blank pages of the dauntingly thorough report. Slouching in defeat, he grumbled his way to the armory at the back of the tent, as Sir Reynald stepped out into the sun and breathed a sigh of relief.

"All right, Jackson. We've got an hour of light left before we head back to camp. No pressure, but your life will depend on your ability to master one of these weapons. Many say that it takes a lifetime. Our conscripts get six weeks. You have three days. Now, I mean no offense, kid, but I figure we can both agree that you wouldn't be any use swinging around a big battle-ax or mace in the frontlines. I want you to try the spear, sword and shield, and crossbow. Ideally, you'd be a more versatile weapon if you learned all three, but let's see how far we get," Tapir gestured to the equipment laid out on the ground.

Remembering Vandexin's advice, Jackson bent and picked up the sword. Taking a test swing through the air, he found it to be lighter than anticipated. Thin and strong, the silver blade shone in the low sun. The edge looked just as meticulously maintained; it wasn't hard to imagine cutting armor, skin and bone with its sharp bite. Next, he lifted the round shield, leaving an indented memory of the pair behind in the grass. Like the sword, it felt light but not brittle, and he maneuvered it easily. With appreciation for the craftsman, he noticed that the shield had a convex bend to better deflect incoming blows, rather than allow them to lodge. Hefting his selection, he turned to Reynald uncertainly. "Should I start with these?"

Reynald shrugged. "Have to start somewhere; might as well start here. How about we leave spear and crossbow for tomorrow and focus on building your sword technique today?"

Jackson nodded in agreement.

Drawing his own sword from an ornate black leather sheath, Reynald pointed its tip at the worn practice dummy in front of them. The mesmerizing silver runes running down the blade and a decorative charm of golden string on the hilt stole Jackson's focus, but the steely rasp of the instructor's voice won back his attention. "This combination is Replacing Thunder—the first technique my Master Jin Iosano taught me. Observe closely."

Sir Reynald exploded forward, slashing across the dummy's midsection to the right inside its guard, then raising his shield arm to block as he reversed his swing into a fast overhead arc. The resounding crack made Jackson flinch as wooden splinters flew from the dummy's scored neck. The instructor stepped back and sheathed his sword, nodding to himself in approval. "Your turn."

Jackson stared blankly at the battered dummy. He felt doomed to look silly, but he decided it wouldn't be for a lack of effort. Imitating Reynald's battle stance, he angled himself to the dummy and, bouncing on the balls of his feet, readied his sword. Purging his lingering self-consciousness with a slow exhale, he focused on his task. A surge of calm cooled his blood. The steel in his hand felt almost weightless as if an extension of his arm. Naturally, as if drawing breath, he stepped forward, slashed, and pivoted into an overhead strike, remembering to replace his shield at the last second. Hoping it was enough to graduate to his next test rather than earn a set of pushups, he stepped back and awaited Reynald's reaction.

A frown wrinkled the instructor's face. Jackson felt his cheeks burn red under the intense scrutiny. He thought he had been paying attention, but had he missed something obvious? Was Reynald so utterly embarrassed on his behalf that he was at a loss for words? A reflective grunt preempted the instructor's question. "First time holding a sword, is it?"

"Yes, sir," Jackson hung his head, abashed and frustrated. Even if he was totally inexperienced, he thought he had done passably for a first attempt. On the other hand, he understood that there would be no such thing as *partial credit* when his life was on the line. He'd just have to do better.

A smile cracked Reynald's stony face, then a deep, bubbling laugh rose from his belly through his throat. "Not bad, kid! Not bad at all. You might just keep that head on its shoulders. Most novices tend to exaggerate their movements or struggle to direct their sword. Different kinds of clumsy, but clumsy either way. You were almost perfect. Shield was too low for a block, mind you—still dead. But, fixable. The technique, I mean. Not death. Again, but bring your shield up parallel to the dummy's hand."

Jackson repeated the sequence, making a deliberate point of demonstrating the correction.

"Again!" called the instructor.

So Jackson did it again, and again, and again. It was almost sundown before Reynald allowed him to rest. By then, he was performing the combination as fast as the instructor had originally demonstrated. Maybe faster.

"I'll admit, you have more than a fair share of natural skill with that sword. If you can think on your feet, you might live to see many a battle yet. Tomorrow I'll gear you up fully. We'll see how you spar against other students—fair warning, most hit harder than that dummy. Survive the morning, and maybe you'll learn a crossbow in the afternoon. Dismissed, soldier." Reynald recollected Jackson's gear and disappeared into the pavilion.

Jackson decided to wait outside for Canon. A minute later, the Cavar stormed outside muttering a gloomy cloud into the air above his head. "The next chap who asks me to count how many helmets he's got lying about will find my steel-tipped boot up his rump," he grumbled, striding toward the camp with Jackson laughing in tow.

# ⚜ Chapter 6 ⚜

The sun was dipping behind the horizon as Jackson strolled into camp with Canon. The alluring smell of wood-fired meat filled the air. His stomach voiced interest with a rumble, reminding him he hadn't eaten all day.

Hunger announced itself as an uneasy knot in his stomach as his thoughts turned to food. For the past year, he had lived off frozen dinner trays, cafeteria food that could not confidently be called fit for human consumption, and off-brand ramen packets. Any camp slop or stew with a bit of smoked meat sounded like a luxury fit for a king, and his nose was eager to guide him to investigate the source of the tantalizing aroma.

The path merged into a main thoroughfare, and they began to pass others coming in from their days. Some caried lumber upon sleds or broad shoulders; others bore meats of varied dress, herbs, and roots. Most common of all were leather training cuirasses and blunted swords. Canon raised his arms over his head and let out a high-pitched grunt as he stretched, startling a comrade into dropping a laundry basket.

Weaving through an increasingly dense throng of people, they soon arrived at a feast, half-attended but rapidly filling, and no less rowdy for the empty benches. The din of conversation resembled jets on an airplane. Uninhibited by surrounding company, one table belted out a proud, patriotic song with a meter and pitch no two singers could agree upon. Finding an empty bench on the periphery, Canon staked his claim and pointed Jackson toward the food line.

"I reckon they have food where you came from. Grab a wooden slab from the end and fill it up with whatever looks good. Stay clear of the dodgy green mush, though—I've been here ages and still haven't a clue what goes in that," Canon wrinkled his nose in distaste.

"You want anything?" Jackson asked, his stomach gurgling an audible growl as he stood.

"Go on ahead," Canon waved him off.

"All right." Jackson followed the thin trail of smoke to the barbecue pit and joined the queue. The line moved fast, suggesting standard fare. Jackson selected a plate instead of the bowl and scanned the spread as the heavyset boy in front of him scooped a double portion of green mush. The long table offered more variety than a cafeteria but less than a buffet. He decided to play it safe, passing over unlabeled stews and mashes for what looked like grilled chicken and steak. A loaf of bread and a handful of blueberries rounded out his plate. His hand hovered over a vine of bright orange berries, supposing them to be like grapes, but he restrained himself from gambling with his digestive system. As good as training was going, he couldn't risk a case of the trots being what takes him out on the battlefield. At the end of the table, an older boy with a wild beard of orange curls like thornbush passed him a mug of lukewarm water. Carefully balancing his board in one hand, Jackson made his way back to the table.

He returned to find Canon had already tucked into a bountiful plate of food, evidenced by saucy red stains on the wood in front of him. Others had appeared at his sides. To his left sat a lanky boy with sharp, square shoulders and braided black hair that looked seldom washed. A shockingly attractive girl sat on his right, laughing at something he had just said. She sat upright like a princess, pristine with her silky blonde hair and crystal blue eyes. The contrast with her neighbor—back hunched, elbows on the table, and sauce dripping from his fingers—was hard to miss. Canon sucked the gravy off his thumb and, as Jackson took his seat across the table, stood to make introductions.

"Jackson! Meet two of my closest mates. This here's my best mate, Tyson," Canon gestured to the warrior-bard, "and this is my *girlmate*, Krystal," he said with a sly wink.

"Nice to meet you both," Jackson said courteously, nodding to each as he shook hands.

He sat back down and prodded his steak a few times before curiosity and a tinge of jealousy took over. "So, how long have you known each other?" he asked in an ostensibly conversational manner.

"I've known Tyson since we were wee lads. Grew up outside of Verden together. I met Krystal about a year ago. She might not look it, but she's a class fighter," Canon said proudly, wrapping an arm around her.

"Speaking of fighters, I heard you made quite the impression on Reynald," Krystal sized Jackson up thoughtfully. A playful grin spread across her face. "I might fix the schedule tomorrow for a chance to fight you—if you think you're ready for it."

Jackson chuckled nervously. As much as he didn't want to admit it, he sensed Krystal was out of his league in more ways than one. He hadn't noticed many girls around the camp; he figured those who were here had both wanted and earned their spots. By the way she held her knife, slicing her meat with precise, efficient strokes, she looked like she'd have no trouble cutting him up into bits as big as berries.

Knocking over and catching his tankard mid-fall as he moved his hand to wipe his chin, Jackson tried his best to play it cool. "I don't know. Fighting may not be the best idea. I mean, that battle's coming up in a few days, and if one of us gets a hand cut off or something... that probably wouldn't be good, would it? Those swords are pretty sharp, after all..." His stammering trailed off as he noticed all three across the table staring, eyebrows raised.

"Well, that's why we come with two hands," Canon shrugged and sipped from his drink.

Krystal swatted his arm but couldn't hold back her laugh. "Pay him no mind, Jackson. We don't spar with real blades—just dulled or wooden ones. You might bruise a bit if I whack your arm, but I promise you won't be permanently disfigured. Wouldn't do the army any good to kill each other off before the battle even begins, now would it?"

Jackson's cheeks flushed with color. He wasn't sure whether he'd turned red because of his obvious mistake or because his mistake had been in front of Krystal. Either way, he lifted his tankard to hide his face and drank a long drink, hoping his skin would quickly revert to its usual color. After emptying his tankard, he sheepishly offered his agreement, "No, I suppose it wouldn't."

He went back to eating with his head bowed, unable to entirely shake off his embarrassment. The conversation across the table turned to reminiscing, and he was grateful to escape the center of attention. He hungrily scarfed down the rest of his plate, relishing the smoky taste of his steak. The blueberries had a sour taste unlike those he was familiar with from home, and after eating several, he decided they weren't to his liking. Five small berries were all that remained of his generous portion, and he leaned back from the table feeling well-fed.

As the others finished their meals, Prince Falcon and King Talon stepped onto the makeshift stage beside the food table. Despite the loud chatter of individual conversations, most heads had turned expectantly toward the stage. Jackson heard the royal brothers' names whispered in anticipation—Falcon's twice as often. Canon's face was unusually serious, and Jackson guessed by his attentiveness that they would be revealing their plan to retake Kanrio.

At the foot of the stage, a short and portly man without a lone hair on his head raised a mallet to the gong. He swung his arm twice, once lightly, then again with some force. The golden gong's wobbling ring commanded silence as it swept over the excited crowd. Anticipation thickened the air as the masses fixed their eyes on the stage; not one conversation continued, not even whispers on the side.

The pudgy man retreated to a cushioned chair off to stage right. For a moment, Jackson imagined unseen tension as the royal brothers stood side by side, looking out at the audience, peers in all measures save perhaps an inch or two. Then, Talon stepped forward, cleared his throat, and smiled as he addressed his subjects.

"Good evening. I trust everyone ate well?" A pause followed, made awkward by the scattered voices of assent breaking the silence of the majority who took the question to be rhetorical. Shifting his demeanor, Talon adopted a mournful expression to remind them of their national grief. "Who can count each sleepless night since we were driven from our homes? They blur together in waking nightmare. Children of Orsadia, sons of Verden—I promise you are not forgotten.

Tonight, however, we declare our plans to retake our beloved city of Kanrio. High though the price of liberation may be, it is nothing compared to the cost of a life in exile and slavery."

"Anyone else hearing plans for our funerals?" Canon whispered darkly. Tyson kept his eyes forward, though he slowly shook his head.

"I won't draw this out in a grand speech with fancy words," Talon said, padding with simple ones instead. "You know what Kanrio means to us all. In your mind, you can still see its streets—its walls, unbroken; you can smell the flowers of the fields and hear the rushing water of the river outside its gates. The enemy believes that victory is theirs, but we have not abandoned our people—nor will we ever. We will drive the Night from our homes and reclaim our birthright, and they shall never return. From today on, this is your sole mission and hope. Falcon will now explain the details," said Talon. A round of muted applause stirred as he stepped back. Falcon moved to replace him at center stage.

"As my dear brother alluded to, we're going to have to bloody our hands a little," he said, stoking a tribal roar of oafish cheering from the table behind Jackson. The bloodthirsty calls died off as Falcon raised his hand, grinning at his loyalists' support.

"The plan is to take the keep before they know we're there. First, we'll smuggle in a few good men in farmer carts on their way to the market. Once inside, they'll jump out and take the gates, opening the way for the rest of us. Then we go straight to the keep. If all goes well, they won't know we're there until I throw that lousy baron off my throne. In fact," Falcon eyed the crowd impishly, "I hear him and his guard spend all day prancing about the keep in frilly pink knickers."

Jeers and barks of laughter rose among most of the tables, but the men sitting behind Jackson took the remark sincerely and were riled to anger. One slammed his palms on the table in rage while another howled, "No son of a milkman's gonna prance around *my* birthplace in his frillies!"

Falcon waited patiently for the noise to settle down, a tumult prolonged by a red-faced gent who shook his table while ululating in fury. Sucking a few calming breaths, aided by soothing pats on the back from his neighbor, the bearded giant settled down enough to let Falcon continue his speech.

The prince looked at the crowd with a gleam in his eye that signaled to Jackson the informational segment of the speech was over. Falcon spoke directly to their hearts. "Even worse, the Baron loves his milk so much, he poured out all the city's mead and ale to be licked up by pussycats—just so he could have his fill!"

That was all it took to send the crowd ballistic.

A deafening shout was lifted throughout the camp as a chorus of voices cried out vows to take Kanrio back from these vile invaders. Many joined in with unvaried but colorful suggestions as to where else the Baron could stick his ale.

*Either Falcon's a world-class speaker, or these men really care for their ale,* thought Jackson. He flinched, then laughed in disbelief as a fully-grown man vaulted onto the far end of his table. The man shook his empty mug in anger, uttering a string of threats that ended in a general mooning toward the southern horizon.

After a considerable show of hoots and hollers, jeers and curses, and the occasional polite applause, the pudgy man stood and waddled over to strike the gong once more. It took noticeably longer to quiet the crowd, but eventually the pandemonium passed, leaving only the crackle of fires and the flapping of tent canvases in the wind.

Falcon had left the stage during the hubbub. Jackson spotted him leaning against a flagpole, grinning coolly as he watched his older brother wait for the crowd's full attention. The king put on an affable smile.

"I share your anticipation, patriots. In three days, we shall march into our city and take down, as the prince put it, that *frill-knickered prancer*." Talon paused to make room for the whoops and cheers he was expecting, which, sure enough, came loud and aplenty. After relishing his speechcraft for a passing moment, he pressed on. "So sleep well tonight, train well tomorrow, and ready your hearts the next day. Once we launch our assault, the wheels of our war machine will not stop nor slow until total victory is ours. The time of waiting is ended; there will be no more long camps, no more hiding in the wilderness. We will press the attack, relentless and un-stoppable, and we shall drive them from our lands with such swiftness that they won't be able to send one ship to carry word of their failure across to the citadel."

The crowd roared in support. Talon watched them with steadfast determination in his eyes. His confident smile darkened as a cloud of malice overshadowed him. Then the king turned away, departing the stage. The masses soon fol-lowed, dispersing back to their own quarters.

As Jackson stood to stretch, a hand came down on his shoulder and pulled him off to the side. Free from the congestion of the crowd, Canon released his grip and exhaled a deep sigh. Tyson was a step behind, but Krystal had split off for her own tent. The boys walked along quiet arteries off the main thoroughfare and soon arrived at their tent.

Inside, Canon unbuckled a belt under his shirt and flung it onto the table beside his bunk. Jackson glanced at the belt and noticed four knives sheathed at various angles. He raised an eyebrow at Canon, who shrugged back. "Doesn't hurt to have extra. Oh, don't give me that look. Not like I've gone and stabbed anyone I weren't s'posed t to, now did I?"

Tyson walked over to Jackson and indicated the bottom bunk on the other side of the room. "That's yours for the next few days. We normally have a third—er, *fourth,* now, I suppose—but he's off an' about tonight. His name's Rein. Nice bloke. Doesn't say much, though."

Jackson thanked him and settled onto his bunk. As he closed his eyes, a strange, dizzying feeling came over him that he couldn't quite explain. All at once, he felt wistful, scared, excited, and awestruck. It was surreal, lying down to sleep for the first time in this other world. What was a dream, and what was reality? He couldn't reconcile that he had been sitting in school earlier that morning, daydreaming while his teacher lectured on some long-passed battle over a hill. He remembered thinking: *Why didn't they just walk around it?* Now, he was about to take part in a battle himself. Would some kid read about him in two hundred years and come up with his own snotty remarks?

What a difference one afternoon had made.

The thought of the approaching battle, not yet real in his mind, made him squirm uneasily in his blankets. He was no killer. Before his lesson with Reynald, he had never even held a weapon. Yet he was expected, depended on, to fight to the death against people he didn't know. People with lives of their own. Hopes and fears. His head ached at the thought of killing a stranger. The Eternai had their reasons—he could sympathize with their fight for freedom—but his heart hadn't steeped in hatred against the Night in the same way.

*They're attacking innocent people*, he told himself, trying to talk down his guilty conscience. The battle was for Eternai lands—the Night were the aggressors. His participation was more than just necessary for his own survival, alone in this foreign land. The facts, as he saw them, made his enlistment seem like a noble cause. What could be more righteous, more virtuous, than someone laying down his life to champion the oppressed? Yet despite all his reasoning, he simply could not bring himself to terms with what he had walked into—and what may be required of him.

Not for the first time, he thought, maybe hoped, that this was all a dream. A long, complicated, bittersweet dream. When he opened his eyes, he'd awake to his ho-hum routine, go back to school—back to boredom and bullies and broken homes—and none of this would have ever happened. It was only his imagination. A crazy escape conjured by a desperate mind in the depths of sleep.

*This is real. This is where you belong,* came a soft whisper in his mind. *You belong,* the whisper echoed as fatigue pulled him into a dreamless sleep.

# ⚜ Chapter 7 ⚜

Adistant trumpet roused him at first light. He blinked groggily as he opened his eyes, swung his legs over the side of the bed, and stretched out his stiff neck. He'd slept funny.

*Better get dressed*, he thought, still half-asleep, starting his morning routine on autopilot. He rubbed his eyes and pressed his hands to his face, feeling like he was forgetting something. What homework was due? For some reason, he couldn't remember getting it done. That wasn't good. It was possible to salvage a semester of partial credit come exam time; zeroes were hard to bounce back from.

"Planning on staying in bed all day, are ya?"

Jackson's head spun as he looked around the room, blinking. Dazed and disoriented by unfamiliar surroundings, he slowly remembered the bizarre events that had brought him here the day before. Far from his childhood bedroom, he awoke to a new day in the faraway realm of the Eternai.

*What in the world?*

He watched Canon sift through the trunk at the foot of his bed, though his mind was too slow to form a cohesive narrative of the images his eyes reported. On some level, he registered that Tyson had already departed from the tent.

Fastening a belt under his shirt, Canon walked over to Jackson's cot and stared with his arms folded and eyebrow raised. "Yoohoo?" he tilted his head. "Is yer bum nailed to the mattress? No? Then time to get a move on, buddy! Brekkie's in ten. You miss that, you'll be hungry till half-noon."

"I'm going, I'm going," Jackson pushed to his feet with a grunt. He looked at his own locker at the foot of his bed, empty, and frowned to himself. As he opened his mouth to form a question he hadn't quite shaped, Canon seemed to follow his glance to its unspoken conclusion, reaching into his chest. He tossed the bundle of clothes to Jackson.

"You can borrow those for now. Should fit fine. I'll look into getting a kit for you while you're out training."

"Thanks," Jackson said with a grateful nod.

"I'll see you later. Good luck today!" Canon waved, ducking halfway out of the tent. "Ah—and if you can help it, I'd appreciate you not chopping off me girlfriend's earlobes. I like 'em. Nice earlobes. Same goes for nose, chin… I'm not as fussed about hair. All good if she ends up trying bangs."

It took Jackson a minute to remember Krystal, then another minute to recall that they had an impending sparring match. His stomach rumbled, urging him to quickly throw on the fresh-*ish* clothes and hurry to breakfast. The shirt was a bit baggy in the arms, but he managed to tighten the fit by rolling up his sleeves.

By the time he arrived at the picnic tables, the cooks had already started tearing down to clean and reset for lunch. He grabbed a bowl of porridge and one of the last red apples from a picked-over basket, then surveyed the tables. Recognizing none of the stragglers, he sat alone and made quick work of his breakfast. He bussed his plate, downed a glass of water, then hurried to muster at Reynald's training tent.

As he approached, he saw a line of trainees formed outside the tent. Reynald stood before them. The instructor seemed to deliberately avoid noticing Jackson as he fell into line, giving both deniability. He cleared his throat deliberately and continued.

"Now, as I was saying, we are going to have a bit of fun today. This will be a great opportunity to demonstrate what you have learned with something on the line—though not yet your lives. For the glory and honor of being crowned this army's best recruit, you'll be competing in a tournament. The winner of this group will get the opportunity to compete against victors from other divisions. Make no mistake, this is a prize—once you step into the arena of war, there's no more featherweight division, and details like age and tenure matter only for gravestones. Better to test your mettle today and see how you measure up.

"For this tournament, you'll use close-range weapons only. Most of you can count, but to be safe, there are a total of eight of you here. Everyone gets a partner. If you lose a single match, you're out. Just like real life. Clear? Good. Our first match will be Josh and Carter. Gear up and step into the ring, please," said Reynald. The boys shared confused looks. Sighing, the instructor indicated a crudely drawn circle in the patch of dirt behind them. The *ring* was roughly fifteen feet in diameter—tight quarters, likely meant to limit running.

Josh and Carter quickly suited up in light armor made from animal hide. Both wore matching shields on their left arms, but they diverged in their choice of weapon. Josh picked up a long, straight sword. Seeing this, Carter opted for a curved one. Though dulled and blunted to prevent cutting, both blades looked to be of true weight and would no doubt hurt to be hit with. Fully equipped, the first two contestants stepped into the ring and squared up, ten feet apart. Reynald held up his hand.

"Ready?" he called out.

Both nodded in turn.

"Fight!" Reynald said, dropping his hand.

Exploding forward from his starting mark, Josh ran two quick steps and lunged. Carter sidestepped and cleanly parried the off-balance thrust but didn't press the opening. Instead, they both backed off a step, circling one another and planning their next move. Then it was Carter's turn to attack. He swung his curved blade at Josh's neck, missing by inches as his opponent leaped backward.

*If he'd have gone with the straight sword, that would've hit,* Jackson thought, frowning to himself. He hadn't yet seen a reason to prefer a sword that traded length for curve, but he figured Josh had one. He had picked second, after all. Then again, maybe he was just used to it.

The duelists circled one another, orbiting closer with every pass. In striking range, Josh made an overly exaggerated feint at Carter's face. It was convincing enough to provoke an overreaction. Carter raised his shield to protect his face but stood still, his lower body fully exposed. Josh stopped his lofty stroke and pivoted into a low, sideways chop.

With a sickening crack, metal striking bone, the blade connected with the inside of Carter's knee. He went down hard, crying out in pain. Josh stepped in to point his sword at Carter's neck, but he underestimated his opponent's resolve.

Carter spun, kicked Josh's legs out from under him, and rolled away. Both took their time getting up. Once they were back on their feet, Josh rushed in and threw his weight into a powerful overhead stroke. Josh barely got his shield up in time to save his skull from being split open, but the force of the blow snapped his arm back and sent him reeling.

Pressing the attack, Carter launched a relentless salvo of furious strokes. It took all that Josh had to deflect the blows and keep behind the cover of his shield. Each time he tried to counter, he was forced to abandon his reprisal to parry a faster backhanded slash. The attacks just kept coming, hard from every angle, darting in and lashing out like a snake.

The barrage was visibly wearing Josh down. The blows raining down on him kept pace, but his tired blocks were slowing, and each stroke came closer to his body. Fairly sure how this would end, Jackson studied the momentum of the fight, hoping to learn a lesson secondhand. He perceived that Carter's thin, curved sword was easier to use, requiring less technical mastery to be useful. Josh had to think through each thrust, parry, and counterattack, while Carter just went to town, hacking and slashing with wily cuts that seemed to never catch on the wooden shield. If both wore heavy armor or, if Josh had finer control, the precision and versatility of the straight sword might have had the advantage—but Carter had chosen well for a fight between novices.

The inevitable happened as one of Carter's overhead swings broke past Josh's shield, clipping him above the ear. The boy staggered sideways and fell ungracefully to his hands and knees, then again onto his face as he tried to get back up. "Mercy!" he cried, dizzily waving a hand to prevent another walloping. Looking quite pleased by his win, Carter backed off and walked over to the instructor.

"Excellent work, Carter!" Reynald patted him on the back. Without waiting for Josh to crawl out of the ring, he called for the next pair to ready themselves: Jamin and Lee.

Lee was bigger by any measure—height, arm length, muscle. Jamin's face showed he knew it. Both chose the same equipment as Josh. The match started. They came hot out of the gate, but Jackson quickly saw Josh was better than either of them. He stopped paying attention, pondering instead how he might beat Carter—assuming he made it that far.

Before he had gotten very far in his thinking, Lee thwacked Jamin's sword hand, causing the boy to drop his weapon. Yipping in pain as he held his bruise, Jamin fled the circle, surrendering the duel. The instructor shook his head, sighed, and called for the next pair.

Nidle and Andarc entered the ring. Short and sorry-looking, poor in muscle but rich in rat-like features, Nidle stood with a roguish hunch, eyeing his opponent with an ill-tempered scowl. He held two blades—one barely a knife, the other a medium-length arming sword.

Across from him, Andarc was his opposite in every respect. A human bulldozer with muscles straining to burst free of his shirt, he had a rugged, cubelike face with a patch of black hair on his chin. In his bearish hands he held a greatsword longer than half of the trainees. Just to show off his abundant might, he twirled the heavy sword around his broad trunk in a neat display. He clearly had no doubt he'd emerge the victor.

"Sure, Reynald? My muscles are much too big for this little boy. What will little boy's mother say when I crush her baby?" Andarc laughed.

"Don't underestimate your enemy," Reynald warned. Muttering to himself, he added, "Especially when your enemy has the cunning of a fox and the compassion of a snake."

Lifting his hand, Reynald called for the fight to start.

It ended just as quickly.

Nidle threw the knife at Andarc's face. Caught off-guard, the giant tried and failed to deflect it with the broad side of his greatsword. The blunted blade hit him above the eye, causing him to howl in pain.

As Andarc raised a hand to nurse his wound, Nidle didn't hesitate to take full advantage of the opening. Rushing in like sidewinder, he rammed his sword's pommel into the wailing giant's temple. Crashing backward like a felled tree, Andarc hit the dirt and stayed there.

Jackson feared he had just witnessed a murder.

Reynald gave Nidle a disapproving look. Through gritted teeth, he declared, "Nidle wins."

Shrugging indifferently, Nidle sat in the grass away from the other boys. He leaned back on his palms and stared off to the south, indifferent to the next round's outcome.

Meanwhile, Josh, Jamin, and Lee teamed up to haul Andarc's body out of the ring. They laid him in the grass on the opposite side, putting six boys between him and Nidle.

"He's alive," Josh reported, feeling his pulse.

"Uh, Sir Reynald? Want us to get him cold water or something?" asked Jamin. The hesitation on their faces said they were hoping not to lug the massive Andarc all the way to the medics' tent.

"Commendable loyalty, Jamin. He'll appreciate that. Dismissed," Reynald nodded, ready to move on with the tournament. "Next: Jackson and Milos."

By process of elimination, Jackson figured out his matchup and was already sizing him up. A thin, wiry boy with flowing blond hair and sea-blue eyes, Milos looked less like a soldier and more like a Gavroche understudy in a community production of *Les Misérables*. He didn't seem as threatening as the others, but after watching Nidle's fight, Jackson wasn't about to let his guard down.

Picking up the sword and shield he'd used in training and strapping on a leather cuirass, Jackson looked over to see what Milos had chosen. The boy had been watching him and, caught staring, hastily copied his equipment. As they stepped into the ring, Jackson was surprised to see that his opponent looked more nervous than he felt.

Reynald raised his hand and looked between them. "I want a clean fight," he said, flashing a disapproving look toward Nidle.

Acting like he hadn't heard, Nidle busied himself by picking the heads off yellow dandelions around him.

"Begin!" Reynald dropped his hand.

Milos struck first, trying a clumsy slash at Jackson's shoulder. Easily blocking with his shield, Jackson disengaged and settled into a calm focus. Instinct took over, sharpening his senses and ridding his mind of distractions. Milos came at him again, but he was ready. The attack telegraphed itself, and Jackson had no trouble moving his shield to block. Each strike that followed felt the same, almost like slow motion. He read the rhythm of the battle, predicting the aim of his enemy even before his sword started its movement.

When Milos struck for the fifth time, Jackson parried and followed up with a swift stroke toward his neck. At the last second, he turned his sword to rest its flat side against Milos' skin.

Milos dropped his sword and tripped backward over himself. He crab-walked away in terror until he found himself at the edge of the ring. Jackson pursued him all the way, then dangled his sword in front of Milos' nose. "Yield!"

"Mercy!" Milos held his neck as if feeling the pain that might've been. Reynald called the match, and Jackson helped him up. "Thanks," he mumbled.

"Welcome." Jackson said, bowing his head to hide a smile. He had done it. His first match.

He was made for this.

# ⚜ Chapter 8 ⚜

W
ell done, Jackson," Reynald whispered to him as he exited the ring. The praise only added to his euphoria. A day ago, he'd never held a weapon. Today, he'd won his first duel. Not just that, but it all felt so natural to him. Every block and counter—they didn't feel like haphazard accidents, but his body's instinctive response. He didn't know he had it in him.

An accomplished smile slipped through as Josh congratulated him. He removed his armor, wiped the sweat off his palms, and sat in the grass to watch the next match.

Nidle and Carter squared off for their second round. Carter looked on edge, and given the trickery of Nidle's first match, Jackson couldn't blame him. He flinched as the match began, anticipating Nidle's ranged attack, but the rattish boy just stood in place, waiting for him.

Carter took initiative and engaged. At first, he looked to have the upper hand. He fought with the high tempo that had won him his match against Josh, keeping Nidle on the back foot. With the disadvantage of a shorter sword, Nidle ducked, dipped, and deflected the flurry of attacks, ceding ground across the ring and returning no answer.

Right up until he ended it.

Nidle deflected Carter's backhand with his knife. As it sailed harmlessly overhead, he lunged low and brought his arming sword crashing against Carter's kneecap. When Carter involuntarily doubled over in pain, Nidle grabbed his breast-plate, stepped to the side, and yanked him forward, throwing him out of the ring. It was enough to win the victory, and yet he pounced and pressed his blades against Carter's neck. Had they been sharp, they might have decapitated him.

"Enough!" Reynald intervened. "Nidle wins."

As the pair disentangled and rose to their feet, Nidle kneed Carter hard in the nose, causing him to fall again.

"Accidents happen," he said unapologetically before returning to his spot in the grass.

Reynald's face darkened with anger. He crossed the ring to check on Carter, kneeling by his side and exchanging a few quiet words. The boy was slow to stand and had blood trickling from his nose but otherwise seemed to be all right. Josh was tasked with watching him, but there were no further delays to the tournament.

Lee and Jackson were called to the ring.

Jackson's adrenaline from the first match had not yet faded; he was ready to keep going. Realizing he'd backed the wrong horse by betting on Carter to make it to the finals, he adjusted to preparing for a matchup with Nidle. Obviously unafraid to fight dirty, Nidle's quickness and cunning made him a formidable foe. Whereas Andarc posed a powerful but predictable threat, Nidle was as hard to grasp as shifting sand. The looming challenge twisted his stomach with nerves, but righteous anger for Carter and Andarc, along with an eager anticipation to test himself, kept him grounded.

"Begin!"

Jackson's attention snapped to the battle at hand. As he prepared to counter Lee's lunge, he wasn't expecting the match to be the second shortest of the day. Lee entered his lunge too early, forcing him to overextend to reach Jackson. As Jackson parried and stepped outside Lee's guard, angling to strike his exposed right flank, Lee tried to halt his forward momentum. He turned his foot to the outside and launched himself backward, twisting his knee with a light *pop*.

Lee dropped his sword and collapsed to the ground, screaming in agony as he clutched his knee. Jackson stood there watching, not knowing how to help. Sir Reynald ended the match immediately and ordered Jamin to help him carry Lee to the medics' tent. Though they moved with speed and care, Lee's screams were audible for at least another minute.

Though he hadn't touched him, Jackson couldn't help but feel a little bad about the injury. He'd like to make it up to Lee somehow, if he ever got the chance.

"What a crybaby," said Nidle.

"What's your problem, dude?" asked Jackson.

"Don't mind him. Been a spiteful little runt as long as I've known him," said Carter. Josh agreed.

"Shh. Dead," Nidle pointed at him. "Dead," he said again, pointing at Josh. "Dead." Milos yelped at his finger. With a mocking laugh, Nidle shifted his gaze to Andarc, who lay stretched out on the grass. "He might actually be dead."

"So you won two rounds. Cool. You're a dirty cheat. You couldn't take any of us in a fair fight," said Josh.

Milos didn't look so sure.

"Idiots," Nidle scoffed. "Don't you get it? You'll be dead for real in two days. All of you will. Fair is worthless."

"Name's Jackson, right?" Carter looked at him.

He nodded.

"Don't go easy on him."

Right on cue, Reynald returned, coming down the path with long, purposeful strides. He explained that Lee was expected to make a swift recovery, but he wouldn't be joining them in the fight for Kanrio. Jamin had stayed behind to give the medics an extra hand—apparently, the other groups had also suffered their share of injuries.

Nidle muttered something in a cough—"Dead," it sounded like.

Jackson ignored him. The win hadn't come the way he'd wanted it, but either way, he was in the finals. Reynald called to prepare for the championship round, and Jackson retrieved his weapons and put on his armor. The competition of the tournament took a backseat in his mind; this would be a fight for survival against a merciless opponent. As twisted as he was, Nidle would be good practice for the real thing.

Stepping into the ring, Jackson took a second to size up his enemy. Even accounting for the slouch, Nidle was half a head shorter. Feeling the full intensity of his gaze, those cold beads of hate and malice fixed on him, he felt a chill run through him. In the lamps of those eyes, his soul reflected no light but utter darkness. Innocence had long been rooted out of him; goodness was nowhere to be found.

Jackson shook his head to free himself of the spell, chastising himself for getting tied up in a runaway narrative. It didn't take much empathy to understand the boy. Nidle didn't have a friend among the group. Sure, he was angry and weird, but maybe his apparent evil came from a lifetime of being ostracized—desperate to be known. It didn't excuse his behavior, but Jackson could understand his pain. Still, he was like a dangerous, feral animal. Jackson would keep his guard up in the fight, but he wouldn't join the others in bullying him afterward, either. Everyone deserved a chance.

"Good luck," Nidle said with a sinister grin, offering his right hand.

As Jackson reached out, Nidle dug his nails into his skin, causing Jackson to yank his arm away. As he walked to his starting mark, Nidle let out a quiet, sadistic laugh.

He'd definitely keep his guard up.

"Ready?" Reynald let them both nod. "Begin!"

Nidle didn't miss a beat.

As soon as Reynald's arm fell, he exploded forward with his arming sword. Jackson parried cleanly, but he wasn't expecting to see Nidle's knife taking flight from his left hand, on course for his head.

In a delayed lurch, Jackson leaned back and raised his shield, deflecting the projectile over his head, skimming his hair as it passed. Reminding himself to keep moving, he hastily retreated, narrowly dodging a cut across his stomach. He swiped his sword across his body, his vision still obscured by his shield. As he recovered, he saw that it had worked; Nidle had dodged backward, buying him a second to think.

Nidle's eyes darted between his sword and shield. Jackson studied him in return, seeking an opening on his left side. He was about to attack when his instincts warned him to pull back. As he did, Nidle hurled himself through the air and barely missed a diving chop at Jackson's front knee. Off-balance, Nidle rolled forward over his shoulder and raised his sword to defend himself.

Jackson was faster, slashing at his sword hand. The metal rapped Nidle's knuckles, and he gave up his grip with a yelp. Jackson booted the arming sword aside, kicked Nidle onto his back, and pointed his sword at his neck. He risked a glance at Reynald, who nodded his head at Nidle.

"Say it," Jackson demanded, pressing his blade into Nidle's throat.

The boy choked out a cough. He seemed close to whimpering, and overall, pretty pathetic.

"Say it."

"Mercy..." sputtered Nidle.

Satisfied, Jackson looked up to Reynald and let his sword off Nidle's throat.

"... is for the weak!"

Nidle kicked Jackson's legs out from under him and rolled for his sword. Jackson fell heavy on his back, gasping for air with the wind knocked out of him.

Jackson looked up to see Nidle crouching over him. "How's this for mercy?" he hissed, slamming the butt of his sword against Jackson's forehead.

His vision went white as pain exploded through his skull. As the sounds of the world faded around him, Jackson thought he heard a man bellowing in rage. A scornful, nasal voice answered him.

*I'll remember that one, Nidle.* His vision faded to black as he slipped into unconsciousness.

# ✤ Chapter 9 ✤

A sharp throbbing pulsed through his head as he attempted to sit up. He moaned in pain and lowered his head back onto the pillow, covering his eyes to block out the light.

A gentle, womanly voice spoke from nearby. It was soft-spoken but felt oddly loud to him. "Good, you're awake. You took a pretty mean knock."

He opened one eye to find a pretty woman staring down at him. She had lithe features from her willowy frame to her thin lips and nose. Raven hair tumbled behind her, tied up in a green velvet band.

"Am I in heaven?" Jackson mumbled inaudibly.

"Hmm? Did you say something?"

His reveries gave way to recollection as his last waking moments came back to him. He had won the finals, but Nidle deceived him and knocked him out after the bell. Rage flared in his chest. He felt stupid for having dropped his guard. For showing mercy.

Opening his eyes and slowly turning his head to look around, he saw that he was lying on a cot in a red canvas tent. Another boy occupied the bed across from him, apparently asleep. He realized he'd been taken to the medics' tent. "How long was I out?"

"You slept through yesterday. It's dinner now."

*I've been asleep for twenty-four hours.*

Jackson eased himself up into a sitting position. The headache was slowly starting to lift. He vaguely remembered dreaming about a red ceiling; perhaps he'd been in and out. The long day before may have also played into his need for rest; he wasn't sure whether jet lag applied to portal travel between planets. "So, am I free to go?"

The medic studied him carefully. "Depends. How are you feeling, firstly?"

He paused to contemplate—first the truth, then the answer he felt he ought to give. Though starting to improve, his head certainly ached. He'd suffered a concussion before, and this time didn't feel quite as bad, but the school nurse had said the odds of a repeat went up after the first one. He could probably manage walking around, but he'd steer clear of any heavy metal concerts. So, the question: *did he want to be cleared to play his part in the coming battle, or did he want a sick note to sit on the sidelines?*

He decided the truth was good enough. Though far from perfect, he wasn't a coward. It wasn't his fight in the way it was theirs, but he didn't like the idea of lying in bed while everyone else fought and died. He felt a deep stirring to be something bigger than himself. Besides, if they failed, who would be left to help him? He would surely join the innocent in their chains, and there would be none left to stand against the invaders. The medic, too, had her future on the line. She deserved the truth and could make a professional judgment from there.

"Head's still a bit sore, but I am feeling better by the minute." His stomach rumbled. "Hunger isn't a symptom of anything worrying, is it?"

"Yes, it's a symptom of not having eaten enough." She smiled at him. "Do me a favor and rest for a little longer; if you're up to joining them in the morning, I'll clear you for duty—assuming you'd want that?"

He hesitated but nodded to confirm his choice.

"Okay then. I'll see if I can track down a little food for you. Take it easy until I'm back." She gave him a parting smile and backed out of the tent.

Turning his eyes to the cot across from him, he saw the boy had sat up and was staring back at him. He looked familiar. Jackson leaned forward to take a better look.

"Fancy meeting you here, Jackson. Heard you won the tournament," the boy moved his long black locks out of his face. "At least, you ought to have…"

*Lee.*

The name popped into Jackson's mind—along with memories of his agonized screams after he'd injured his knee. He still felt guilty about accepting a victory he hadn't earned. "How's your knee?"

"They say I got lucky. Dodged a tear that might've hobbled me for life. It's swollen, but they're going to give me crutches and a leg brace in a few days to help me get around. Then it's a month or more until I'm back training with you guys. Hate that I'll miss tomorrow's battle." Disappointment showed on his face.

*Tomorrow.*

Out loud, that sounded a lot sooner. Jackson felt his nerves coming undone. He hadn't had much time to prepare himself. Was he ready? Or was he hurrying off to his death? He shook his head to push away his spiraling thoughts and immediately regretted it as nausea from his injury flared up.

"I'm sure there'll be another one," Jackson tried to sound convincing.

"Won't be the same. I've got family from Kanrio. I signed up for this fight." Lee looked down at his knee and frowned. "Wish I could be there to see it happen. To see our flag flying above the city walls. I get giddy about the plan— the surprise that'll be on those Nights' faces when we come bursting out of the vegetable cart, take the gates, and storm the city. Er, not we… You and the others, I mean. Tear one of the enemy's banners down for me, will you?"

"Sure thing, Lee," Jackson offered him a tired smile. Acutely feeling the throbbing in his head, he lay back on the soft pillow. "Think I'm going to try to sleep," he said.

Lee didn't answer.

It felt as though he had only just closed his eyes by the time morning arrived.

Jackson awoke to a soothing and melodic voice that fell like a harp on the ear. "Feeling any better?"

He opened his eyes to see the young medic who had been tending to him. She wore a gentle smile and didn't hurry his answer. Stretching as he sat up, he realized his headache had passed in his sleep. At worst he felt a little dizzy, though that in part was lingering anxiety at the coming battle.

"Much," he said truthfully, swinging his legs over the side of his bed. "Am I good to go?"

"If you say so," she allowed. As he began to rise, she pointed to a sandwich on his nightstand. "But I insist you eat something."

Wobbling on his first step, he decided that was sage advice. The smoked meat between two slabs of rye was still warm; the medic must've gone out for it just before waking him. He nibbled a few more appreciative bites, downed a jug of water, and decided he'd take the rest of the meal to go. He passed her as he crossed to the exit, pausing with one hand on the canvas. "Thanks," he looked back to tell her. "Take good care of him, will you?" he asked, his eyes sweeping to a sleeping Lee.

"Let's plan on seeing him rejoin you, rather than you rejoining him," she warned gently.

Stepping out into the morning sun, already hot and intense against his fair skin, Jackson longed for the modern wonder of air conditioning. Evidently, he was among the last to awaken. The grounds were abuzz with the sounds of tents being struck and packed up. Past the outermost row of tents, the lawn was littered with carts and wagons. Stocky horses and disobedient mules were strapped into harnesses to pull them. As Jackson began to turn, something big and purple caught his eye. His head snapped back for a better look. He couldn't be sure what he saw—it looked like a giant purple beetle and seemed to wink at him as it trotted on by.

*Maybe I'd best stay in bed,* he thought, rubbing his eyes.

Navigating through the camp with all the skill of a drunken homing pigeon, he eventually reached his assigned tent. Neither Canon nor Tyson were there. Instead, he found short but sturdy man rummaging through a footlocker. The stranger wore a brown cowl over his head and at least two knives on his hip. The bulges inside his cloak suggested he had another pair concealed within. Perhaps sensing he was being watched, he paused what he was doing and turned to look at Jackson. The grit and determination in his stare didn't match his youthful face, free of lines or facial hair. Equally mismatched were his striking eyes—one green, one blue.

"Hello," said Jackson.

The boy barely nodded, returning to his packing.

Jackson stood awkwardly in the entryway. Stepping inside, he gave conversation another shot. "Are you Rein?"

The boy paused stiffly, nodded, then resumed.

Jackson opened his own footlocker. "You don't say much, do you?" he joked.

Rein snapped his chest closed and heaved it up onto his shoulder. "I'd say you do enough for the both of us," he said in a surprisingly deep voice. He exited the tent, leaving Jackson in stunned silence.

*He seemed like a nice boy.*

Shaking off the lukewarm interaction, Jackson put on the clean uniform that had been left in his trunk. After stowing his loaner outfit, he latched the chest shut and tried to heave it onto his shoulder. Even half-empty, it proved too heavy. Lifting it by the rings on either side, he shuffled out of the tent like a crab.

As he stepped out into the sunlight, he saw a familiar figure strolling towards him.

"Oi, Jack! That box too heavy for ya?" Canon said with a goofy grin. As if it were paper mâché, he scooped it out of Jackson's hands and rested it on his shoulder. "Come along, Jack. We can walk and talk."

"Miss me?" Jackson followed along beside him as he started toward the loading area outside camp.

"'Course I did. How's a man s'posed to get any sleep without the white noise of your snoring?" he said without missing a beat.

"Right, now listen," he continued, shifting the chest to his other shoulder so they could talk face to face. "I want you on my squad, Jack. There're five 'farmer carts' set to go through the gates. We'll be riding in cart four. Oh, don't give me that look—I ain't asking you to drive. Just listen to me; I'll let ya know when to pop out and start with the whacking. Krystal, Tyson, and Rein will be with us, too. Our own little party wagon! I take it you've met Rein?"

"Yeah, a few minutes ago. He seemed… reserved."

"Aw, Rein don't bite. Except if you wind up on the wrong end of his knife… Then he's a right nasty biter, he is. Good man to have at your back, though. Loyal. Capable and dependable when it counts. Just not a *people person,* per se. Once you get to know the surly porcupine, he'll warm right up to ya, I'm sure. Quite confident, actually."

"I'll look forward to that." Jackson was curious how their five distinct personalities would fare in a cart together, but he figured if anyone could bring them together, it would be Canon.

"Anyway—what I really wanted to talk about is that conniving rotter, Nidle. I heard you torched him handily, then that sore loser suckered you without warning after the fact. The bloody cheek! Someone ought to wring out his cocky chicken neck," Canon squeezed the air with one hand.

"Know if he's part of today's mission?" Jackson asked. The idea of fighting alongside him didn't instill much confidence.

"No clue. I haven't seen him around, anyhow. Name didn't come up at this morning's briefing for wagon team leaders. Must be loitering someplace around here, though… ah well. Maybe a bear got to him," said Canon, unconcerned.

Jackson laughed at the mental image of a roving bear happening upon the camp and dragging Nidle away. They'd both probably find the experience equally unpleasant.

Clearing the tents and reaching the open grass with the carts, Canon rested the chest among others and scrawled *Jackson* across the top using a piece of charcoal. "Right," he turned, starting off toward a cluster of five carts set apart from the bustle. "Time to say farewell to camp and put on your best potato impression. The other spuds are waiting for us in the farmer's cart."

Jackson eyed the pairs of brown horses hitched to each cart. He couldn't tell what breed they were; he had a shallow knowledge when it came to wildlife. Still, he'd gone on enough field trips to the petting zoo to know they weren't ducks.

"How long's the ride?" he asked.

"We'll be flying about as fast as wagons go. These here are some of the best shire horses in the country. Roads are good, flat all the way. I'd bet under eight hours, barring incident. We can always borrow a horse from the battalions that went ahead at dawn, if need be. So, settle in, get yourself comfy—the yams don't mind a snuggle."

"Good to depart in five?" a man asked Canon as he fed the tallest horse an apple.

"Ready in four," Canon raised with a smile, leading Jackson around the side of a worn cart. Though the horses looked healthy, the wagon was destined for the trash heap. Peeling grey paint hung off a splintering wooden frame, and the once-white canvas covering was yellowed with dust and pollen. Canon slapped the sideboard, and Jackson flinched with worry that it would all fall apart.

"This is our chariot for the day. I need a quick word with Ethan, but you can go on and get yourself situated."

Delaying entering, Jackson looked back across the grass at the other, less dilapidated wagons. "What about the carts over there with all our stuff? The ones being pulled by mules and those big beetle things?"

As if it had overheard, a purply-blue beetle shuffled around and stared him down from afar.

"The logistics vehicles are following behind. If all goes well, they'll get to the city after we're done handling business. Oh, and that's not a beetle you're looking at. That's a Beffle."

"A... Beffle?"

"Yeah. Beffle," Canon sniffed the air of the country-side and wrinkled his nose. "Easy to tame—less easy to clean up after. Strong creatures, though. One can do the work of five mules, I'd reckon."

"Good to know," Jackson accepted, surprised only that he was still surprised. "I'll head on in?"

"I'll join you in a minute," Canon waved.

Shrugging to himself, Jackson walked around to the back and carefully climbed in, trying his best not to think of the carriage as a hearse. Picking his way past a few loose bags of vegetables and stacked crates secured in place, he found Krystal and Tyson in the back. Rein was there, too, lying off to the side with his head resting on a bag of potatoes.

"Welcome aboard, Jackson. Your head feeling any better?" Tyson asked as he sat beside him.

"Not feeling any worse, at least."

"Good to hear. Shame we didn't get our chance to spar, though," Krystal teased. "A fight between champions is always a nice spectacle for regular people like Tyson."

"Sod off," Tyson rolled his eyes. "Mine was harder."

"Harder? The winner of your division got a bye after the trainee champion got pulled."

"Because Canon complained he was being shorted a match and they had to rejigger everything around. You sailed through beating the second-year I would have stomped in the original bracket."

Krystal turned to loop Jackson back in. "What he's really saying is that he's a sore loser. I get it—no judgment here. I hate losing, too."

"I mean, I just don't understand how either of you feel comfortable calling yourselves champions when I'm the only one here who's undefeated," he said, successfully getting a rise out of both of them.

"That there's a cold bowl of facts. Hard to swallow, Krystal?"

"As if!"

"How about we have a match after Kanrio? Winner takes all," suggested Jackson. He still didn't actually feel like fighting Krystal, but he figured it would be fun banter now and a forgotten promise later.

"I'm in. We can get Canon to ref," she agreed.

"That's hardly fair, now is it? Jackson might be his new army mate, but let's not pretend his date to the snog-fest wouldn't get any special treatment."

Krystal made an offended face as if she might argue but lost her composure and snorted out a guilty laugh. "Fine, fine. You can ref, Tyson. All better?"

Tyson shook his head, indignant. "Still don't see why I wasn't the obvious first choice."

Canon chose that moment to vault into the cart. The wooden bed squeaked for mercy as he landed. "Seven short hours till we fly our flag over Kanrio. Getting excited, Rein?" Canon asked, with enough pep to put a cheerleader to shame.

Lifting his head, Rein gave a dry smile. "I can barely contain myself," he said tonelessly.

"Announcement! Captain Canon says it's time to get this buggy rolling," Canon said importantly. He stowed his sword in the corner, saluted, and rearranged a couple bags to make the aisle to the back of the cart less apparent.

Tyson snorted. "Captain? I wouldn't let you pilot a dinghy."

Canon stared at him, then dropped his hands to his hips and huffed. "Fine. I'll be driving this crumbling wooden box held together by scrap, spit, and prayer three-dozen miles to Kanrio while the lot of you hope I don't steer us off a cliff. How's that? Do you feel better, now that I've abandoned the majestic airs of a mariner? Is anyone impressed? Awe-struck, perhaps? Nary a one?" He draped a tarp across the wagon to better conceal them, ensuring anyone glancing inside would see only a false back.

The wagon rocked as he clambered out of the cart, then again as he climbed onto the jockey box up front.

A moment later, the cart lurched forward.

They were on their way.

Once the dregs of conversation died down, everyone settled in for the long ride. Jackson snuggled against a tall bag of wheat and rested his eyes. The wagon rocked as the horses trotted out a rhythmic beat with their hooves.

Despite the fear he should've felt about the coming battle, his eyelids grew heavy, and he drifted off into a series of fitful naps.

## Chapter 10

T he cart groaned to a hard stop. Jolted awake, he took inventory of his surroundings. The others all looked tense, crouching with their weapons drawn, waiting anxiously to see if their plan worked. Sensing the danger, he sat up slowly and reached for the comfort of his sword.

"Halt! Do you have your papers?" demanded a deep voice outside the cart. "State your business."

"Papers? No papers. I farmer! I farm," Canon said in what could only be an offensive imitation of a local farmer. Jackson felt sorry for the reputation of the *hill-folk* he'd once been lumped in with. He really hoped Canon wasn't outside pantomiming how to till a field.

"A farmer? What do you have in there, then?"

"Peas, potatoes, carrots. You buy my peas, potatoes, carrots?" Canon asked expectantly.

"All right. In you go."

The cart jerked forward. The sound of the hoofbeats changed as the road turned to stone, from soft clops to sharp taps. Through a tear in the canvas, Jackson watched the gates pass overhead.

Once inside, the cart slowed, then crawled to a stop. Canon thumped three times on the jockey box, then jumped down, making the wagon wobble. In the back, Tyson gripped his sword in one hand and grabbed the concealing cloth with the other, ready to spring out. Krystal lined up behind, and Jackson followed. Looking none too concerned, Rein stood off to the side and stretched out his legs.

"Oi! You can't park there."

"Me, sir?"

"Both of you. Move along."

"I sorry! Many apology. Where to go?"

The guard grunted. "There's a stable just around the corner where you can rent a stall. Otherwise, you can try your luck finding an extra patch of grass in the open-air market— assuming you don't have an assigned lot."

"I stall! Many thanks!"

"Yes, stall!" a second voice said in a different accent.

Close to the first guard, another voice chuckled. "Is today your nation's onions holiday or something? Look at you all—two here, two there... another one, coming through now! What, is everyone trying to beat the evening rush?"

Canon gave the cart two slaps.

Throwing aside the cloth, Tyson jumped out of the back and swung his greatsword into the nearest guard's chest. Before the second could draw a weapon, Tyson pirouetted and slammed his blade against the side of his head. The blow rang out against the guard's iron helmet, and he folded in a boneless heap.

Tumbling out after Krystal, Jackson took a second to let his eyes adjust to the sunlight. The skirmish ended as fast as it had begun. Canon and another cart driver prevailed over two more guards, while cart five's team looked to have the upper hand against the defenders outside the gate. Six bodies lay strewn beneath the portcullis. No Eternai among them.

Meanwhile, soldiers from carts one and two battled for control of the winches in the guardhouse above the gates.

"Quickly! Up here with me!" Canon shouted to his team, leading the way up the steps and onto the outer wall.

Jackson followed Tyson to the battlements. Looking over the parapets, he reeled at the sight of the armed horde before breathing in relief, remembering that they were on his side. A thousand or more, they charged forth in a shapeless sea devoid of row or column. When the Night flags were cut down from the outer wall, the warriors raised their weapons and lifted up a thunderous roar. The battle cry of this violent wave crashed over the walls and flooded the city, bringing citizens out of their homes—confused at first, then inspired to join in. A unified voice cried out for the liberation of the city; hope for freedom and bloodlust for retribution filled the air, the song of thousands of men and women ready to fight and die for the city they love.

Before the army reached the gates, their unorganized mass swiftly conformed into four columns. Once inside, the two outer lines split off into side streets while the middle two surged through the main drag. Many citizens watched outside their homes, cheering them on. Some took up weapons; the boldest ran ahead on their own, while most of them formed a mob of torches, knives, and pitchforks behind the columns. A few just watched, merely curious about the noise.

In every direction, the city of Kanrio came alive. Its citizens swarmed the streets like locusts. Every Night soldier unlucky enough to be caught out alone was swallowed by the hateful mob.

"This way," Canon signaled for his team to join him. "We'll cut through the backstreets to get ahead of them."

"Know where you're going?" Tyson checked.

"A thousand percent. I went over this a dozen times in my mind last night."

Down the stairs, Canon led them into an alley and up a narrow set of stairs. The path forked into a wider street. By the signs above the shuttered shops, the area appeared to have once been a charming row of restaurants. They turned left, running parallel to the main road. A tall castle appeared ahead now and then between the rooftops.

A patrol of four Night soldiers stepped into the alley, barring their path. Surprised at first to see the enemy here, they soon recovered and formed a line covering the width of the alley.

Before Canon's strike team could engage them, a strong, warbling voice echoed through the alley from above. "Gardyloo!"

Jackson looked up to see a portly woman leaning out of her second-story window to deposit the contents of her chamber pot on the Night below.

The afflicted Night swore at their tormentor, their faces twisting in disgust. As they tried to wipe the foul sludge off themselves, Canon and Tyson rushed in to engage them. The patrol's attention was further divided when a door burst open to their left. Six drunken, middle-aged men who looked to have been in the middle of a poker game spilled out with fire pokers, kitchenware, and shovels. The shortest of them threw empty bottles to varying effects.

Two Night turned to defend themselves against the poker players. Canon and Tyson separated and attacked the other two from the outside. The Night stepped back as they fought, bumping into one another and throwing themselves off balance. Both were dispatched—Canon's blade only just the faster—and their comrades fared little better. One had dropped his sword when a wooden stool, followed by a cast-iron skillet, struck him in the head. Tyson gave the other a great kick in the back, toppling him to the ground. The rabid townsfolk piled on to batter and beat him.

"Go on! Give that Baron my regards!" spat one of the rebels as he pinned the swordless Night.

"This way!" Canon continued down the alley.

The backstreet narrowed as it merged back into the main thoroughfare, one edge curving more suddenly than the other. The wall-to-wall houses, dark and silent within, leaned over the alley at a precarious angle. Fortunately, the impending collapse held off for a later day, and Canon's detachment emerged into the failing sunlight unscathed.

Jackson followed Canon's gaze to their right. They had reached the literal end of the road. A deep moat about twenty feet wide separated them and the walls of the castle courtyard. The unclimbable sheer stone ensured the only way inside was across the imposing drawbridge. The problem was immediately clear—the bridge was raised.

"I was wondering when you'd join us."

They turned to find Prince Falcon leading two lines of soldiers. He stood gallantly in extravagant golden armor and an orange cape with his signature black bird. The grisly evidence in the street behind him marked the last stand of a Night platoon that had failed to stop the rebel army, perhaps slowing them just enough for their comrades to retreat across the drawbridge. Falcon stared across the moat at the dark and defiant banners of his enemy. "Thoughts?"

Growing restless as they waited, the men turned to grumbling and cursing. Canon looked at Rein, who appeared to hesitate before hurrying over to whisper in Falcon's ear.

Falcon called two men forward and sent them into a butcher's shop. They emerged a minute later with four meat hooks bound together with knots of wire. A rope of braided cords was looped over one end of the hooks.

"Big John, get up here!"

A bear of a man stepped out of line and approached Falcon to receive his orders. He accepted the hooks and rope and made his way to the edge of the moat. Swinging his burly arm in a loop, he launched the bundle up and over the moat, landing it past the wall. Pulling the rope taut, he leaned back with his considerable weight to form a steady anchor.

At first, Jackson thought he meant to pull the entire wall down. A second strongman wrapped his arms around the first, reinforcing the picture of an impossible game of tug of war. Then Rein stepped up to the edge. Turning his back to the chasm, he grabbed the rope with two hands and swung up his feet to hang like a sloth. Wasting no time, he started to shimmy across the cold, fetid waters of the moat below.

He suddenly dropped a yard in the air as one of the anchors' feet slipped and the rope slackened, but the second redoubled his effort and tightened the line once again. Eyeing the far end of the rope, where the makeshift grappling hook could be found and dislodged at any second, Rein doubled his pace.

The rest of the vanguard could only watch and hope. Their ambition of retaking Kanrio rested on that drawbridge coming down. If Rein failed, the enemy would stay holed up in the keep. Doubtlessly, they would have enough provisions stored to endure the siege until reinforcements arrived. The Eternai would be caught in the middle, trying to defend the city from within and outside. If Rein failed, so would their campaign. They all knew it, so they watched without a word, willing him onward.

Voices rose from beyond the wall. Rein didn't stop. Five feet away. Four. Three. Another second, and his hands would be on the stone ledge.

But he didn't get it.

He entered a freefall as the rope snapped back from the wall, its frayed end writhing like a snake, cut loose from the grappling hook. The anchors spilled backward, and the crowd gasped in despair.

Twisting in midair, Rein pulled out a long knife and slammed it into the thick wood of the drawbridge, arresting his fall. Dangling from one arm, he looked down as the rope rebounded off the exposed, jagged rock and splashed into the water. Then he drew a second dagger with his free hand and plunged it beside the first, beginning his ascent.

Carefully, methodically, he worked his way up the door, reaching higher with his right hand and stabilizing with his left. The wood cracked and creaked under each thrust. Reaching the top of the wooden bridge, still another foot of stone between him and safety, he hammered each hilt in as deep as he could. With a burst of strength, he pulled himself up like a gymnast on rings. One arm, then the other he threw onto the stone ledge. Finally, his foot found the hilt of his knife, and he kicked himself up, rolling onto his back. He rested there for a second, staring up at the twilit sky, then glanced down at the bridge as if debating whether he could retrieve his knives. Deciding against it, he drew himself into a crouch, reached into his shirt, and dropped down into the courtyard on the other side.

Urgent voices. Panicked yells. A scream of pain here and there. These were the only clues available to the anxious crowd. Jackson shared their worry. Unable to bear it alone, he turned to confer with Canon. Surprisingly, the Cavar had a big smile on his face.

"Sure lives for the drama, doesn't he?" Canon mused to himself.

The metallic rattle of chains broke the silence, and the drawbridge fell into place. Astonished applause erupted from the company as Rein walked into view. Leaning against the side of the gate, the hero of the hour sheathed his knife and gave a nonchalant nod toward the Falcon.

"Show-off," Canon grumbled in amusement as he mimed clapping for his friend's triumph.

"Move out!" the prince ordered, leading his century across the bridge.

A few men lingered on either side of the bridge to stand guard. Canon's team joined the rest of the company in the castle courtyard. The tension built throughout their ranks as they waited for the prince to address them from the foot of the keep—the steps that would bring them to their final test where history would be written. One way or the other, the Battle for Kanrio would be decided inside those walls.

"All right!" Falcon looked over the company he had hand-selected for this day—the finest soldiers the Eternai had to offer. After months of planning and hoping, the weight of the hour showed on his face. Yet the prince did not shrink from the moment but bore the burden as a king should. "Here we are. Many have fought bravely to win us this final trial. I expect no less from all of you now. Put on the hearts of lions and fight with honor and valor.

"You all have your teams. Follow your leaders. One more time, here's the plan: Vector's group will join mine in front. Cut down anyone or anything in our way. There are fifty of us, so we'll cycle our freshest to the front where it narrows and spread out to overwhelm them where it widens. Sweep every floor and cleanse the castle of filth. Dersul's group will sneak behind their defenses, taking the sewers to the kitchens. Deal with the entrenchments, then make your way upstairs to join us. Statol's team, go around back and cut their retreat. Lastly, Reynald's group will keep watch. Make sure no one escapes from under our noses. Clear? Good. Let's do this. For the Eternai!"

"For the Eternai!" they all answered in unison.

The assembly dissolved as each group got in place. Jackson was following Canon and Tyson to Falcon's group when a strong hand gripped his shoulder from behind.

"Jackson, right?"

He turned to find a terrifying man looming over him with unblinking eyes and at least twenty scars. His breath was hot and stung with the sharpness of onions. "I'm Dersul. We lost too many getting here. Reynald says he hasn't a man to spare but thinks you can handle yourself. Come with me."

Dersul pulled him to the side to join five battle-worn men huddled around an open sewer grate. One offered a few pleasantries, but something in the corner of Jackson's eye stole his attention. He did a double take and watched Nidle slinking behind the group assigned to enter around back. The anger he felt at the sight of the honorless rat surprised him. Even after Nidle and the rest of Staton's group were gone from sight, a bile of disgust lingered in his throat.

Dersul's gravelly voice won back his focus. "If this is your first time in a sewer, I'd recommend holding your nose till you're through."

Their leader turned and dropped himself down into the pipe without hesitation. The others looked around the circle, waiting to see who would volunteer. One did, then another, and, begrudgingly, so did Jackson.

He landed in the shallow slurry, splashing his pant legs with the grimy drainage. Though he held his nose, he could smell the foul air with every breath he took through his mouth. He kept his eyes on the man in front of him and put one foot in front of the other, trying not to think about what might be brushing against his boots.

A dim light broke the utter darkness right as his back began to ache from hunching over. Up ahead, the faint outline of Dersul motioned for them to stay silent and raised his weapon. He counted his fingers down from three, then cast away the overhead grate and sprung out of the pipe, inviting a beam of light into the gloom.

The next two eagerly followed his escape from the drain. Jackson's exit was less agile; his clunky shield blocked his view, and he couldn't put enough weight on his other hand without losing his grip on his sword. Fortunately, his struggle was shortened by help from both above and below. After his ally fished him out of the sewer, he reclaimed his sword and prepared to redeem himself in combat.

As the last of the strike team vaulted out onto the floor, Jackson realized why the scene felt eerie. The kitchen was empty. Instead of soldiers, cooks, or servants laboring to prepare an evening meal, the place looked abandoned.

"Something's not right," said Dersul, breaking the tense silence. He cautiously circled the large prep table before returning to the group. "Nothing."

Jackson jumped at the sound of glass breaking. He hastily scanned the room but couldn't tell where it had come from. Then it repeated, twice more in rapid succession.

His vision blurred, gradually at first, then all at once. The air turned thick and hostile. An acrid burn attacked his nose and lungs.

The smallest on the strike team, a boy about his age, started coughing and didn't stop. He sank to his knees, then collapsed onto the floor. The older, sturdier boy next to him stumbled into the wall.

Jackson felt his own strength deserting him. He tried to cover his mouth with his sleeve, but it didn't stop the fire spreading in his chest. Leaning on the table for support, he looked across the room through blurry eyes to see a mystery.

A living horror entered the room. Its fur black as coal, muscles rippling around its sleek shoulders, the creature inched closer like a shadow at sunset. Long white fangs hung beneath its glowing eyes. If panthers could grow to the size of bears, this beast might have resembled one, though it was unmistakably of its own order. Most peculiar was the ghostly purple haze that seemed to rise from its body, dancing over its fur like a flame.

Jackson's grip on the table slipped and he fell to his knees, losing sight of the creature. As he glanced around, he realized he was the last one awake. The others were all face down, motionless.

Rounding the table, the beast fixed its eyes on him. It stalked closer, snarling, until its menacing fangs hovered over his face. It leaned forward and sniffed. A deep, guttural growl bubbled in its throat.

A cough racked his body, dropping him to the floor. His vision failed. Unable to fend off the threat, he could only wonder: *What is that thing?*

A woman's soothing voice echoed in his head.

*"That, my dear, is a Nocturne."*

# ⚜ Chapter 11 ⚜

Outside, Captain Vector ordered ten men to take up positions on either side of the battering ram. He walked among them, making sure they were ready. Making sure he was ready. The rest of his team waited with the prince's a few yards back from the keeps' front doors, ready to charge as soon as the way was opened.

"On my mark," he squeezed the leather grip of his shield. "Breach!"

In unison, his men swung the heavy log against the door. The iron head crashed against the wood, causing the whole frame of the great gate to jump.

"Again!"

The ram boomed over and over, thundering like the creaking death knell of impending doom. The door endured the assault, groaning at each blow, but the stalwart defender could not hold forever. A loud crack heralded the inevitable as a split ripped down the center of the door.

"Finish it!"

Rallying a final display of strength with a valiant cry, the tired besiegers drove the ram into the weak point. The planks finally gave way in a shower of dust and splinters, and the door crashed inwards. A short-lived cheer came from the onlookers.

"Fire!"

A volley of bolts departed from the crossbows of the kneeling and standing Night troops lined up inside. Fourteen quarrels ripped through the air. Most found a mark.

The brave men at the front of the ram never stood a chance. Others behind them yelled out in pain, falling and gripping their wounds.

"Don't let them reload!" shouted Vector.

The unscathed survivors by the door recovered from the shock first. Invigorated by avenging wrath, they stepped over their fallen allies and the door's debris and engaged the enemy lines. Others of Vector's men, friends and brothers, hurried into the fray to lend their aid. Their swords' thirst for retribution was slaked by the blood of the Night.

Vector and Prince Falcon followed them in, but the skirmish was short-lived, and there was no more to be done. Passing by two men with superficial wounds, Vector quietly tasked them with finding a medic for the injured and taking the bodies of the fallen outside. Once he had given orders, he joined the prince in front where the corridor split.

"You and your men go right. I'll take left. We'll meet outside the throne room and confront the Baron together," said Falcon. He turned and led his team left down the hall, and Vector signaled for his own to follow him to the right.

The way forward was straight, no doors or branching paths until they rounded the corner. At the end of the next hallway stood a purple door. "Be vigilant, now," Vector said to the men around him as he took the lead.

Readying his sword, he stepped up to the door. With a mighty kick, he sent it crashing against the wall and stormed inside, ready for a fight.

To his surprise, there wasn't one. No trap sprung, no scrambling defenders—just another purple door in a narrow hall, five feet ahead.

He checked behind him to make sure his men were with him. They were, dependable as ever. He psyched himself up, then kicked in the next door.

It slammed open to reveal another identical purple door, five feet ahead of the last.

"What devilry is this," Vector grumbled.

"Want me to kick one?" offered Rosco.

"I'm fine," Vector said, though he already felt it in his knee. He moved to the next door, growing increasingly irritated. Throwing his shoulder against it, he stumbled into a wide room with a grand staircase rising in the center.

This time, they were waiting for him.

A small Night platoon had taken up position on the staircase, crossbows aimed and loaded.

"Cover!" shouted Vector, diving behind one of the pillars to the side of the landing.

The Night officer had his arbalists fire in thirds—first the bottom rank, scoring hits past the vanguard's shields; then the middle, exploiting the disarray as the Eternai tripped over bodies at the door; finally, the top, trading shots with the crossbowmen pushing in to oppose them.

Vector yelled orders to his men, but the din of battle and screams of the dying drowned out his instructions. Some had made it to the pillar on the far end of the carpet; others crouched behind their shields, advancing slowly in pairs. The surviving crossbowmen retreated to reload outside in the hall, gumming up the works and blocking the way of others trying to stream in.

The enemy shieldmen protected their arbalists while they reloaded, fending off the brave Eternai who dared cross the killing floor. A practiced team, each third took fewer than twenty seconds to ready their crossbows and fire another volley, cycling so that there were mere seconds between hails of bolts.

Vector despaired at the bloody toll the ambush had taken on his men. The dead and the dying were many. As he looked back, he saw a black bolt pierce the side of Olliver—his nephew, only just sixteen. Despair twisted into a reckless vengeance, and he could bear it no longer.

Raising a defiant roar, he stepped out from the pillar, raised his shield, and charged. The defenders at the foot of the stairs could not withstand him—he slammed his shield into the nearest, bowling him over. Vector did not stop or slow but raced up the steps to cut down the closest arbalists.

His boldness took them by surprise. Too slow did they abandon their crossbows to reach for their knives. With the fury of a tempest, he slashed and stabbed and threw them down. Those above could not shoot without fear of hitting their own, and below, Rosco gave the surviving shieldman no quarter. Others joined in claiming the steps, running down those who turned to flee.

By the time he reached the top of the stairs, Night blood drenched his sword and raiment. Half or more of their number had died by his hand. He added another to his count upon the upper landing. There, defiant before him, stood one last challenger.

Another purple door.

He swore at the infernal mockery but wasn't ready to confront it. Instead, he summoned Rosco to his side. "How many did we lose?"

"Nine." A curt reply. Though Rosco was among his most trusted men, even a friend in many respects, the death of their brothers in arms pressed on old pains between them. That Vector, stout and intrepid warrior, should be promoted to lead these men instead of he, a careful and strategic mind. The words they'd exchanged that afternoon were unpleasant ones, but, evidently, Rosco did not feel this was the time to rehash that issue. For that at least, Vector was grateful.

"Injuries?"

"Kim, Jake, and Nicholas… Sir."

Vector sighed deeply. The words Rosco chose not to say weighed heavily upon his shoulders. He turned to address the survivors. "Rosco will see the wounded out safely to the medics. Everyone else, with me."

"What?" Rosco demanded. "Why me? The way out is clear and two can walk. Let them go—or let it be another."

"That's an order," Vector gave him a warning look. Though his mask was one of anger, he truly couldn't bear the death of another close friend that hour. The rest of these men were comrades and his duty to lead well, but he did not know them. These were strangers whose lives were given to him, being a stranger himself, only in the past month. The rest he'd known, even his brother's son, lay in the grave that was this city. Gem of the North, and a priceless one at that. Had this battle ended the day, he might have wept instead; but still more lay ahead, and this burden was his duty to bear, however heavy.

Rosco's face twisted. For a moment, Vector thought he'd let it all out. Perhaps strike him. Instead, he saluted and hissed through clenched teeth: "Sir."

"I can still fight," Nicholas protested, clutching his bleeding arm at the bottom of the stairs.

"Go!" Vector commanded him.

Vector turned his back to them, positioning himself in front of the purple door. The survivors joined him on the upper landing. One vainglorious lad—an excellent duelist but a known hothead—stepped up, silently volunteering himself to be first through the breach.

"Hold," Vector whispered, restraining him. He slung his sword over his back, then scavenged one of the Night's crossbows. After reloading, he turned to the accursed purple door. "Let's see how they like it."

He channeled all his rage and grief into his foot as he kicked in the door. Stepping through, he scanned for a target but found none. He cautiously lowered his weapon.

"What is that?" the duelist—Werner or Warner was the boy's name—asked from beside him.

Vector followed his gaze to the end of the hall. On an oddly shaped table resembling a birdbath rested an orange phial. As he drew closer, he noticed the liquid shifting inside the glass like unsettled sediment in a storm-battered lake. It had a faint glow, if not a trick of the light, reflecting softly off the surface of the table.

Taking note of the imposing doors on either side of the curious table, he cautiously lifted his crossbow. His hand rested on the trigger, ready to shoot the first thing to move in front of him. The others fanned out behind him, their own crossbows and swords at the ready.

Reaching the table, Vector stared at the phial as if it might explain itself. No answer came from the mysterious liquid, which danced in delight of his ignorance.

A low growl came from the other end of the hallway, reverberating off the stone and blackening the air with terror.

Stalking out from around the corner, an eerie beast of shadow and dark flame fixed its gaze on Vector. He fired a shot, but the creature shifted its shoulders and ducked. The bolt skittered across the floor behind it, clattering to a stop against the wall. The creature—a Nocturne, he'd heard them called—bared its fearsome fangs.

Following behind it, a human came into view. The rest of Vector's team responded, firing their crossbows at the pair. None hit. Vector watched the last bolt sail through the man's chest. Disbelieving his eyes, he focused on the enemy and realized the figure was incorporeal—a ghastly projection, pale like a plague-stricken corpse.

With a shock, Vector recognized the image; he was one of Reynald's trainees.

Nidle.

The projection spoke in a wispy, think voice. "The hour turns late! Night is upon us, Vector."

"That's a Shade!" an older soldier identified, as much in awe as in fear.

*A Shade. That's right.*

As he recalled, some Night had the ability to conjure ghostly images of themselves nearby and even speak through them. An unnatural ventriloquism and another reminder that these monsters were no regular men. Legend had a lot to say about these Shadecasters, but seeing this example firsthand filled him with nothing but disdain. Their kind was a blight on the world.

"Oh, and this was a trap, by the way—just in case you were too stupid to figure that out."

The Shade threw back its head and broke into a high cackle that raised the hairs on Vector's arms. The Nocturne dashed forward in a burst of speed. Vector readied his shield and stepped back, joining his men in a defensive line, but the

Nocturne didn't charge them. Instead, it swiped its great paw against the table, knocking it sideways.

The crystal containing the orange liquid shattered against the floor. Noxious gas permeated the air as the liquid violently bubbled, choking the Eternai and stealing ragged coughs from their lungs.

A fog poured into Vector's mind. His head, heavy, started to spin, throwing him off balance.

The two doors flanking the toppled table burst open and a stream of Night soldiers flooded the hall.

As Vector's cheek hit the cold stone floor, he felt a deep pang of regret. He had led these men to their graves.

*We should have known.*

Nidle made passing eye contact with Jackson as he slunk back to rejoin his group assigned to the far side of the castle. A bitter malice surged through him at the sight of that entitled blockhead. He felt almost beside himself with anger. *I'll show him. I'll show them all.*

He forced himself to take a breath. He couldn't blow it now. *Temper, temper,* his mother would tell him—if she were still alive. He crossed his arms across his chest and stared at his team lead from the back of the pack.

Statol, tall and proud, turned to face his team of ten. Evidently thinking their instructions clear and having no need for further words, he nodded at each of them. Nidle looked away uncomfortable at his eye contact when it was his turn.

Fortunately, he moved on and lifted a hand to signal they were to begin their infiltration.

Moss, a dumb brute with a head like a melon, stood below the open window and folded his hands above his knee, ready to boost the rest of them up. It was a fitting role as he was always lugging around weights for more skilled cooks at the evening meal.

They all climbed in, one at a time. Before long, it was down to Moss, Statol, and Nidle on the back lawn. "In you go," Statol ordered. Nidle obeyed.

Inside the carpeted corridor, two tall men stood with loaded crossbows, waiting for instructions. Mindless drones. The rest carried swords. Nidle had his own pair—at last with sharpened edges. He naturally managed not to draw attention to himself, keeping to the side as they loitered and slipping into the middle of the pack once they began to move.

They paused after a short walk, stopping at the deserted walkway leading across to the great tower.

*Mission accomplished.*

"Nothing?" Statol asked despite the obvious.

Corey tilted his head sideways like a dog. "Nothing," he echoed, just to look like he was contributing.

*Mangy mutt.*

"Doesn't look locked," said a one who smelled like a sweat towel. His name didn't matter.

Statol looked to be in thought. "All right. Four of you scope it out and make sure it's empty, then stay posted at the door until we bring word that the battle's ended. Corey, Moss, Aster, Bill. Everyone else, we're pushing on and quietly tilting the scales in our favor. Send word if there's trouble."

"Heard," said Corey.

*A shame they won't be there,* Nidle thought malevolently as he followed Statol into a room with a tall staircase. At the summit, Statol scanned the walls for danger. Finding nothing, he continued into the hallway beyond. The corridor stretched on for a long while, but they stopped in front of an ornate blue door about midway.

Holding a finger to his lips, the fearless leader quietly cracked open the door for two other men to take the lead. The crossbowmen were light on their feet and would have crept forward almost silently, if not for their clanking metal armor. Nidle followed them in.

The library was two stories, doubly impressive given the limited real estate in the keep. Towering bookshelves doubled as a museum and morgue for thousands of books, scrolls, and tablets. A few near eye-level seemed to have been perused on occasion, but most lay forgotten under a shroud of dust, words and their authors lost to disinterest. Moths were the final audience for those relics of self-importance. A dozen dioramas and pictures decorated the first floor, adding to the desperately imposed sense that any guests should feel a sense of grandeur—and just a hint of envy. The second floor featured a small balcony overlooking the first. The reading nook was a thoughtful design, though presently unoccupied.

Nidle was no more enamored with the library than the others, but he told himself that he had a different reason. They lacked the basic faculty to read, whereas he was smart enough to realize the *intellectual* writings that nobility loved to collect and pretended to love were vain absurdities. Memoirs, philosophy, history, literary essays and their critiques. These soldiers would wipe their backsides with them all—and in this case, they'd be right to do so.

Nidle bit his tongue as two Night walked into view on the balcony, immersed in conversation. The crossbowmen had spotted them and one more, the third flipping through an illustrated children's book on the first floor. The Eternai arbalists took up aim. Nidle coughed, trying to alert the Night soldiers, but they were too slow to react. Theirs were fitting fates for sluggards derelict in their duty.

The arbalists fired up at the balcony. The first hit his mark in the throat—a lucky shot, to be sure. He was dead before he hit the ground. The second pierced the other's arm. Howling in pain with a sound unbecoming of his station, he turned and ran for the adjoining room, calling for help.

Meanwhile, the Night on the first floor dropped his book, clearly surprised that intruders had found their way to the library. Statol sprang forward like a wolf and butchered the reader where he stood. Still, he was too slow to load the crossbow. The man on the balcony had escaped.

A chorus of familiar growls drifted into the library. He had forgotten how few Eternai had seen Nocturnes until he saw the face of the arbalist beside him, terror in his eyes as he imagined what terrible creature was behind those snarls.

Statol handed off the looted crossbow, favoring his sword. "They're sending in Nocturnes. Split into pairs and hunt them down the rows. Look out for each other and don't let them sneak up behind you."

As he broke off with one of the arbalists into the maze of tall shelves, Nidle walked toward a row with a *Young Romance* sign above it. His partner, a slightly older boy named Seth, followed behind.

"Nidle, stop running ahead!" Seth hissed. "You take the crossbow. I've had more sword training."

Nidle sheathed his swords, stepped to the side, and faked a smile as he accepted the crossbow. *We'll see who's giving orders when the Nocturnes find us.* Spite flashed in his eyes, but he looked away to conceal it.

They crept through two rows without any sign of the Nocturnes. The snarls seemed to come from all around them. A short-lived scream rose from the far corner of the room.

He was pleased to imagine their dread.

As they rounded the corner into *Artistic Poetry,* at last the magnificent beast revealed itself. The Nocturne prowled toward them slowly from the end of the row as if thinking itself concealed in the tall grasses of the wilds. Hatred burned in its eyes. He knew the feeling well.

"Shoot it, Nidle," Seth whispered, stock-still, his voice quavering.

Nidle tapped the side of the trigger, faking a firing mechanism jam. "I can't—it won't fire!" he said, putting on a frantic and panicky voice to hide his maniacal excitement.

*Crossbow isn't working, Seth! Big kitty's going to rip you up, Seth!* Nidle grinned in anticipation.

Seth exhaled slowly, inching closer to the Nocturne. The beast mirrored his pace, inching toward him. As soon as it was within fifteen feet, the Nocturne broke into a sprint and pounced, claws outstretched and teeth bared.

Seth flung himself against the shelf to dodge the feral lunge, but the beast's claws tore through his pants just below his chainmail shirt. He cried out in pain as his blood dripped to the carpet, but the Nocturne didn't let him recover.

As soon as it landed, the Nocturne wheeled around to load its powerful legs for another lunge. It launched into the air, sure to land a killing blow.

Reacting in panic, Seth stumbled backward, swinging his sword up as he lost his balance and fell onto his back.

It was foul luck.

The tip of his sword caught the Nocturne at the base of its neck. The force of their landing drove the blade home, the hilt bracing against the carpet like a pike digging in for a cavalry charge. He gasped and coughed as the massive paw bore down on his chest. Despite his pitiful writhing, his armor had spared him any lasting damage.

A true tragedy, the beautiful Nocturne lurched sideways into the shelf, yowling a strained note. It fought to rise, to stand on its feet once more. Then it collapsed, and there it remained, motionless.

Nidle hated them.

Panting hard, Seth turned over onto his hands and knees. "That mongrel didn't seem too interested to chew on your bones, did it?" he commented.

Nidle shrugged. "Maybe it realized my weapon was a dud? That or it liked the look of all that extra meat on you." As Seth frowned at him, he slapped his perfectly good crossbow as if disciplining it for its disobedience.

Seth's face lit up. Excited, he spoke in hurried tones to breathe life into his idea. "We'll cut them off at the source. Come on, I think I know where that injured Night ran off."

Forgetting his injuries, Seth started toward the back stairwell leading up to the second floor. Still, every few steps he would wince or grab his leg in pain. He held it together until the end of the row, where he blundered sideways into a bookshelf. Unfortunately, he recovered.

Nidle patted the dying Nocturne's blood-matted fur. The creature's eyes flashed open in bestial fear. Its chest rose and fell in shallow breaths. Watching Seth round the corner, he drew his knife and put the animal out of its misery.

He caught up to Seth at the top of the stairwell. The boy soldier was crouching outside an ajar door. Motioning him over, Seth pushed open the door and tiptoed through.

Following him in, Nidle spotted a Night across the room. The handler was fumbling with the lock on a cage, his back to the door.

"Stop clawing at me, you dumb cat! I'm trying to get it open for you," the handler attempted to reason with the unpersuaded beast.

Seth silently crept across the room, determined to eliminate him before he could release another Nocturne. As he neared, he lifted his sword, poised to cut the Night down with a decisive stroke.

A sharp yell ripped from his throat, followed by the clatter of his sword falling to the ground. Seth crashed onto his face. Weakly reaching behind him with a trembling hand, his fingers brushed the black shaft protruding from his back. Breathless, tears in his eyes, he turned to look behind him.

Nidle smiled down at him. "Good news—looks like I got it unjammed."

Betrayal and hatred were the last emotions to cross Seth's face before death softened his stare. He had exhaled a final word with his dying breath, but Nidle hadn't heard it. Whatever it was didn't matter.

"Took your time, didn't you, boy? I was starting to think you were going to let him kill me after all," the handler said gruffly, still facing the Nocturne.

"Don't be cruel. You know I wouldn't let him do that to you, Father," Nidle assured him.

He turned to face his son, resting his calloused hands on his hips as he considered his boy. "Yeah, well—you've still got other business to attend to. I suppose you best be getting on with it."

"I suppose I shall," agreed Nidle. He stopped by the table on the way out to grab a few vials. After pocketing four, he released three Nocturnes from their cages and led them down the stairwell Seth had brought him up.

He searched the library for Statol. Row number five turned out to be the winner—*Modern History*. He found the captain hunched over the disfigured body of the tall arbalist. Three Nocturnes lay dead around him. Butchered. At least they hadn't gone without a fight. He leaned to one side with his hands clutching his ribs. As he looked up, blood dripped down from his forehead into his eye. He had done a sloppy job staunching the wound.

"Nidle… help me," Statol begged, shuddering as he drew a breath.

Nidle gave a humorless laugh. "No. You'll die here, but don't worry—the rest will join you soon."

"Fool," Statol wheezed out a cough. "You're Eternai as much as me or anyone else. Don't let them trick you into thinking you're one of them."

"I am Night—I have always been Night. I was never one of you," Nidle spat.

Statol shook his head. "You lived and trained with us for more than a year. Many would call you their brother. The Eternai took you in when you had nowhere else to go. We made you one of us."

"You still don't get it, do you? I lied. My father is alive," Nidle scoffed. "Ever the fool, Statol. A prime example of the pestilence that is the Eternai. I reject you and all that you are. I'll never be you, and I look forward to the day your kind ceases to exist."

"If that's how you feel, then I have no choice. You'll die with me!" Statol drew a knife and threw it awkwardly.

Nidle sidestepped the pathetic attempt. "It's never a pity to see a fool die." One of the Nocturnes began to circle the helpless captain as he slumped to the floor. Nidle turned to leave with the other two Nocturnes at his heels. "Oh, and Statol? A word of advice—don't resist; it only riles them up."

He shut the library doors behind him, pausing just long enough to hear the Eternai commander's screams. He couldn't enjoy it for long. One of the Nocturnes fixed on a scent and sprinted off down the hall. Nidle let it go, figuring it had sniffed out a target. The other sat patiently awaiting instructions.

Composing himself, Nidle cleared his thoughts and stared into the eyes of the Nocturne, cupping its big head as he imprinted his will. "The hour turns late! Night is upon us, Vector." He cackled with delight.

He looked away, ending his message. "One will find all sorts of surprises in the Night, won't one, my pet?" Nidle mused to the Nocturne. The creature bowed its head, then sprinted off toward the barracks.

*The arrogant fools haven't a clue what they're up against,* he thought proudly as he marched to the Baron's throne room.

# ✤ Chapter 12 ✤

J ackson's senses gradually returned. He realized he was
leaning against a wall, his hands loosely bound behind his
back. The rest of Dersul's team were similarly restrained
along the wall—unconscious, but alive. They appeared to be
in a cramped, makeshift cell.

"Sweet dreams, I hope?"

Jackson shifted his gaze to locate the source of the
voice. With a start, he realized their captor was sitting just a
few feet away on a low wooden stool. A black Nocturne lay
on either side of the Night, both watching Jackson in silence.
One yawned, as if debating whether it could squeeze in a nap
before its next meal. Lazily scratching its ear with a paw, the
beast decided to stay awake for now.

"Can't imagine anyone could sleep through all this
excitement. Must be a battle for the ages happening upstairs
right about now. Of course, *battle* wouldn't really be the right
word... *Ambush* is a more suitable term. Yes, an ambush for
the ages," the Night rambled on with a crooked smile.

As their jailor entertained himself, Jackson noticed their weapons were lying out on the table to his right. Three steps away—if he could get that far. He liked his odds against the distracted soldier, but the two Nocturnes hadn't once taken their eyes off him.

He tested the knot around his wrists as subtly as he could. His bindings loosened with each jerk, half an inch at a time. Keeping his elbows tight against his body, he managed to wriggle a hand free. Before he slipped the other out, he paused and took careful stock of the situation, planning his every move. He'd only get one chance.

The rest of his squad was still unconscious. No help there; he'd have to take on the soldier and both beasts alone. The odds weren't in his favor, but they also weren't likely to improve. At least for the moment, the Night seemed wholly distracted, lamenting his inability to get a promotion.

*Push off: right foot. Step left, right, left again. Grab sword, turn. Lunge at closest enemy.* He took a deep breath, preparing for the dash and clash.

He slipped his bindings and leaped into action.

Springing to his feet, he dashed to snatch his sword from the table before his adversaries could challenge him.

"Attack!" ordered the soldier.

Jackson spun and faced the approaching Nocturne. He debated reaching for his shield, but as the beast loaded back on its legs, he knew it would take too long to put on.

The Nocturne pounced, snarling. Stepping forward to meet it, Jackson drove his sword with both hands into the beast's mouth. The force of the lunge knocked him against the table, but the thrust had done its job. He leaned back and yanked his sword free, expecting the second Nocturne to be upon him.

The Nocturne hadn't stirred. Resting at its master's feet, it raised an eyelid at the commotion, scratched its ear, and yawned sleepily.

"Get him, you useless animal!" the soldier spurred the beast in the ribs with the toe of his boot.

Seeming to roll its eyes, the pestered Nocturne got up, walked a few paces toward the door, and lay down again with an exaggerated sigh.

The Night let out a frustrated groan. "Fine. I'll do it myself. No dinner for you, cat," he said as he drew his sword. The Nocturne raised its ears at the word *dinner* but otherwise looked unperturbed.

Brandishing a gleaming sword, the soldier bared his teeth in a malevolent smile as he crept closer. "This will only hurt a lot."

As he double-stepped to take a swing, Jackson tried to beat him with a lunge. The Night danced back to avoid the tip of his sword and beat it aside to forestall any follow-up. His smile was gone now, replaced by an uneasy look of surprise that this boy had dared attack him.

Sensing the change in dynamics, Jackson seized the advantage, pressing his offense with a flurry of strikes. The frustration on the Night's face turned to fear as he struggled to defend against the unyielding assault. Finally, as the soldier backed up into the stool and almost tripped over it, Jackson saw his opportunity. He delivered an arcing strike down at the man's head.

Barely deflecting the blow with his sword, the Night crouched and threw a desperate roundhouse kick at Jackson's knee. It connected hard, sweeping his leg out sideways and sending him crashing to the floor. Jackson tried to scramble to his feet, but his enemy had gained the advantage. Jumping on top of him, The Night pinned him down and pressed his sword against his neck.

"Help!" Jackson cried to anyone who might hear.

Laughing, the Night tapped the flat side of his blade against Jackson's forehead. "Pitiable fool. Who do you think will save you? Your friends—tied up and asleep? No one's coming to help you."

Realizing these panicked gasps were to be his final breaths, Jackson's eyes went wide with fear. *This can't be the end... Not like this. I'm not ready.*

"You don't know anything worthwhile. Too young. A foot soldier," said the Night. "I'll get my answers out of someone else."

The soldier lifted his sword to deliver the fatal blow.

Suddenly, a black blur shot across Jacksons' eyes and the soldier's weight vanished from his chest. Taking the unexpected reprieve, Jackson rolled away and found his footing.

The lethargic Nocturne had come alive and was now bearing down on the soldier. The Night tried to grapple with the traitorous beast but couldn't free himself from under its weight. Before long, the Nocturne found an opening in the soldier's frantic defense. Jackson looked away squeamishly as its fangs tore into the Night's throat, ending his life.

Teeth dripping with crimson, the Nocturne prowled over to Jackson. Fear gripped his chest. He slowly scooted backward, his sword hand stilled by the fear the fresh carnage had awakened.

The Nocturne made a sound that made him pause— more of a purr than a growl. He stayed still as the cat walked over and affectionately nuzzled his hand.

Staring in surprise at his furry new companion, he cautiously scratched the Nocturne behind the ear. "Hi there.

You're not so scary, huh? Want to be friends? I'm Jackson. What's your name?"

Unsurprisingly, the beast didn't answer.

Jackson considered the big cat. "How about we call you Leon. Do you like that name?"

The Nocturne purred in agreement. Giving Jackson's hand one final lick—an appreciated gesture despite its tongue being as rough as sandpaper—the creature turned to face the door. A warning growl rose from its throat, forcing Jackson back to his senses.

"Right. Time to play later—the others need us. Now, how are we going to get them awake?" Jackson asked the cat.

Leon walked over to the nearest prisoner and bit the rope bindings. Violently shaking his head, he managed to rip loose the knot. He paused and looked expectantly at Jackson.

"Oh. I suppose I could use this," he said, hefting his sword. He got to work and freed the rest, one by one.

As he worked, the Nocturne walked over to an oak cabinet in the corner. When Jackson looked up, Leon got on his hind legs and scratched the door. Taking the hint, Jackson looked inside the cabinet and found a multicolored collection of crystal vials. They looked sorted, but the cryptic labels did little to explain their purpose. The Nocturne sniffed at a cluster of vials filled with blue liquid on the bottom shelf. The label said *Release*, but there were no further instructions.

Jackson picked up a vial, handling it gingerly. Using mysterious liquids his pet had sniffed on unconscious allies probably wasn't the wisest thing to do, but he was short on time. He decided to trust in his insistent companion.

Uncorking a vial, he worked his way down the line, administering a drop onto the lips of each sleeping comrade. Within seconds, each began to stir. The first to come to his

senses was Dersul, who started in fright at the sight of the Nocturne. In turn, Leon gave him a wet lick.

"It's all right, Dersul! That's Leon. He's a good boy," Jackson said with unfounded confidence. He had met the animal just minutes ago—and had seen it maul its previous handler to death—yet somehow he felt he could trust the big cat. He abandoned his initial perception that Nocturnes were mere killing machines—useful tools used by Night soldiers. This one, at least, was different. He couldn't explain it, but he was sure Leon understood him. Strangely, he trusted the cat's personal loyalty more than that of his entire strike team.

Dersul didn't seem convinced, but as he got up, he mumbled, "If you say so."

The captain retrieved his equipment from the table, and Jackson walked over to grab his shield. As he did, Dersul asked about the cabinet full of vials.

"Not sure," Jackson said. "I used one marked *Release* to wake you up. No idea what the others do."

Grunting, Dersul pocketed a *Release* vial. "Right, so where are we now?"

As soon as they finished reequipping, the Nocturne barked to get their attention, then walked out of the room. Jackson was the first to follow. Exchanging uneasy looks, the others reluctantly joined him, allowing the cat to guide them through a winding labyrinth of corridors. At last, they found themselves back in the kitchens.

"Glad to put that detour behind us. Hard to say how much time we've lost, but we should try to find the others," said Dersul.

As he made his way toward the stairwell at the back of the kitchen, Leon darted past him, slowing once he had taken the lead. The Nocturne seemed intent on guiding them and, surprisingly, they were willing to follow.

At the top of the stairs, Jackson heard a sharp crash of shattering crystal. Leon heard it too and set off in a loping, silent run toward the sound.

As he raced down the hallway behind the Nocturne, Jackson heard soldiers running up ahead. At the end of the hall, just before it turned, they stopped and pressed against the wall. Leaning around the corner, they stole a glance into the corridor beyond.

Night soldiers were moving Eternai bodies. Jackson thought them all dead at first but realized it wasn't entirely so. The pierced and bloodied were taken through the left door. The bodies dragged through the right looked unharmed but unconscious—likely the same alchemic trickery that subdued Dersul's team. Borne by two men, Captain Vector's immense frame was among the living.

"They slayed his unit," Dersul despaired, shrinking back around the corner.

"But he's still alive," Jackson reported.

Dersul looked at Jackson gravely, as if he had just been ordered into a hopeless battle. "Then we'll do all we can to rescue him."

"Any idea where they're taking them?" asked the man on Jackson's left.

"One way to find out," Dersul said with a grim face. He rounded the corner into the deserted corridor and led on.

The narrow stairwell through the door to the right led up to an inornate black door. Leon drifted to the back of the pack, allowing Dersul to be their guide into battle. The captain counted his men, then turned and breached the door.

Inside, the prisoners were few, and the captors were many. Vector was deposited in a heap in the middle of the room. Smug and all too comfortable delegating directions, the betrayer stood over him.

Nidle.

Rage frothed in Jackson's heart at seeing the traitor. Such betrayal of one's kin filled him with a righteous anger. Giving rein to his wrath, he ripped the crossbow out of the hands of the soldier beside him, aimed, and let the bolt fly.

Vector felt the tendrils of sleep toying with his mind, but he refused to yield to them. Fighting to stay conscious, he managed to resist the sudden onset of torpor, but it had already seeped into the rest of his body. He could not turn his head, but he saw his comrades. Most had fallen asleep. A few others twitched, desperately struggling against their bodies to defend themselves.

The Night soldiers were clinical in dispatching them. Only a handful—those deemed important—were temporarily spared. Like a sack of tubers, he was hoisted into the air and hauled roughly through the door. He felt the stairs strike his back time and again as he was carried up, but he was numb to the pain. Far worse was the shame of having failed his men. His family. His kingdom. *Haste makes waste*, his father had always told him. In his hurry, he had led his men into a devastating trap that could cost the Eternai everything they had fought for.

Fatigue piled on to his woeful state, tempting his mind to succumb to nothingness. His deep guilt was all that kept him awake. It was his duty to suffer knowingly until the end. He was unsure what awaited him after—eternity, if the stories were true, but of what kind? For all the blood on his hands, he deserved an endless age to reflect on his ill choices and failures. This final, fatal error that cost the lives of those who trusted him was one of many.

They threw him to the floor. His existential brooding fled before the brutal immediacy of his worldly fate. Looking down on him with a satisfied smirk was the wolf in sheep's clothing—Nidle.

"Nice of you to drop in, Vector," Nidle laughed as the other survivors were dumped on the floor.

"Get on with it, dog," Vector spat. He refused to play their games. He wanted it to end as quickly as possible—before his grief consumed him.

"Aw. I'd hoped you'd be in a more sporting mood. Fine—I will get on with it. You'll be the first to die, coward that you are. The rest you brought here will also perish, don't you worry, but I'll be taking my time with them."

The traitor lifted his sword. Vector didn't blink.

"I'm going to enjoy this," Nidle sneered.

Shrieking as an arrow pierced his right side, Nidle reeled backward and fell to the ground. He writhed in pain, staring at the protruding black shaft in shock. Screaming, he gripped the bolt lodged between his ribs and yanked it free. Blood spurted as the stop came loose. He hastily covered it with his shirt.

Vector wished he could have finished the job.

Nidle's vision blurred between the pain and the tears in his eyes. He shouted frantically to the Night in the room, ordering them to execute the Eternai prisoners. Few listened to him; they were swarming to engage the enemies who had followed them into the chamber. A clever trap. He hadn't seen any sign of a second squad hiding in wait.

Screaming as he peeled himself off the floor, Nidle found his feet and fled to the hidden stairwell in the corner of the room, away from the fighting. Leaning on his sword as a crutch, he struggled up the steep steps with a painful limp. A trail of blood painted his wake.

At the top, he fell against the door, staggering into the throne room. The Baron stood and called an attendant to aid him.

"Nidle! What happened?"

"Eternai rats are swarming us! One of those dirty vermin shot me. Either they held a team back in reserve, or Mihir screwed up and let them crawl in through the sewers," said Nidle. The words took tremendous effort to voice.

An aide hastened over to clean and stitch his wound. Nidle bit into his shirt to deal with the pain, but he breathed a sigh of relief once blood stopped oozing from his sides. It still hurt, but he wouldn't let that show in front of the Baron.

"Ryland, bring me my shield," said the Baron.

Dread sunk into Nidle's heart. "Sir Baron—we need to leave right now! We don't have the people to stay and fight, and the prince broke through. He and their extra men will be here any minute, and we weren't able to find out their positions in the city."

The Baron thought carefully before answering. "No, Nidle. You must leave now. Do not argue! They will have guarded the exits and will not relent until they have my life. We cannot go. The others will stand here with me, but you will not. You must make your way into the moat and out to the river. It is night—stay still and float; they won't see you."

"No! I can't abandon you and Father. I won't!"

"You will do as you're told, Nidle!"

"But Uncle…"

"Cease! Say no more. Someone must bring news to Orsadia and Verden. It must be you, Nidle. If we fail to warn them, they will surely suffer the same fate. Go, nephew. Time is not on our side tonight," said the Baron, ushering Nidle toward the trap door.

Nidle fought back tears as his uncle pulled him into a hug—too brief—and said goodbye. "Make us proud, boy," he whispered. He squeezed Nidle's shoulder, then sent him down into the hatch.

Nidle raced down the dim and spiraling stairs, wiping away the tears that blurred his vision. His feet carried him away from the only family he had left, abandoning his father and uncle to near certain death. *I don't have a choice,* he told himself sternly, fortifying his will to go on.

He snuck through the side door, out into the night air. The enemy had patrols everywhere, but he'd always had a knack for avoiding attention. Slipping through the shadows, he climbed onto the outer wall and, without pause, leaped into the frigid water.

No one noticed as he splashed in, feet first.

Gasping for breath against the icy touch of the filthy water, Nidle flattened his back and floated down the slow current. The night concealed him as he passed by the bridge and into the pipes that carried the city's filth out to the river.

He heard voices in the streets above. Laughing. He hardened his heart and swore to himself.

*I will make my family proud.*

# ✤ Chapter 13 ✤

When Jackson took his shot, he threw the chamber into chaos. The Night frantically searched the prisoners for weapons, then, shouting over one another, realized the enemy was rushing in from the stairwell.

The skirmish was over within a minute, thanks to the confusion and disarray. Dersul's men got the jump on the first few from behind, helping even the odds. Overestimating the size of the attacking force, half of the platoon fled after Nidle through a concealed stairwell at the back. While others battled, Jackson focused on freeing captives, administering *Release* to each. The first to wake rearmed themselves from fallen Night and joined the short-lived fight.

Thirteen casualties total. Both sides contributed.

Only three Night surrendered—two involuntarily on account of their injuries. The Eternai soldiers dragged them to their knees on the spot Vector had occupied minutes ago. A few of those who had been incapacitated moved toward the Nocturne eyeing them from the back wall, intending it harm. Jackson interceded, barring their path and advocating for the cat's good nature. Remembering his face as the one who restored them to life, they relented, albeit uneasily.

Vector stood in the center of the room and took command of the remnants of their two teams. "This is it—our second and last chance. This day has little left to ask of you all, but it asks at least one more fight. Captain Dersul, on behalf of me and the men you saved, thank you. We'll take the lead and finish what we started—we owe that to your team. Grake, find the opening the Night slipped through," he directed a man with bloodshot eyes to the back wall.

The Eternai were haggard—some, haunted by the day—and grew anxious as they waited. Jackson shared their exhaustion. Fighting for survival, he'd had no time to unpack what had taken place, but he could not think about rest. Not until they were done. They all waited for Vector's orders.

The captain sensed his burden to lead and accepted it dutifully. "I don't know what's happened to the prince and his team. They may already be ahead of us, or they may never appear. Either way, he would want us to carry our banner and reclaim Kanrio."

On edge as they were, many lifted shouts of approval and demands for battle. Grake found the false wall, and some began shuffling toward the hidden stairwell, determined not to be tasked to stay behind and guard their prisoners.

Jackson heard a faint clang—metal against metal—somewhere in the distance. At first he thought it was residual ringing in his ear, but as it repeated and multiplied, he turned to face the stairwell.

Vector tasked two to watch over the prisoners, then raised a fist and shouted, "For the Eternai!"

The soldiers echoed his cry and poured into the hole in the wall. Jackson filed in at the end of the line with Leon at his heels. They flew up the stairs at dizzying speed, fueled by adrenaline for the final battle. Jackson held his sword tightly but quietly hoped he wouldn't need it. Despite death raging around him, he had fought but not yet killed. The thought comforted him, though he knew everything could change in a heartbeat—he also hadn't died, and that felt more fortunate with each passing hour. He had Leon to thank for surviving the closest call. He didn't know what the battle would bring, but his stomach churned with nausea at the possibilities.

Stumbling into the Baron's throne room, he stopped his brooding and called back his wits. He had stepped into the heart of madness. Shouting and ringing blades conspired in a horrible din. Violence engulfed the room. Crossbows unloaded, and bodies fell with bloodcurdling screams. Rage played out an eerie, almost dreamlike melody.

He had entered a warzone.

It was impossible to tell who was winning—if that term could be used at all. Casualties from both sides were mounting. Everywhere he looked, people were fighting for their lives. The grandeur of their shared causes paled before their personal struggles against death. Friend and foe alike looked human in their fear and striving and wrath—and all the more in their dying gasps and frail mortality.

One of eight Nocturnes finished savaging an Eternai and turned, fangs dripping with blood. Fixing its wild eyes on Jackson, it lunged from a running start. Leon didn't hesitate to meet his twisted kin in the air. The Nocturnes crashed to the floor, rolling and flipping in a tangle of teeth and claws.

Jackson stalled, wanting to help but finding no opening to strike. His eyes drifted past the bestial fray, distracted by the gleaming armor of a solitary Night beyond them.

With no one left to oppose him but a circle of corpses who had evidently tried, the grizzled soldier surveyed the battle with an unflinching stare. Standing by the window, moonlight glinting off his polished armor, he looked like a final-boss supervillain ripped out of a comic book. Encased in a crimson and gold breastplate, silver vambraces, and an ebony helmet, he was half moving fortress, half scaly dragon, and all but impenetrable. Caped, of course, he wore a dark blue cloak with golden trim. Judging by the rip, tears, and patches sewn over them, the cloak had seen more than its share of battle. One hand wielded a colossal sword; the other wore a red glove, each finger tipped with clawlike gold.

Meeting Jackson's eye, the Night shed his cold stare and smiled warmly, as if seeing an old friend. He pointed his broadsword, issuing a challenge. For a long moment, Jackson could only stare, transfixed by the indecipherable scrawl of silver symbols that glowing down the face of the blade. The symbols slowly faded back into the metal, leaving only the sword's sharp edges and devastating point.

It was a bad idea. It could only be a bad idea.

Feeling a rush of energy, Jackson scanned the room, working out a path to meet his challenger. On some level, he realized he was probably choosing the worst possible match-up—but at least this way, he'd feel a little more in control of his fate. With the unpredictable fighting between Nocturnes and men all around him, and unseen arrows flying through the air, standing still felt like giving up and waiting for death to find him. Impulsively, he darted straight for his opponent through the heart of the chaos.

Mindful to avoid the clashing blades and falling bodies, he reached the pocket of space won by his challenger and slowed to a walk. Smiling, the man bowed his head in respect for his acceptance of the duel. The Night held out his sword once more. The long blade stretched over half the distance between them. Jackson mirrored his pose.

After their swords touched, his foe leaped backward and dropped into a low crouch. Jackson stepped after him to close the gap, intending to try a probing strike.

The Night sprang his trap.

Whirling like a top, the man brought his sword down in an impossibly fast arc aimed at his head. Jackson raised his shield to block, but the astonishing force of the one-handed blow sent him staggering. As he stumbled back, off-balance, the Night followed up with a dive, rolling into another strike. At the last second before he would have cleaved Jackson in two at the hip, he disengaged, narrowly dodging a stray arrow shot from across the room.

The Night settled back into a crouch. Not only did he have uncanny speed and power, but he was evidently too patient and composed to rush his duel.

Still feeling the aftershocks of the blow buzzing through his shield arm, Jackson eyed his opponent and felt his stomach drop. He was fully, hopelessly outmatched. Panic began to creep in. Why had he thought he'd stand a chance? Here he was, not even three days of bootcamp under his belt, fighting against a swordsman who had lived a life of battle.

He wasn't left to his dismal thoughts for long.

The Night exploded forward. Getting out of his own head, Jackson relied on instinct and sidestepped to narrowly dodge the lunge. Moving his arm before his eyes saw it, he surprised himself by parrying the lighting-fast backhand that followed. Disengaging and dropping back into his crouch, the man smiled with the same troubling, warm approval he'd started the fight with.

*I can't win by defense alone,* Jackson thought, trying to build up his nerve. With a hoarse yell, he shot forward and lunged with everything he had.

The Night lazily parried his thrust aside using his gloved hand, then countered with a high stroke. Jackson was lucky to deflect it with his shield, since he was solely focused on executing a follow-up cut at his ribs.

The resonant ring of metal sang as the man brought his sword down at the last second, halting the blow inches from his body. Emboldened by near success, Jackson kept up his aggression in even measure, answering each strike with a counter. For a minute, they might have appeared almost evenly matched, probing, attacking, parrying.

Jackson's luck ran out. He backed up onto the stray blade of a fallen soldier, slick with blood from another duel. His foot slipped, and in an instant, he was flat on his back. His sword came loose from his hand as he fell. Scrambling, he searched for it on the floor around him. His face fell as he looked up.

His sword was in his opponent's clawed hand.

"Standard issue. Ah, well. We all start somewhere," the Night commented to himself. Seeing the mortal fear on Jackson's face, he laughed sportingly. "Up on your feet, lad. We're not done yet."

Cautiously, Jackson picked himself up off the floor, keeping his shield half-raised all the while. Once he was up, the man tossed his sword back to him, hilt-first. Jackson caught it and gave the man a quizzical look.

"There may be much worth living for and little worth dying for, but death is not my master. I would rather lose than win dishonorably," he explained in an avuncular tone as if teaching his son valuable life lessons. The reprieve was only fleeting. He resumed his crouch. "Prepare yourself! En garde!"

Jackson launched into the fray, unleashing a barrage of devastating blows from every angle. Surprising himself, he executed each strike with new purpose and power. The Night looked equally surprised, and though he managed to defend each incoming attack, he found no opportunity to reply with his own. The longer Jackson continued his relentless assault, the more apparent it became that the man's defense was weakening.

Fear gave way to unassailable courage, founded upon undeserved confidence. Noticing his flagging opponent's slowing counters and glimpsing the gray locks of hair under his helmet, Jackson boldly set up a hopeful gambit. Feigning a backhanded stroke, he drew back his sword to avoid the Night's parry and struck like a viper—an efficient slice down through the gap between his pauldron and helmet. His blade bit into the man's neck, drawing an agonized yell from the hardened warrior.

The Night reeled backward, holding his gloved hand to his wound. When he lifted it, he and Jackson both stared at the crimson spot staining the metal. He clenched his teeth, and something that looked like surprise crossed his eyes.

Surprise must have been on Jackson's face, too.

"We're not finished yet, boy. To the death!"

The Night came in fast with a two-handed swing. In one fluid motion, Jackson stepped forward, ducked under the attack, and drove his sword through the chinks in the man's breastplate, hitting flesh. He pulled his sword free, stepping back as the Night dropped to his knees.

The blood from his neck ran down the front of his armor, joining the stream from his midsection. Despite his grave wounds and a voice heavy from years of command, his words come out untroubled. He spoke lightly, as if he were a coach giving praise at the end of practice. "Well done, lad. You showed remarkable promise for one so young."

The man doffed his helmet, freeing his graying black hair, which was longer than Jackson would've guessed and damp with sweat. His dark green eyes looked tired, and his gray face appeared weary in the dim torchlight. Choking out a cough, he held his black helmet out toward Jackson. "You have bested the Baron. This belongs to you."

Jackson felt stunned and unequipped to comprehend the moment. He had just killed a man. This priceless life, lost because of him. More, he was the Baron of Night—enemy of the Eternai. Did this make him a hero or a monster? Who was fit to judge? That the Baron was now offering his helmet in congratulations was all too much.

Numbly, he accepted the heavy burden in his hands. The battle still raged around them, but he felt disconnected from it like a movie playing on mute in the background. He could not tear his eyes away from the Baron. Strangely, he wanted to know him.

The Baron thought of something and laughed, but it turned into a ragged cough. As the light faded from his eyes, he forced a smile, whispering: "You must really be her son."

Then the Baron sank to the floor, adding one more lifeless body to the collection of death and gore that defiled his throne room.

His final words struck a chord in Jackson. Shaking the Baron's shoulders, he demanded: "What? Whose son? What did you mean? Tell me!"

But the dead man offered no reply.

Breathing a sigh of frustration, he turned the black helmet over in his hands. Heavy was the crown. The dense, hard metal added to its weight. Its shape and detail should have been impressive, and they in part were, but the symbol felt cold and foreign. The Baron surely had not intended for him to rule in his stead, had he?

No, this was not his crown to take.

Leaving that burden behind for a greater man elected by destiny, he rested the black helmet on the Baron's chest. As he stood, he looked around the room and realized a victor had been decided. Soldiers from both sides lay motionless on the floor, but a majority of those still standing belonged to the faction Jackson had lived among for the past few days. As the last Night fell, ending the bloody battle just short of midnight, Jackson thought of his friends. His eyes darted around the room, searching for a familiar face.

Relief washed over him as he spotted Canon hugging Krystal off to the side. They both looked exhausted but also understandably happy to be alive.

Closer, Falcon was staring out the window. He raised a hand to signal Vector over, then said, "Sound the bells and gather everyone in the courtyard—we've taken back Kanrio." It was a joyous statement, but he sounded exhausted. He left the throne room without stopping to talk to others.

Vector seemed just as tired. Instead of yelling for their attention, he walked from huddle to huddle among the survivors to pass along the message. One by one, they slowly drifted toward the exit.

Standing on his own, Jackson became acutely aware of the fact he didn't have a huddle to join and commiserate with. As he headed for the door, he was interrupted by a black blur that rose to place its paws on his chest.

"Leon!" he beamed, happily scratching the Nocturne behind its ears. He was the only one among his kind to have survived—a miracle given that both sides could have counted him as their enemy. Yawning, the big cat returned to all fours and waited expectantly for him to lead.

*I really should get him a tag so he doesn't get mistaken for an enemy.* Jackson made a mental note as he led his new companion through the exit.

Within half an hour, the survivors assembled in the same courtyard where they had divided into teams before breaching the castle. Many had stood in the sunlight; few had returned to the moonlight. Each absence was sorely felt by someone, though Jackson hadn't known many of them and could only marvel at the empty space in the crowd.

Vector laid a crate at the prince's feet. Falcon eyed the box wearily, then stepped on to address them. There was no need to call for their attention; no one else was speaking.

"We've all lost friends tonight. Too many. I lost one of my commanders and a lifelong friend. The best I can tell you is that he did not die in vain. None of them did. Those who died did so willingly. They sacrificed everything so that we could be here. So we could take our land back from the Night and free the citizens of Kanrio. We fought for them, and they will fight with us for our kingdom's future. In this, though we have suffered, we've also gained much. Tonight, we mourn those we have lost, but let us take more comfort in the friends and family still among us. We all survived to see another day."

"Tomorrow, we'll rest and recover here. Eat, sleep, be merry if you're able. We'll enjoy a week of peace before we carry on this war we must fight. The caravans will have arrived by morning, and as long as you meet in this courtyard after dinner, you may do as you please during the day. Well done, brave heroes—you fought well!" Falcon concluded. He waited out their polite applause before walking off to speak with Vector alone.

Jackson strolled over to the side of the castle. The night was pleasantly warm, and he'd get no rest tonight inside the walls of the blood-soaked keep. Finding a place in the grass, he lay and stared up at the sky. Occasionally, he'd catch a break in the clouds and glimpse the starry night beyond.

He mulled over the Baron's words. *Had the Baron mistaken him for another boy? And who was 'she'?* Questions swirled around his head, but he came no closer to answers.

Jackson smiled as Leon curled up by his side. Fatigue replaced curiosity, and by the time the cat began to snore, his eyelids had become heavy. Breathing in the fresh night air, he shut out his thoughts and worries and drifted off to sleep.

# ✢ Chapter 14 ✢

The next few days blurred together, rest and recovery filling the uneventful hours. Vector was appointed Lord of Kanrio, and after the castle was thoroughly cleaned, he moved into the Baron's residence. With no formal assignments for lodging, the rest of the Eternai army made their own arrangements—some rented rooms at the inns, others slept on cots in the castle barracks, and many claimed a few square feet in parks or side streets to spread out bedrolls or lie in the grass.

It had been days since Jackson last saw anyone he knew. Canon and Krystal had seemingly vanished, not even making appearances at the evening muster. Falcon, as one might expect from a prince, was much too busy repairing the city and planning logistics for the next campaign to dawdle and chat. He hadn't seen Tyson or Rein since the battle, and he was afraid to ask.

Surprisingly, Jackson enjoyed the slow days: rest and privacy. Leon proved a faithful companion. Together, they roamed the city, sat by the water, and perused the market—

up until they were ejected following an incident involving a disappearing crate of fish. They couldn't prove it was Leon who had wolfishly devoured the fishmonger's merchandise, but the circumstantial evidence was incriminating.

That incident aside, those quiet pursuits brought him some of the most serene days of his life.

But the war still loomed, and the pause couldn't last forever. Life began to pick up again by the end of the week— thankfully, just gradually. Lying by the waterside, Jackson was watching Leon pursue a startled butterfly through the grass when Canon finally reappeared, hand in hand with Krystal.

"Jack! Been a minute, hasn't it? How've you been?" Canon plopped himself down onto the grass beside him.

"Playing with your cat, I see," Krystal observed as she sat on the other side of Jackson.

"Nocturne," Jackson corrected in defense of Leon's honor. He also thought of Leon as a big cat, but one mustn't forget his majesty.

"If you say so," Krystal grinned. "By the way, wasn't there something you owed me, Jackson?"

"I do?" He frowned, unsure what she meant.

"When are we having our duel?"

Ah… that. He was hoping she'd forgotten. Poorly, he fished for an excuse. "Soon, I hope—but all the training gear's packed away in the wagons, right? We obviously can't fight with real swords… So, I guess we'll just have to do it sometime before Orsadia?" Jackson promised emptily.

Krystal rolled her eyes. "If you're too scared, you can just forfeit." Canon snorted a laugh.

"I'm not! It's just, we don't have equipment. Besides, we've got time. Who knows how long it'll be before we leave for Orsadia?" Jackson asked, hoping neither of them did.

"Maybe another week or so. But some exciting news just became official: tomorrow, we're putting on the Festival of Light! Everyone thought it'd be canceled this year, so the whole city's buzzing with excitement. It only comes around every four years," Canon said cheerily.

"What's the Festival of Light?" asked Jackson.

"A day of celebration—to remember all the good in our lives. It'll have games, contests, exotic foods, and when night falls, we'll gather outside the city to watch fireworks," Krystal said dreamily.

Jackson wasn't exactly convinced by the phrase *exotic foods*. The last thing he wanted to sample was local traditions of Beffle stew. Still, at least the fireworks were something to look forward to.

"Tomorrow at noon, we'll meet up by the food stalls and proceed to have a lovely time together. Any objections?" Krystal prompted, looking from Jackson to Canon. "Good!" She clapped, rose to her feet, and started off for the bustling city streets. "Let's go, you two! Daylight's burning!"

"How do you keep up with her?" Jackson did a sit-up and let the momentum help him to his feet.

"No idea," Canon shook his head with a grunt.

Trumpets sounded above the city gates as the clock struck twelve. Citizens and soldiers alike packed in around the makeshift stage, eager to hear from their prince. A hush rippled through the crowd as Falcon approached the podium, but the excited chatter couldn't be fully quelled.

"My friends," Falcon began his address, beaming at the sea of expectant Eternai faces. "Today, we celebrate the Festival of Light!"

A deafening wave of applause broke out. Each voice seemed to be in a hard-fought competition to be heard above the rest. Without waiting for the rowdy crowd to settle down, Falcon continued.

"Unfortunately, King Talon could not join us today on account of a head cold, though he sends his regrets. In his stead, I will kick off this year's Festival."

The audience fell silent with anticipation.

"The air we breathe and the people we see are two of countless daily gifts. Though some sit in high places and others in low, we all receive the same day, and no one may borrow or give an hour beyond the appointed time. Let us enjoy the mystery of this day and give thanks for the light of hope we see, if dimly, in the present darkness. Now—eating and brewing of world renown await us. Let the Festival of Light begin!"

The masses cheered in approval as the prince waved and left the stage. The crowd slowly broke off, each after their own fancy—children racing to be first in line for their favorite carnival games, mothers keeping mostly watchful eyes from nearby shops, and men flocking with their buddies into the colorful beer tents. Enjoying a slower pace, Jackson followed Krystal and Canon to the market square.

He remembered visiting a funfair as a kid once, but the scale of the festivities filled him with awe. Standing in the heart of the music and revelry, he felt ten years younger. He paused, slowly turning in awe of the dazzling array of food and drink stands.

"Here," Krystal handed him a small brown pouch. "This should be enough for you to buy any food you want. Once you grab a bite, meet us down by the water. And… Hey! Canon! Where'd you go?"

Jackson spotted his friend devouring a turkey leg at a nearby stand, hunched over his prize like a vulture. Though he tried not to give him away, Krystal followed his eyes. She marched over to confront her boyfriend, demanding that he share his find.

Left to wander on his own, Jackson began the hunt for a worthwhile lunch. He passed more than a few stands hawking questionable meats, ranging from fried mountain yak to grilled eel *sur la* tree bark. Finally, a wooden stand with a proud red banner caught his eye. He approached the stall and was greeted by a small man with an impossibly bushy mustache that looked like a squirrel tail glued to his upper lip.

"Want to try some Vla'kish, neh? My Vla'kish is far more digestible than Bagh's," boasted the short man.

A ceramic plate whizzed past Jackson's ear and over the vendor's head, narrowly missing both before shattering against the back of the stall.

"Babanoosh lies! Try Bagh's instead; Bagh's Vla'kish is best Vla'kish!" yelled the belligerent vendor across the way. Short, stout, and hairy, he was Babanoosh's spitting image in every way except his moustache—his was clearly bushier.

"Bagh's Vla'kish? Do you not hear yourself? What a disgusting name for product! Even the sound of it is enough to make you ill. Who in their right mind would eat Bagh's anything?"

"You're simply jealous of my superior quality! I would not feed your Vla'kish to a dog."

"Your moustache looks like an ox's backside!"

"At least I have a moustache, caterpillar-lip!"

"You take that back!"

"Caterpillar-lip!"

Jackson made a quick exit before another plate could threaten his life. Fortunately, he had plenty of other stands to pick from. The variety was both wonderful and intimidating. Merchants of unique, intriguing, and outright bizarre dishes called out to him as he walked, each offering their own menu of adventure. He was open to trying something new, but he wasn't daring enough to sample mystery meats. One seafood stand raised his hopes, but the proprietor had unfortunately sold out just minutes ago. Poor logistical planning given the circumstances, really.

Eventually, he stumbled upon a booth marked by a striped yellow-and-red banner. A woman with rosy cheeks and a yellow dress that matched her bright smile greeted him. "Hiya! Want to try our soup of the day?" she offered in a bouncy drawl.

"I'd love to," Jackson said, won over by her smile. At least he managed to stop himself short of asking her to marry him.

She danced to the back of the stall and rang a loud gong that jarred him out of his reveries. In a warbling voice, she harmonized, singing, "Mooshi!"

Continuing her bizarre song and dance, she spun and grabbed a porcelain bowl from a box, then dipped a ladle into a pot to measure out three shakes. Rocking her hips at him high and low, she hopped to the counter and deposited the steaming bowl in front of him. Jackson looked around, struck by second-hand embarrassment, but no one else had stopped to watch the spectacle. He reached for the bowl, but she moved it out of his reach, unwilling to let him cut short her finale. Finally, she dropped in a spoon, clapped her hands twice, three times, and slid it back to him. "Careful, it's hot," she whispered creepily.

Jackson stared at the bowl ruefully. Chunks of purple meat swam around the opaque broth, mixing with sickly pale carrots and onions. A big bubble rose up with an unsettling gurgle, though he had no idea what might have caused it. He took an apprehensive whiff of the concoction and gagged.

"Try it," the woman flashed an expectant grin.

Reluctantly, Jackson lifted the bowl to his lips and took a sip.

The taste ranked between rancid milk and hot horse dung. Worse, the sourness burned his tongue like a mouthful of pickled cucumbers and old kimchi. His lips curled back in disgust as he looked for somewhere—anywhere—to spit it out. Turning his head, he spewed a violent spray onto the dirt street, then shoved the vile bowl back across the counter.

"Do you like it?" she asked hopefully.

"How could anyone like that? It's putrid!" Jackson clawed the residual seaweed off his tongue.

"I guess it's an acquired taste," the woman shrugged before knocking back the rest of his bowl.

"What's in there?" Jackson demanded, still scrubbing his tongue with his shirt like sandpaper.

"It's my famous Mooshi Surprise!"

"And what the blazes is Mooshi?"

"Oh, now I get it—you loved it so much, you want my recipe! I'm flattered, but just between us, it's all the usual stuff everyone puts in their Mooshi. The only difference is I add a little parsley—that's the surprise!" she said with a wink.

"Yeah? What's the ingredient that makes it taste like death?" he asked bluntly.

"Onion? You just boil water, chop up some onions and carrots, then plop them right in. Parsley, if you like. Add a generous helping of the main ingredient—chunked Beffle loins—and voila! In ten hours, you've got Mooshi!"

His face blanched as realization dawned. He'd done the one thing he'd sworn to avoid this day. He'd eaten Beffle stew, and it tasted just as he'd feared. "You're sick, lady," he shook his head with contempt as he stormed away from the booth. "Sick!" he repeated over his shoulder.

"Don't forget to tell your friends about my Mooshi Surprise! Have a nice day!" she hollered after him.

Disgusted by the lack of appetizing or editable food, Jackson resolved to leave the marketplace behind. Before he could make his exit, a man in a green apron called out to him, "Wait, my child! You must try my dish; it appeals to even the harshest of critics."

Jackson approached him cagily, unwilling to subject himself to another Mooshi Surprise. "And just what kind of poisonous swill are you selling?" he challenged the hawker.

"Poison? I thought everyone liked chicken and rice," the merchant said, bewildered.

Jackson popped the last cube of grilled chicken into his mouth and chewed happily. Like the dozen before, it was perfectly cooked. Not at all stringy. It may even have earned the title of the best dang chicken he'd ever tasted. After his outburst, he could only feel embarrassed by how he'd treated the merchant.

And all at an affordable price, too.

Canon and Krystal were lounging in the grass beside him. Krystal had finished her noodles before he arrived, but the telltale signs of red tomato sauce still marked her plate.

Meanwhile, Canon was doing his best impression of a feral dog, chomping down on skewered meat of some kind. Jackson asked, and he answered, but little was revealed in his grunted reply. "Wildfowl" might have slipped out.

After a loud belch, Canon straightened his hunched back and cried out, "Oh, honey! You *must* try this meat. It's just so... meaty. And the flavor! It's so... flavorful!" he raved with his mouth full.

Krystal looked at Jackson and shook her head. "No, that's all right, dear. Enjoy," she said, sighing as she wiped sauce from his chin.

"Thanks," he mumbled, barely pausing for air.

Leon stalked over with an entire pheasant in his teeth. He dropped the bird next to Jackson and sat proudly behind his find.

"Leon!" Jackson chastised reflexively, looking over his shoulder. With no angry merchant in sight, he grinned and joked, "Looks tasty. How much did you pay for that?"

Leon sneezed at this paltry display of humor, then proceeded to sink his teeth into the roasted bird and barbarically thrash his head to rip off chunks of meat. The big cat stared at Jackson as it chewed.

"Such elegance," he remarked sarcastically.

"At least the cat has an excuse," Krystal raised an eyebrow at Canon.

Canon didn't notice—he and Leon were busy eyeing each other's poultry.

# ⚜ Chapter 15 ⚜

K rystal squealed with girlish delight as Igor launched
another challenger out of the ring. Another scream
followed, coming from the unlucky melon vendor
whose stand was flattened by the human discus. He sounded
less delighted.

"Woo! Go Igor!" Krystal cheered, indifferent to the
plights of a melon man.

The strongman competition was a simple game. Two
men entered a ring and tried to knock the other out. The first
to step out lost. The competition lasted until they ran out of
challengers.

Igor, a certifiably enormous specimen of a man and
the undefeated champion of the ring, let out a bestial roar as
the announcer counted to eight—the number of challengers
dispatched so far, the latest being melon man's bane.

"Yes, Uncle! Smash those puny weaklings with your
hulking muscles!" cheered Andarc, the boy-giant Jackson had
met on his first day of training.

*Size runs in the family*, Jackson observed.

"He's so strong!" came a shrill voice from the gaggle of women behind Jackson. Krystal giggled along, earning a grumpy look from Canon.

"Are there any other challengers? Any at all?" The announcer searched the crowd with a hand over his eyes to keep the sun out.

Canon snorted and, shooting a sideways glance at Krystal, raised his hand. "I'll take a crack," he said, pushing his way through the crowd.

"Excellent, excellent! What's your name, good sir?" the announcer asked.

"Does it matter?" Igor retorted. His voice matched his imposing frame, loud and deep. As he joined the outbreak of laughter, his whole body bounced with each mighty laugh.

"Canon," his challenger answered gruffly.

"Well then, we have our boy Caneland—"

"Canon!" he corrected angrily.

"Yes, yes. We have our challenger here against the reigning champion, Igor! He's strong, he's fast, and he'll kick your derriere twenty feet into the air! Are! You! Ready!?" The announcer looked between the combatants.

They eyed each other across the ring.

"Begin!"

Canon charged at Igor, dropping his shoulder as if to ram him out of the ring. Igor bent his knee and grabbed Canon by the ankle, lifting him into the air. Just for show, he spun Canon in circles above his head before slamming him into the ground like a bag of mulch. Groaning in pain and slow to recover, Canon desperately tried to crawl away, but Igor was already on him. Grabbing him by the feet, Igor spun round and round like a discus thrower, laughing all the while with a hearty guffaw. The only surprise in the ending was Canon's high-pitched yelp as Igor flung him into the melon stand. Only beginning to recover his surviving merchandise, the vendor cried out in dismay as yet another contestant sent his fruit scattering across the ground.

"Yowch! That one's going to hurt in the morning. Unsurprisingly, Canine loses—"

"Canon!" he shouted indignantly from among the wreckage of the watermelon cart.

"And Igor wins! Are there any other suckers—uh, I mean, *challengers?*"

"Poor Canon," Krystal said without much concern, barely keeping herself from drooling as she watched Igor rip off his shirt and flex his rippling, sweat-glistened back.

With apparent difficulty and several false starts, Canon disentangled himself from the wrecked cart and glowered at Jackson. Trying to look innocent, Jackson raised his hand, smiled, and waved.

"Another volunteer—that'll make a clean ten! Please, sir, come on down to the front," invited the announcer.

Jackson looked around, wondering who could be so foolish to volunteer against this human catapult. A few heads turned his way. Many laughed when they saw the challenger.

*Is he behind me?*

Jackson swiveled his head but couldn't see anyone moving toward the stage.

"Yes boy, you!" the announcer pointed at him. The crowd began pushing and prodding him toward the ring. His feet briefly left the ground as he was passed to the front and set down before Igor.

"Challenger, tell us your... Sorry, sorry! I can't keep a straight face," The announcer doubled over, unable to hold back the laughter. Trying to regain his composure, he wiped a tear from his eye and asked, "What's your name, boy?"

"Jackson." He winced as his voice cracked.

The announcer repeated his name in the same high inflection, to the crowd's great amusement. "Well, Jackson, if nothing else, you're certainly a spirited fellow. I'd commend you, but I'm not quite sure if you're brave or dimwitted. I'll tell you what, folks! Seeing as we're down to the dregs of the volunteers, and this being Igor's tenth consecutive win—if he wins, of course—I'll enter into a wager with you. If Jackson here wins this fight, not only will he be our *Strongest Man*, but I'll eat twenty bowls of Mooshi Surprise while you count! How's that for a deal?"

The crowd's roar of laughter told Jackson he wasn't the favorite—and neither was the Mooshi.

"Okay now Igor, I'm going to need you to be at the top of your game. This is an important fight… oh, who am I kidding?" Falling victim to his own humor, the announcer reeled sideways with laughter. Sighing, he looked between the unevenly matched combatants. "Ready, Jackson?"

Nodding, Jackson held his fists up in the self-defense stance he learned in gym class.

"Wait—let the melon man fix his cart," Igor grinned maliciously.

Grumbling against the plain injustice, the disgruntled watermelon vendor slapped a "closed" sign on the wreckage.

"Ready, Igor?"

He grunted.

"Begin!"

With a guttural roar, Igor charged forward with his arms stretched wide. Adopting the instinct of a startled turtle, Jackson hit the deck and curled into a ball, shielding his head with his arms. Igor was coming too fast to stop. Surprised by the sudden turtling, he tripped on Jackson's folded body and crashed onto the ground.

Outside the ring.

The crowd fell silent. Every head turned to look at the announcer, waiting to see if he'd confirm the impossible. The shock was heavy in his voice. "Igor... loses?"

Groaning as he sat up, Igor gingerly scratched his head, searching for the lump that was starting to form.

"The belt!" demanded a voice in the crowd.

Visibly stunned, the announcer retrieved a large belt with golden buckles glinting with images of flexing muscle-men. "Congratulations, Jackson. You are the strongest man."

As Jackson accepted the belt, his arms bobbed under the unexpected weight. After a brief struggle, he managed to hoist the trophy overhead. The men in the crowd erupted in hearty applause and triumphant laughter. The women were less enthusiastic. With incredible speed, someone had already retrieved a bowl of Mooshi Surprise and was shoving it under the announcer's nose, who in turn started to tear up—likely at the thought of consuming twenty bowls.

As Jackson returned to the crowd, he received many congratulations and a few pats on the back from strangers. Krystal gave him a loud whoop as he walked up with his belt over his shoulder. Canon muttered something like "congrats" while flicking stray pieces of watermelon out of his hair.

"Nice, Jackson! You're officially the strongest man!" Krystal laughed as she inspected the belt.

Canon motioned for them to move along. "We all own belts—chuffed you'll be keeping your pants on—now, what other games are there?"

Canon headed for the games pavilion. With one last look over his shoulder, Jackson watched the crowd carry the announcer off to the market despite his protests. Smiling, he turned and followed Canon to the heart of the carnival.

The games reminded Jackson of the fair from his childhood—once again, and now in more vivid detail. His eighth birthday. He remembered playing the ring toss with his mom. They must have spent at least forty dollars before he'd finally landed one on the bottle and won the two-dollar toy lion. Though long-forgotten, the stuffed animal was most likely still tucked away in his room, maybe under his bed or in a sock drawer.

In addition to the ring game, he recognized a few other staples he had belatedly learned were rigged against the player. Hanging ladders, the upside-down pyramids of jars, dunk tanks—he'd played them all, but they never rewarded his effort. Across the way, he spotted a familiar figure leaning back against the counter of the knife-throwing game. Though a cowl hid his face, his discreet posture and compact frame gave him away.

It was good to see that Rein had survived the battle.

Jackson elbowed Canon to point him out, but the barker in charge of the station got to Rein first.

"You there! You look like you know your way about a knife. Care to take a chance throwing one?" invited the greasy barker with a crooked smile.

The wooden target was barely fifteen feet from the counter. From the little Jackson knew about the mysterious operator, that was a distance Rein could bullseye in his sleep. Regardless, Rein didn't seem interested. He'd taken notice of a little boy who had just lost at ring toss. "No thanks."

Cutting his losses, the little boy gave up on ring toss and approached the knife-throwing game. His voice was shy and small like a mouse. "Excuse me, sir, how much to play?"

"Just one bronze Kronyx!" answered the barker. He followed the boy's wide eyes. "Ah, I see you'd like to win that fancy blue cape, wouldn't you? That just so happens to be the finest material in the kingdom, and it could be yours! All you have to do is hit the red bullseye in the center of the target."

The boy got on his tiptoes, his eyes barely reaching over the counter even still, then nodded. He turned his small purse upside down, and a single bronze pellet dropped into his hand. The boy held his last piece uncertainly, a conflicted look on his face. One more look at the blue cape decided it—he laid the money on the counter.

"A stool might help you see better," suggested the carnie, handing him a wobbly three-legged one.

The kid climbed onto the stool and accepted the knife the carnie handed him. The knife was dulled, but of course, the boy didn't know any better. He pulled back his arm, closed one eye, and threw the knife.

It bounced off the target—hilt first—and clattered to the ground.

"A shame! Better luck next time, eh, boy?" said the man as he reclaimed the knife, then the stool.

Dejected, the boy turned to leave, but a strong hand on his shoulder stopped him. He looked up at the hooded man, who offered a reassuring smile.

"I decided I'd like to play after all," Rein said, laying a bronze Kronyx on the table.

The little boy looked on curiously. The carnie barked a laugh, snatched up the pellet, and slapped a knife onto the counter. A smug grin spread across his face. "Same rules. Hit the bullseye, win a cape."

Rein tested the weight of the knife in his hand. He had probably figured out that it was too dull to stick in the wooden target, even if thrown perfectly. Tilting his head, he grabbed the knife by the blade and took a shot. It dipped unexpectedly and bounced off the bottom of the target, well below the bullseye.

"Unlucky, there! How about another try?" the carnie offered, sounding unsurprised.

Rein tossed another bronze pellet on the table. With a broad smile, the carnie slid him another knife.

"I'll take that one," Rein declined, pointing to the one on the floor.

"Suit yourself," the carnie complied, shrugging.

This time, Rein calibrated the weight perfectly and aimed higher to compensate for the drop. His knife hit the bullseye dead center, tip-first.

And then rebounded lamely off the wood.

"I hit the mark. I'll take my cape," said Rein.

The carnie laughed nefariously. "Sorry, but it only counts if your knife sticks in the bullseye! In case you haven't noticed, your knife is on the floor. Good try, though—maybe you'll get it with another throw?" He offered the knife with a taunting smirk.

Rein paid the man and took the knife.

Turning to watch the target, the carnie chuckled to himself. "Whenever you're ready," he said as he preemptively placed another knife on the counter.

Rein passed the rigged knife to the little boy with a wink, then held a finger to his lips. The boy nodded and hid it behind his back, watching in awe as Rein drew a glinting dagger from his belt. With practiced ease, Rein flicked his wrist, and his knife punched a hole in the middle of the red bullseye.

"So close! Care to go again?" the carnie tapped the knife on the counter.

"No thanks. I'll take my cape and be on my way."

Confused by his confidence, the carnie glanced at the target and realized a knife was buried an inch deep into the target. "But that's impossible! I made sure that—" he cut himself off.

"Go on. What did you make sure of?" Rein invited innocently, drawing a second, sharpened blade from his belt.

The carnie stammered nervously. Realizing he had already said too much, he sheepishly presented the cape to Rein. "Congratulations! Your prize, sir."

Rein draped the blue cape over his shoulder but kept staring down the crooked carnie, making him squirm. The man tripped over himself to praise Rein's skill and apologize for any misunderstanding that might have occurred. Rein gestured to his knife embedded in the target.

"Ah, your knife, of course! Where are my manners?" The carnie ripped the blade out of the target and gently laid it on the counter. "Is there anything else I can do for you? No? Then I wish you a happy Festival!" he said, closing the blinds on his stand.

"That was amazing!" the boy marveled at Rein.

Kneeling to be eye-level, Rein tied the cape around the kid's shoulders. "It belongs to you."

"Really?" The boy's eyes lit up as a big smile spread across his face. "Thanks, mister! You're the best—I want to be just like you when I grow up!"

Rein smiled back. "I don't recommend it. Mine isn't as glorious a life as you'd think. Become a knight instead—at least those guys get free horses."

"Kay," the boy laughed. Giving one last wave, he took off running, his cape flowing behind him.

"Aww. That was super sweet of you, man. Tender," Canon said, wrapping an arm around Rein's shoulder.

"If you say so," Rein brushed him off, replacing his mask of stone.

"Methinks someone ain't keen on others seeing their sensitive side," Canon teased.

"Don't you have a strongman contest to lose?" Rein replied evenly.

"Already did," Canon mumbled.

"What's that?" Rein cupped a hand to his ear.

"Already did!" Canon shouted testily.

"I know."

"Then why'd you ask?"

"Making conversation," Rein said casually, pulling a piece of watermelon out of Canon's hair.

The evening was brighter than usual. Moon and stars brightened the cloudless night. Torches lining the city walls poured a warm glow over the stone.

Outside the city gates, long tables were set for a bountiful supper. Every Eternai soldier was invited, along with a generous contingent of Kanrio citizens. Although the citizens had been selected by a lottery system, there was a conspicuous overrepresentation of fighting-aged men. Over the course of the hearty meal—with every food and drink imaginable, save for Mooshi—many heroic tales about the liberation were shared, along with jokes ranging from clever to downright strange. As the pace of eating slowed, Falcon stepped onto the elevated platform to deliver his address.

"I hope you all enjoyed a wonderful Festival. I know Igor did," he added slyly, sparking hoots and hollers at the expense of the runner-up strongman. "I just wanted to take a moment to say: this is what makes us Eternai. In times of peace and prosperity, in war and hardship, we remember our traditions. The spirit of our kingdom will never fade. Given our present circumstances, I believe this Festival may be the most important we've ever held. In celebrating, we remind ourselves the Eternai are not a war machine by nature. We are a nation of hope, united under one crown in peace and harmony. We are a proud people, rich in culture and history. Above all, we are free. As you enjoy the fireworks, remember why we fight. Why those heroes before you fought. Freedom. The Night shall not prevail; darkness will never overcome us. We fight for the glory of the Eternai."

"Glory to the Eternai!" citizens and soldiers shouted back in unison.

Falcon nodded his approval. "As is tradition, I now invite our Strongman to the stage to commence our firework finale. Jackson, the honors are yours."

Canon nudged him forward. Jackson stood from the benches and walked to the stage, very aware that every eye was on him. Managing not to trip, he reached the stage. One aide presented him with a torch, while another set a bucket at his feet. Inside, a single firework with a concerningly short fuse was planted in wet sand.

Falcon stepped back and motioned for him to light the fuse. Carefully, Jackson extended the torch until the cord sparked to life, then hastily retreated off the stage.

The firework shot up with a *woosh-hiss*. Higher and higher it climbed, its shrill whistle carrying through the silent night. Above the city walls, it exploded in a *crack!* A fabulous flower of red rained down.

The small army of pyrotechnicians on the city walls saw the signal to begin the show. To the delight of Kanrio's children, the sky was enveloped in color. All ages shared a common word: "Wow."

Canon wrapped a brotherly arm around Jackson and said, "Happy Festival, Strongman."

# ⚜ Chapter 16 ⚜

The joy of the Festival lingered for days, even after the games were packed up and the market returned to its usual rhythm. By the morning, plans for the next phase of the war were already finalized. The army would have mobilized sooner, but evidently Talon truly was sick. The king insisted the Eternai army wait for his recovery, so they did, delaying the inevitable by another week.

Once the king was fit to travel, his edict went out to every soldier and able-bodied man to gather outside Kanrio's gates. Making up for his lack of visibility in recent days, he personally briefed them on their next target: the seaside city of Orsadia. While many had suspected as much, most were taken by surprise when he called for an immediate march to avoid further delay to their assault. Though the logistics had been prepared during his bed rest, many in the infantry had to leave with goodbyes left unsaid.

The caravan marched twelve hours straight before stopping for dinner that night. Though the pace was grueling, any attempts at maintaining the neat four-wide columns were abandoned within the first two hours. The only hard rule—and corporeally enforced—was not to fall behind the cavalry at the rearguard.

The next day, and indeed the next week, consisted of long hours under the same harsh regimen. Each morning and night, Jackson's sore muscles groaned with pain. Somehow, he endured the long hours between, growing stronger every day. The forests grew thinner the farther south they traveled, briefly giving way to bare, rolling hills before yielding again to a timber-lined dirt road. Conversation, too, became sparse.

On the sixth day, their march slowed, columns were once again required, and they halted early to make camp. The reason was revealed at supper—they were within a day's walk from Orsadia.

They established their camp at the edge of the forest, clearing a few trees around the glade to make space for their neat rows of tents. Eternai banners were planted in the center of camp to boost morale, and the meagre wine reserves were opened to be served with dinner. A few resourceful hill-folk snuck away to hunt, but any reprimand they might've earned was forgotten when they returned with three feral hogs on spits, ready to roast over the evening fires.

By the twilight hour shared by both sun and moon, Jackson was ready to devour a plate of wood-fired meat and call it a night. He strolled past rows of crowded tables—with hungry patrons strategically positioning themselves close to the food pit—and eventually found a seat at an empty table on the edge of camp. Muscles aching, he sat on the backless bench and groaned.

Leon had decided to stay in the tent, unsurprisingly preferring a nap—his go-to pastime. Jackson sullenly wished he'd dragged him along. The food was just starting to cook, and he was sitting alone at a big table, incurably bored. His strongman celebrity status had evidently been short-lived, as he had already faded into obscurity within the ranks.

Out of the corner of his eye, he imagined he saw something moving among the trees. He turned his head and stared at the trees, searching for confirmation.

There it was again.

Just beyond the edge of the woods, a hunched figure prowled through the bushes. From Jackson's seat, the dark shape looked like a large animal—possibly a bear. He stood uneasily, debating whether to get a closer look or find help.

Another shadow darted through the trees.

Jackson subconsciously reached for his sword. The touch of its hilt comforted him; he was thankful not to have left it behind in the tent. Spotting two more shadows moving in the trees, he decided against investigating alone. He looked around for someone, anyone, he could report the anomaly to.

He recognized someone poring over a piece of paper at a nearby table. A focused frown creased Rein's forehead as he read. Jackson ran to him, stopping his momentum with both palms slapping the table. Rein looked up in surprise.

"Easy, tiger. How much do I owe you?" he asked jokingly, his hands up in mock surrender.

Jackson shook his head, refusing to be deterred from reporting the possible threat. "I saw someone—something— out there in the forest! Two or more, at least!"

"I see," Rein scratched his chin with a deadpan look. "Big ears? Bushy tail? Goes by *squirrel?*"

Jackson raised his hands out in front of his face and growled in frustration. As he turned to look at the forest, he caught another shadow advancing into a bush at the edge of the trees. "There! Another one! Whatever it was, it wasn't a squirrel, Rein, and it's not one of us. Just watch, will you?"

Sighing, Rein folded the missive and tucked it into a pocket inside his shirt. For a minute or longer, he stared into the forest without blinking. He remained stock still, barely appearing to breathe. Aside from trees dancing in the gentle breeze, nothing moved. Not even a squirrel.

The stillness made Jackson think he was going crazy. He felt on edge, full of dread and paranoia. As they watched, he wished the creeping shadows would return—not just so Rein could see them, but so he could reassure himself they had ever existed. Another uneventful minute stretched on. At last, Rein shook his head.

"Sorry, Jackson. I don't see anything out there. Have you eaten today?"

"I'm not having hunger hallucinations!" Jackson said irritably. "I swear, it's not just one—there were five at least. I saw them," he said, unable to explain.

Suddenly, five shadows moved as one, diving into the low bush closest to camp.

"There!" Jackson pointed at the bush, as though that would make the lurkers reveal themselves.

Frowning, Rein followed his gaze. "You sure you saw something moving? Or just shadows?"

"I'm not freaking out over trees and shadows!"

Rein focused his gaze on the trees. He looked a little less certain, his brow furrowing in concentration. They stared at the forest together in silence. Nothing. Still nothing. Then, finally, a shadow dashed from the trees into the bushes.

"Did you—"

"I saw it," Rein said, sharing Jackson's unease.

"What was—"

"Not an animal. It was carrying something. A satchel on its back, maybe. He had on a black tunic or uniform," Rein analyzed.

Jackson was amazed at the depth of his report. His calm focus was equally impressive. The shape had only been visible for a second, and all Jackson could discern was that it was dark. In contrast, he was not at all calm. Very uncalm. Frazzled, even.

"We should either engage now or alert Falcon. The Cavar and a veteran team could neutralize the threat and take prisoners for questioning. How many did you say you saw?" asked Rein.

"At least six now. Maybe eleven or more?"

"We should get Falcon. Wait here and keep an eye on them. I'll return quickly," instructed Rein. He stood and weaved through the crowd like water, drawing no attention to himself as he sped toward the tall blue tent.

Jackson debated yelling out to warn the surrounding tables, but he sensed Rein wanted to avoid raising the alarm and potentially scaring the watchers off.

Something glinted in the bush.

Jackson looked over his shoulder, but Rein had not yet returned. The nearby tables were completely vulnerable. Largely unarmored, they were caught up in conversation and oblivious to the danger lurking outside the camp. No patrols had come by recently. Realizing he alone knew of the threat, he found himself rising from his table. He had to be sure the shadows were only there to observe. If a rain of arrows burst from the trees while he sat on his hands, their deaths would be on his conscience.

Using a roundabout approach to avoid cutting across the open grass, he crept away from the tables and toward the bushes. He had no intention of being seen, and certainly did not plan to engage, but he was resolved to catch a glimpse of the watchers and find out how they were armed. Moving in a crouch, he kept one eye on the trees to his left as he closed in on the crowded bushes ahead.

He stopped as another trio of shadows entered the bushes. Two had satchels on their backs, just like Rein had said, but otherwise they appeared to be lightly armored. No warbows, at least, but they may have had swords. Away from the light, his eyes adjusted enough to spot their dark outlines lying under the bushes. A dozen or more. He kicked himself for leaving his armor with Leon in the tent.

After cursorily scanning the trees one final time, he decided he'd seen all he needed to. They seemed to be scouts or raiders, but they certainly weren't an entire army prepared to spring an ambush. He'd pass along what he'd learned once Rein came back with reinforcements.

As he turned to retreat, he glimpsed a glinting object launch from the bush, tracing a high arc through the air. He looked up and caught it in the light of the moon—heading straight for him.

As the object fell, he identified it as a crystal vial of orange liquid. Just like the one in the castle. He stepped aside, dodging, but the glass shattered on a rock behind him and began spewing its gas.

Covering his mouth with his sleeve, Jackson backed away from the gas—and toward the bushes. Two crouched shadows traded quick words. Their argument was resolved as one shoved the other out of the bush. Black clothes. Gray skin. Rope in hand.

*Night.*

Jackson drew his sword to defend himself, but his first step forward turned into a clumsy stumble. The effects of the gas had already started seeping in. His groggy limbs refused to obey. His chest heaved up a sputtering cough. Though he was putting up a valiant fight for consciousness—

better than before, at least—he couldn't maintain his grip on his sword. His weapon slipped out of his hand and bounced off the ground, rendered useless.

A cold bead of sweat dripped down his neck as fear took over. The Night drew closer. Jackson tried with all his strength to will his legs into motion. He pleaded with them to carry him back to the camp—back to Rein and Falcon. Still, he could not move.

His eyelids grew heavy. His mind screamed at his body to run, but his feet stayed in place. Even as they bound him with rope, he couldn't break free of the drowsy spell. With his bonds secured, the man half-carried, half-dragged Jackson into the bushes.

The urge to sleep was overwhelming. It took all that he had to keep his eyes open. Branches and twigs scraped his skin as he went through the bush, but he barely felt them. His body was already numb.

Twenty men or more waited on the other side. Black clothing, gray skin. They spoke a language that sounded like English, but he couldn't understand a word they said.

Laughter.

His vision went black.

*This can't be happening*, he thought. Overcome by the orange liquid once again. This time, he'd have no one there to help him when he woke up.

*That is, if I ever wake up again.*

# ✤ Chapter 17 ✤

R rough jostling woke him. Before anything else could register, he felt a nettlesome itch on his head. Trying to scratch it, he found his movement impaired. His hands were tied behind his back at an uncomfortable angle. If he had to guess, the rope was biting into his skin. Squirming, he sat up awkwardly and took in his surroundings.

Rays of late-day sunlight filtered through metal bars overhead. The rhythmic clop of hoofbeats repeated outside. Through the slits, he saw trees passing over him.

*Great. I landed in a moving prison cell.*

He shared his captivity with three others: a woman and two men, all visibly older. The prisoners were similarly bound and still asleep—not moving, at any rate. The black material padding the walls shut out any light from the sides. A suspicious row of sealed crates lined one wall. Fortunately, the cage was spacious enough to hold everything without its cargo being crammed together. The vehicle must have been something to behold from outside.

The wagon shook violently as its wheels passed over rough terrain, knocking him onto his back. His head swam with a weird déjà vu. He had dreamed about stormy waves tossing him about at sea, and his body seemed to remember. Slow to rise, he entered a squat and pressed his face against the bars. He was trying to steal a look at his captor's face, but all he could make out was the back of a black hat, resting upon a gray head.

"Where are you taking me?" Jackson asked, his voice quivering weakly. His throat felt bone dry.

The driver laughed coldly. His voice was like leather, old and raspy. "Awake, are you? Let me learn you the rules. You ain't home anymore, boy. In fact, you'll never be home again. Your future is in the land of Night. Forget your old life. None of it matters now. You'll live as a slave, dutiful and hard-working, or you won't live at all."

"You didn't answer my question," Jackson put some defiance in his voice this time, though his dry throat left him sounding weak and scared. It was an accurate portrayal of his current state.

The driver snorted. "I don't answer your questions, boy. Slaves don't get no say. Now, unless you want a beating, you'll call me 'Master'. You're my property—until I sell you."

Jackson said nothing. He refused to bow down to this slimy smuggler.

Apparently dissatisfied by the silence, the man gave another snort. "Fine, I'll tell you. We're going to a magical place called the slave auction! There, you'll get to enjoy brief but magnificent views of the coast before being locked inside a factory or iron mine for the rest of your miserable days."

Jackson tried to mentally recreate the map he'd seen in Canon's tent. Orsadia's dot was close to the coast. That seemed like a probable destination. Another possibility was

Verden, the capital. Either way, he figured he was somewhere on the continent. There was hope in that. He wondered just how far they'd traveled while he slept.

His thoughts were interrupted by a violent lurch to the side that nearly tipped the cart over.

"Whoa!" called the driver.

The cart halted immediately with another lurch.

Jackson peered through the bars, trying to get a look at what had caused the abrupt stop. As he looked up, he saw a girl drop onto their vehicle from the trees above. Her dark brown hair was tied back in a black band that matched her ebony-and-green armor. She held what looked like a katana in each hand.

"Hey! What do you think you—"

His inquiry was silenced by her swords. She climbed over the body and dropped down to the horses. The receding drum of hoofbeats suggested that she set them free. Working quickly, she vaulted back onto the roof and made her way to the hatch. After assessing the knot keeping the hatch shut, she sawed through the rope with practiced ease. Finally, she slammed the heel of her boot against the hatch and followed the broken wood into the cage.

Without a minute to waste, she went straight for the crates. After brief deliberation, she toppled over the stacks, spilling their contents onto the floor. She got on her hands and knees and rifled through the mess, in and out of boxes, flinging jewelry, coins, papers, and more across the floor in her frantic search. Growing increasingly frustrated, she over-turned another few crates but still couldn't find what she was looking for. Soon there was just one box left unopened, long and low against the wall. She ripped off the lid and threw it over like the others. A dozen fish flopped onto the floor.

Defeated, she sunk to her knees.

Feeling his eyes, the girl lifted her head and returned his stare. Her lip was drawn tight in a thoughtful line. Despite her vexed state, a light shone in her piercing blue eyes, sharp and bright. Her skin was a mystery, fair and beautiful—even flawless—but for a gray streak marring her neck.

She was unquestionably the most attractive girl he had ever seen, completely natural and effortless. This girl had totally confounded his understanding of what a Night should look like. Some might have called him gullible, but his heart decided: there was no way she could be his enemy.

Somber and silent, the girl walked over and stopped a foot away. His heartbeat quickened as she studied him. She looked to his age. About the same height, too.

Jackson felt his cheeks turn red.

"Hi," she said in a surprisingly soft voice.

Suddenly, he forgot how to speak.

*Howdy?*—Nah, too country.

*Hajimemashite?*—No, too Japanese.

*Hubba Hubba?*—What does that even mean?

"Hi," he stammered after an awkward pause.

*Hi? Smooth. Better than "Ahoy!", I guess.*

They stood in silence a minute longer, each studying the other. Then she moved first, stepping behind him. His heart leaped as her breath brushed his shoulder. His severed bonds fell to the floor.

"Thanks," he said, feeling his tender wrists. His brain felt slow, though he doubted it was a lingering effect of the gas. He told himself to pull it together. "I'm Jackson."

"Cate," she said, scanning the other captives.

"We should help them," Jackson suggested.

Her face fell with sorrow. "I don't think they can be helped anymore."

"What do you mean?"

"They look like they're … gone. You haven't spoken with any of them recently, have you?"

He knew he hadn't. Even in indirect light, their faces looked pale. Not one of them was at all familiar. Although definitely Eternai, they weren't dressed like soldiers. Whether they were recruits from Kanrio or citizens from elsewhere, they helped to fill in a few blanks for Jackson—his captors hadn't come to fight the army, but to snatch up anyone who strayed too far from the camp. For all he knew, the raiders weren't even affiliated with the Night army.

He knew she was right, but he couldn't leave them like this. "What if we cut their bonds, in case they wake up?"

"Sure," Cate agreed quietly. She severed their bonds, but they still did not stir. Moving on, she lifted herself out of the cart. "Coming?"

Eyeing the abandoned spoils, Jackson climbed out of the hatch after her. Before he jumped down from the wagon, he noticed a flask on the driver's bench. He greedily sucked down the water, then followed Cate into the lush forest.

"How far is Orsadia?" he asked.

"Where?"

"Orsadia?" he tried another pronunciation.

"Did you hit your head?"

He frowned, puzzled by her response. Even if they had veered north or gone south toward Verden, she ought to know the name of such a large city. Remembering Canon's reaction to his own geographical confusion, he wondered if she was one of those hill-ham folk.

An impossible, terrible thought came to mind.

"We're not in the land of Night, are we?" he said, half-jokingly.

"Of course we are." She returned a bemused look. "Where else would we be?"

His head spun, and his heart skipped a beat as he saw the forest through new eyes. Teeming with life, this place was nothing like the ever-dark, desolate wasteland he had imagined the Nightlands to be. It was like nothing he'd ever seen. Beautiful birds darted overhead, perching among the dense, dark green leaves of towering trees. Purple and yellow plants filled the underbrush. A sloth-like animal hung upside down from a nearby branch, watching Jackson with curious eyes. Despite all the biodiversity, there wasn't one grotesque monster ripped out of Greek mythology parading around the jungle. Although he'd formed his own mental picture of the dreaded land of Night, he couldn't help but feel lied to—the reality couldn't have been further from the truth.

How had he come so far?

"I was living with the Eternai," he said in disbelief.

Cate walked on in silence. Finally, she revealed her mind. "My father was an Eternai. Mom was a Night. I guess that makes me half of each—or all of neither. I've never been to the Eternai lands, but I've always wondered what it's like."

"Honestly, it doesn't seem all that different," Jackson said, wondering if that was also true of its people.

"Still, I'd like to see it someday," she said, a fanciful smile on her face. She surprised him by taking his hand. He hoped she hadn't noticed the color rushing into his cheeks. "Here, stay close."

Cate led him through densely packed woods into a small clearing. In the center, a ratty knapsack lay alone in the grass. Letting go of his hand—too soon, he thought—she walked ahead and looked around the glade. "I've been living here for a while. Welcome home."

It reminded Jackson of the place where he had met Voldroun, the gatekeeper who had transported him into this strange world. Weirdly, the association made him feel safe.

"It's a nice place," he said without much thought. It did seem odd for a girl to be living out here alone, though. Eventually, the obvious question came to mind. "Where's your family?"

Her smile faltered, and she dropped her gaze to her feet. "My village was destroyed." She fell back into the grass and stared up at the sky. The memory played behind her eyes.

"I grew up in a village of fighters. It's what they had to be. The governor was lazy and greedy and never left his city on the other side of the province. When his soldiers did come around, it was to demand money. They never stayed to protect us from the bandits or beasts that plagued the area. Eventually, my village got fed up and started pushing back against the tax collectors. It worked—for a little while.

"Every villager trained every day, from the youngest to the oldest. And it worked. Not only did we scare off the governor's envoys, but we also sent a message to the bandits: the days of easy scores were over. Of course, some tested us on from time to time, trying to steal food or money. Night patrols would stop by and tell us we weren't acting like good citizens. For the most part, though, we left the world alone, and it left us alone. When war broke out between the Night and the Eternai, that all changed.

"Because our disobedient village was on the coast, the Night feared we'd give the Eternai a landing site for an invasion. So, they attacked us. A legion of soldiers. We didn't stand a chance. My dad hid me in a haystack behind our house and told me to stay put no matter what. I watched them kill my friends and burn down my home, and I stayed put," she said, her voice bitter with regret. She paused and took a deep breath, trying to steady herself. Tears welled in her eyes, but she bit her lip, refusing to let them fall.

"When the attack was over and the last screams died down, I ran into the woods. For hours, I didn't stop, and I didn't look back. I couldn't. Eventually, I wound up here. I was so tired, I just stopped, sat in the grass, and… I cried."

He didn't know what to say. He couldn't think of any wise proverbs or profound words of comfort. Instead, he lay down beside her. As she turned and buried her face in his chest, hiding her tears, he pulled her into a gentle embrace.

Intertwined in the light of the moon, neither spoke for a while. Jackson felt her breathing relax, every rise and fall of her chest slower than the pair before. Finally, she steadied herself enough to speak. "You're the first person I've talked to in months. Really talked to, I mean."

He felt he owed her a deep answer to show that he had heard her, that he cared, and that everything was going to be all right. He searched for words to console her, something clever to make her smile, but he found none. In the end, he realized he didn't need them. Listening was enough.

"So… what's your story?" she asked, wiping tears from her eyes.

"Don't have one, really. Life was pretty dull before I ended up here," said Jackson.

"You've been in the Nightlands for less than a day," Cate said, not buying his downplaying.

"I meant before I wound up in this world."

Cate raised an eyebrow. "This *world?*" she repeated as a question.

"So, the thing is, I'm not exactly from here. I'm from Canada—which I'm guessing you don't know a thing about, because why would you? It's a land in this other world they call Earth. I know this sounds crazy, but stay with me for a minute. I walked into a clearing—that looked a lot like this one—and came into your world through a door that turned out to be a magic portal across space. Some Eternai guy ran into me, we became friends, and I got drafted into their army.

Then there's this thing about a giant cat who I swear can read my thoughts—or understands me, at least—some disgusting Beffle stew called Mooshi, getting kidnapped across the sea by slavers… and here we are. Pretty crazy, huh?"

"I don't think you're crazy. My dad used to tell me stories about a portal to another world hidden in the Citadel of Night. What's your world like?" she asked, her eyes wide with wonder.

"Different in some ways; similar in others, I guess. We have nature like yours. Clouds and trees and bugs. Plenty of people and conflicts, too. More than here, even. Weapons that kill people on the far side of the world, all by themselves. Honestly, even though we have machines small enough to carry in your pocket that let you talk to anyone, anytime, or play any song you want, or record any moment so you can relive it forever… huh. I think I like your world better." He felt weird saying he preferred one world over another, but he knew it was true.

"Yeah, pass. I don't ever want to visit your world."

"What? Why? It's not *that* bad," he said half-jokingly, though he was unsure why he defended it.

"I don't know. I just feel my place is in this world. I really don't need to look anywhere else."

He considered that for a moment, reflecting on his past life. The brief time he'd spent in this world was far more exciting than anything that had come before. His supporting role as a dancing tree in the sixth-grade musical wasn't even close. Here, with Cate by his side, he felt more alive than ever before. "You know, I don't think I really want to visit my world again, either."

They lay watching the stars, sharing a peaceful smile.

Jackson voiced the question on his mind but realized as soon as he spoke how many presumptions he was making. "So, how are we getting back to the Eternai?"

With a crafty grin, Cate readily expressed her support for his proposal. "Isn't it obvious? We'll get the Night to take us there. I'll show you tomorrow."

He was intrigued by her vague response, but he was satisfied to leave tomorrow as a mystery for now. He closed his eyes and squeezed her hand, butterflies fluttering through his stomach. The soft grass was comfortable, and the distant buzz of crickets lulled him to ease. It was just them, away from the world, together. They fell asleep, hand in hand, their fingers clasped until the morning light.

# ⚜ Chapter 18 ⚜

T he warm sun woke Jackson from his dream. As he sat up, he realized Cate's hand was still intertwined with his. Listening to the slow rhythm of her quiet breaths, her face serene in sleep, he gently let go of her hand.

A lost cow stumbled into the clearing. Cate shot up, immediately shaking off her lethargy and leaping to her feet. Identifying the threat as a harmless bovine, she sheepishly sat back down and laughed at herself, clearly embarrassed he had seen her total overreaction to the dopey cow. Quick to dispel any discomfort, Jackson spread his hands and laughed at the strange visitor.

The cow stopped, chewed some grass, then moved on, cutting through the glade to continue its aimless roaming on the other side. Jackson's stomach growled. His mind daydreamed about the cow wandering back to throw itself on a grill after slathering itself in a tantalizing tomato-based sauce.

Reading the look on his face, Cate reached into her bag and pulled out two haunches of smoked and salted meat. Jackson accepted a leg and thanked her before devouring his breakfast with wolfish speed. After they both chased down their meat with water, Cate fastened both flasks to her belt, gave her bag of worldly possessions a final once-over, then discarded it beside a tree.

"We won't need anything else. I'm out of food, and blankets won't help much on the boat," she said, preparing to leave her homeland behind.

"Oh, sweet! You got us a boat?" he asked hopefully.

"Sure—courtesy of the imperial forces. I booked us passage in cargo, but fair warning: if they catch us, we might need to persuade them that our tickets are legitimate," she said, tapping her sheathed swords.

Less encouraging, to be sure, but it was a way back.

They set off into the woods. Cate led, thankfully—each turn felt wholly random to Jackson. Comfortable silence fell over them as they walked. Leaves rustled in the gentle breeze. Birds warbled. The morning was cool, the sun finding their skin only in scattered shafts through the tight canopy.

After almost an hour, Cate came to a sudden halt at the edge of the forest. Jackson quietly came alongside her, following her gaze into the distance. Half a mile away, a fleet of iron and wooden ships crowded a smaller harbor. Night soldiers scrambled up and down the docks with the urgency of imminent departure. Final preparations involved repacking a large wagon shipment for transport. Big crates were hauled onto the ships, packed with a bounty of practical necessities, materials, and food. Dozens of Nocturne cages were carefully loaded, but one cage twice as tall and twice as wide as all others stole his attention.

They dragged the colossal carrier onto the deck of an ironclad ship at the end of the pier. The whole boat appeared to sink a foot lower in the water. His eyes tried to make sense of the monstrous creature behind those feeble metal bars, but the cage reached the central elevator and was lowered below deck. Whatever *thing* was being smuggled into the land of the Eternai, it would surely be the deadliest, most sinister battle pet they'd seen yet.

He turned to ask Cate about the caged creature, but she was already halfway down the slope. He ran after her as fast as he was able, but when she broke through the last of the brush and hit the road, she accelerated, widening the gap. Trying to stay low, he ducked his head and crossed the road after her.

Finally catching up, he crouched next to her in the shadow of a parked wagon at the edge of the docks. It looked almost empty, suggesting its contents had already been largely loaded onto the boats. Breathless, Jackson started a question, but Cate shushed him and motioned for him to follow.

She silently crept around to the side of the dock and slipped down onto the rocky beach. Following a brief pause to make sure Jackson hadn't been seen crossing over to her, she waded into the water, pushing against the waves. Once she was in past her knees, she surged forward and began to swim under the pier. Night soldiers walked three feet above her head, but no one looked down to see her through the cracks in the floorboards.

Not entirely without hesitation, Jackson decided he'd be better off under the docks than standing out in the open. Reluctantly, he followed her into the water, wondering if any sharks were watching him. His fears were washed away by a freezing wave that surged up his thighs. A muted yelp slipped out before he could stop it, though he managed to stifle a full shriek of surprise. Cate passed the halfway point of the pier, leaving him no time to ease himself in. He pushed forward, against the tireless waves that battered his chest. He thought he was a decent swimmer, but the combination of the current and trying to kick with boots on made the effort exhausting. Despite his exertion, the gap grew as he fell farther behind.

A Night soldier halted his step right above him. If he hadn't been in conversation, he would've seen Jackson as he knelt, then stooped forward to fill his bucket. As the bucket dipped past the floorboards, Jackson plunged beneath the icy waves, wrapping himself in the dark waters. Cold needled his bones as he sank deeper. After the bucket entered and exited the water above, he spurred himself into motion, propelling forward with strong breast strokes. In case the soldier came back for another look or had a second bucket, Jackson aimed to surface as far away as possible. The salty ocean stung as he opened his eyes to gauge his progress. Slow. Too slow. When his lungs could bear it no longer, he kicked and clawed up to the surface, gasping for air as he broke through.

With the imminent danger of exploding lungs behind him, he tilted his head, anxious to hear if any alarms had been raised. Evidently, his delve into the deep had gone unnoticed. The dockhands were still sharing jokes with the sailors.

Pushing through discomfort and exhaustion, Jackson paddled to the end of the dock. Looking equally soaked and miserable, Cate clung to a thin piling as she waited for him. She whispered something as she observed the iron ship, but a wave splashed off the supports and threw water into his ear. Struggling to stay afloat, he sputtered, "Sorry?"

"The ladder on the side of the ship! We'll get on and stow away while the crew is loading," she repeated forcefully.

Four soldiers arrived at the end of the dock lugging another big crate. Once the last of them made it up the ramp and stepped onboard, she swam like her life depended on it, rounding to the far side of the ship. Still out of breath from the first leg of the swim, he ordered his body to keep up with her by any means necessary.

A rope ladder with wooden slats hung from the far side of the boat. Without hesitation, Cate started climbing the ladder's weathered rungs. Jackson went next. As he pulled himself up onto the fourth rung, his head bumped into her foot, though she seemed not to notice. Focused, she peered over the rail. Her opportunity came, and she vaulted onto the deck with the grace of a cat.

Jackson forbade himself from falling or causing a scene as he dashed across the sea-sprayed deck. Cate dropped into the hatch where the colossal cage had disappeared into. He jumped in blindly, trusting that she had scouted out the landing for both their sakes.

He landed in time to see her hurrying down a narrow stairwell to the bottommost deck. Reaching the cargo hold, she cracked open a horse-sized crate in the corner. Satisfied, she waved him over before climbing inside.

Incredibly, the crate was full of woven fabrics and soft blankets, some even silk. There was a foot or two of space above the fabrics. Enough for them to lie down. He moved the top back into place but left a crack open on the side against the wall for air. Apparently thinking along similar lines, Cate bored a small hole into the side wall facing the room. She looked out from the dark box into the dim hold to check her work, then loosely plugged the hole with the piece she had chipped out.

As the adrenaline faded, Jackson realized his body was still shivering from the chilly water. He tore off his wet shirt and soggy boots and stashed them in the corner. Having enough sense to know it'd be inappropriate to take off the rest of his sopping wet clothes, no matter how dark the crate, he wrung out the water dried himself with the ample cloth around him. Deciding that *damp* was better than *soaked,* he wrapped himself in soft blankets.

Wriggling like a caterpillar, he found Cate in the dark and lay beside her. She was shivering too. Whether that was from the water or fear of their hiding place being discovered, he didn't know. He reached an arm out of his cocoon and protectively wrapped it around her. She shrank closer to him.

"I'm sure we'll make it there just fine," he said to comfort her. "There's plenty of food around here if we get hungry, and beds don't get any softer than this."

"It's not that I'm worried about. We tracked in a lot of water with us, didn't we? We're completely soaked. How long do you think it'll take for them to find a trail leading straight to us?" she said shakily.

She had a point. *Not much we can do about it now,* he thought grimly. He chose words very unlike the thoughts in his head. "I'm sure they'll think it was a wet sailor loading cargo. They aren't exactly expecting us. Plus, water splashes onto ships all the time, right? Nothing suspicious about that."

They lay in the darkness for what felt like an eternity. Neither spoke. The passage of time was marked by the gentle sway of waves lapping against the hull, the creaking bones of the ship, the scuff of boots on the upper deck, and the scrape of crates being dragged into the cargo hold. Cate risked one glance through the hole, but otherwise, they hid in stillness.

Finally, the ship banked away from port, out to sea.

Outside, somewhere close by in the cargo hold, four very distinct voices carried out a quiet conversation. Jackson became aware of them when one let out a cackling laugh like an animated hyena. Overcome by curiosity, Jackson crawled to the carved hole and peeked through.

It took his eyes a minute to register anything. While the floor above had a deck prism in addition to the elevator hatch, the cargo hold was lit only by cracks in the ceiling and a precarious lamp hanging from a rotting post. Beyond the lamp, half in shadow, sat the colossal cage Jackson had spied from the forest. It was just to the left of the staircase—they must have missed it on the way in, and fortunately, it had missed them too. The creature was a living terror. A massive black bird resembling a half-molted phoenix slept facing him. Its feathers looked rigid and hard like scales or battle armor. Each hooked talon stretched a foot long. It was a wonder the bird hadn't sliced through the metal bars.

Three of the four handlers sitting in front of the cage—far enough away that the creature wouldn't catch any with beak or claws if it woke—shared a laugh at the fourth's expense.

The pudgy handler swatted a hand to dismiss the wisecrack. His voice was surprisingly deep. "Never mind that, now. If any sensible man should lay eyes on this incredible beast, let him feel a rightful dread. This here's a natural killer. Its offspring will be bred and raised as flawless weapons of war. In the wild, one of these would be near impossible to take down. Just imagine the carnage he'll do in our service!"

"I still don't see what the big deal is. What, is it going to peck the enemy's eyes out like a big hen?"

"Quiet, fool. You know not what you speak."

"A mount like no other—far more than an obedient carnivorous beast. We'll rule the skies, raining poison and fire down from above the enemy's defenses. So much for a fair fight! Who could withstand the destruction even one of these beasts will unleash? Not even the Ancients could survive!"

"You should've seen the carnage Ol' Buck wrought when we captured him at his nest. Oh yes, I was there. He's a fighter like nothing you've ever seen. Mean and vicious, too. Bit Jeff's head clean off and would've clawed my eyes out if the captain had been a hair slower with the net," the lankiest soldier said, oddly prideful about the memory.

"Try to keep it down, will you? You know Ol' Buck gets grouchy when he's tired. Best let him sleep."

The one with the hyena cackle laughed again. The bespectacled man on his left gave him a stern nudge to quiet down, then said in a dutiful voice, "Everything appears to be in order here. We should report in. Captain will be waiting."

"Might as well. Got a few days to kill. Plenty of time to goof off out at open sea," the tall man said with a laugh.

One by one, the men filed up the stairs, exiting the cargo hold. The last one out stopped on the first step, turned, and retrieved a chunk of bread from a box. Reaching through the bars, he threw it square into Buck's face. Ol' Buck awoke violently, lunging and screeching in anger. The soldier backed up a step from the bars, out of the talons' reach, and laughed.

"Donald! What possessed you to do that?" scolded the pudgy one, returning to see the cause of the commotion.

"Thought he might be hungry," he said, playing at innocence.

The soldiers headed upstairs, leaving Jackson, Cate, and the enraged beast alone in the dim room.

As frightening as Ol' Buck had been in sleep, awake it was monstrous. Behind its sharp beak, two wild red eyes darted around the room, never blinking, searching for its next meal. Fighting to break free, it lashed out unpredictably. The metal bars cried out in terrible screeches as its mighty talons raked them. It tried to stretch its wings, but its cavernous cell was too small to allow a full wingspan.

Calming down enough to stop its thrashing, the bird spotted the bread loaf in its cage. With a menacing squawk, it swallowed the loaf in a single bite. Buck looked for more, but with nothing else to consume, the bird settled back onto the cage floor and rested its eyes.

Afraid of being heard, Jackson and Cate lay silently for a long time. They took turns staring through the hole at the monster, hoping it would never stir again. At last, Jackson had to say something.

"What is that thing?"

"I'm not sure. I've never seen anything like it," Cate said, equally lost for words.

*If they have more of these, that soldier might've been right— the Eternai wouldn't stand a chance.*

As Jackson dwelled on the morbid thought, an idea entered his mind and refused to leave. Foolish and crazy as it was, he felt compelled to say it—not as a suggestion, but as a fact that allowed no other course of action. "Cate, we need to kill that thing."

She stared at him, then nodded. "I know."

He wracked his brain for a solution that didn't end with him going hand-to-beak with the monster. "They must have their doom vials in one of these crates—poison, bombs, whatever. We'll toss the whole box at it till it stops moving."

"We can't. Not today. That one guy said we're out at sea for days, remember? If we do it now, they'll tear the place apart looking for us. We'd never make it to the Eternai."

"We'll do it tomorrow then."

"There's no rush. We can take our time. We'll sneak out once we're sure it's asleep, find something deadly, then make a quick exit."

"Perfect. We can work out the details after getting some rest. That swim really took it out of me," he said, his eyelids growing heavy.

Cate didn't reply. Apparently, the swim had drained her too—she was already asleep on their soft bed of silks.

# ✦ Chapter 19 ✦

Angry screeching served as Jackson's alarm—again. Already awake, Cate was monitoring the situation through the hole. She scooched over to let Jackson watch. The nightmare bird viciously ripped the heads off the fish its handler tossed into the cage, showing a preference for mackerel. It intercepted most before they hit the floor. When the handler was too slow to throw the next one, Buck settled for swallowing the leftovers, bones and all.

The handler tossed one more fish into the cage, then revealed his empty palms to signal there would be no more. "Sorry, old boy. Another couple hours, and then we'll get you out of that cramped cage. You be good now, Buck."

Its handler started up the stairs, and Buck redoubled its efforts to break out of the cage. Long after it was clear the creature wouldn't escape, it settled down for another nap.

"How long was I out?" Jackson said through a yawn. He crawled back from the hole.

"You slept in. I didn't want to wake you, but I was tempted when you started to snore," she teased.

"I didn't actually… did I?" Jackson asked, thankful she couldn't see him blushing in the dark.

Cate's teeth shone in a smile. "Not *that* loudly."

Jackson forced out a laugh, then quickly changed the subject. "When are we going to take out that bird?"

"Now's probably as good a time as ever. It just ate and looks like it's asleep. I'd guess the handlers won't be back for an hour. We should search for the alchemy crate. Oh, and here—I grabbed it from the crate beside ours while you were snoring," she said, prodding him with a hunk of bread.

He hungrily devoured the loaf with a speed that may have rivaled even Ol' Buck. Working up the nerve to face the monster—and possibly a ship full of enemy combatants—he whispered in support of her plan, then joined her in lifting the lid off the container as quietly as they could.

Landing softly, Jackson scanned for movement, then focused on the stacks of unmarked crates littering the room. "Fragile" was painted on a handful along the wall. He silently pointed them out to Cate. She nodded, then they crept over and began to comb through their contents.

The first two crates he checked contained hundreds of bottles of amber liquid that smelled like alcohol. The third held weird teapots labeled with slogans like "This pot is hot!" and "I decree we all drink tea!" Eventually, it was Cate who located the crystal vials. She waved him over, frowning as she contemplated which ones they needed.

Jackson peered inside. A long wooden rack spanned the inside of the shallow box with individual holders for each vial, all resting on a bed of hay. Fortunately, they were clearly organized and labeled. He counted three of each of the four mixtures, distinguishable by their colors. Twelve in total. The blue liquid was labeled *Release*. Beside it was a haunting green mixture called *Explosive*, then a red one called *Fear*, and, lastly, a familiar orange liquid called *Slumber*.

"You pick." Cate backed away from the box.

Jackson pondered the selection. He knew two from experience, and he figured he could take a reasonable guess at the others. Deciding one of each should suffice, he pocketed a *Slumber* and a *Release,* keeping the other two in hand.

"Ready?" he asked Cate.

She gave his left hand a quick squeeze of support.

"Ready."

Quietly, carefully, Jackson crossed the floor to the cage, afraid of breathing too loud. Outside the bars, he drew in a deep breath to steady himself. Then, like a professional pitcher, he threw the vial marked *Explosive* through the bars at the monstrous beast.

The glass bounced off the bird's face and clattered to the metal floor.

The bird snapped to life in a violent rage.

It came for Jackson first, springing forth and trying to claw through the bars. Thwarted by the cage, it shrieked in anger and switched up its tactics, bashing its beak against the unyielding iron instead. Though the bars seemed to be withholding the assault, Jackson instinctively backed away from the crazed animal bent on killing him. He weighed the other vial in his hand, debating whether to throw it now or keep it in case Ol' Buck got free.

The bird paused its attack, spotting the strange green vial resting in the corner of its cage. It turned, tilted its head, then smashed the vial with its foot.

A roaring explosion instantly erupted from the vial. The blast force was strong enough to throw Jackson onto his back. Miraculously, neither the two vials in his pocket nor the other eight in the crate were activated.

When he lifted his head, he discovered that the cage had been destroyed. Remnants of metal rods stood twisted and bent. Several were ripped in two. A gaping hole now split the floor, having ripped through the wooden boards beneath to expose the hull. Suffice it to say, skipping the needlessly gory details of the creature's dismemberment, Ol' Buck never stood a chance against violent chemistry. If anyone should doubt the fact, they need only look up to see feathers ripped from the bird's body and fashioned into throwing darts.

Jackson's ears were ringing. Still, he could make out voices rising in alarm from the upper decks. Their work had not gone unnoticed.

"Jackson! Time to go," Cate said, frantically scanning between the hole in the hull and the stairs, trying to come up with their next move.

Jackson rushed into action, returning to the crate to pick up another *Explosive*. "Come on!" he yelled, taking her by the hand and leading her across the room. He risked a fretful glance at the stairwell. No one yet—but he heard them coming. Cocking back his arm, he threw the glass vial with all his strength at the alchemy crate.

The glass burst, starting a chain reaction. Without the nightmarish bird's dense body to soak up the blast, the explosion was immense. The seven remaining vials detonated in a deafening rumble as a plume of fire burst through the freshly torn hole in the ship's iron hull. Flames leaped onto the nearby wooden boxes, swiftly finding fuel to grow. As the heat wave stretched across the cargo hold, Jackson turned and shielded Cate. His back took the worst of it, and he cried out as the heat licked his exposed neck. The pressure wave caused them to sway and stagger, but they kept on their feet.

"Are you okay?" Jackson asked, concerned.

"Yeah," she murmured, staring across the hold.

Water rushed in through the bottom half of the hole, soaking through the floorboards into the bowels of the ship. It was coming fast enough to form a rapidly rising pool. The ship listed with a groan, and metal screeched across the deck above. The invading stream would certainly win before long, condemning the vessel to the bottom of the sea.

The *Feir* mixtures revealed their purpose. Even the floor now covered by water burned in eerie red flames. The strange fire swept across the room like fog, silent but for its growing crackle of destruction. Smoke began to fill the air.

Cate found her wits first and pulled him into motion, leading him to the stairs. She drew her sword and dropped his hand. He followed behind, unarmed, acutely feeling the loss of the sword and shield his captors had stolen from him.

How embarrassing.

At the top of the stairs, Cate stopped abruptly and yanked him into a compact supply closet. She left the door cracked open, just enough to peek through. A team of eight Night soldiers hurried by a second later, heading downstairs to investigate.

Before he could breathe a sigh of relief, Cate shoved him back into the hall and broke into a run.

Frantic and confused shouts tumbled down from the main deck. Jackson thought he heard someone say "Iceberg." Instead of heading for the main hatch in the middle of the ship, Cate rounded the corner and started up another set of stairs. The rising clamor suggested they were moving in the right direction to escape.

They met their first adversary at the top of the stairs. Unfortunately for him, he was unarmed and unprepared for

Cate's lightning-fast strike. He crumpled to the floor, his eyes frozen forever in a final expression of shock.

Thankfully, no one else impeded their path.

Up another flight, they ascended a short ladder and popped out a hatch onto the quarter deck. She slayed the officer before he could finish drawing his sword, then engaged the helmsman at the steering wheel. Their screams were lost in the chaos.

On the quarter deck, Jackson realized the extent of the damage he'd caused. The ship leaned hard, thirty degrees to port. Water was already lapping at the low side railings. Dozens of seamen, desperate but doomed, jettisoned every deadweight they could find—barrels, boxes, beds—anything to lighten the ship and keep her afloat a little longer. Within minutes, several gross tons of cargo littered the waves around the vessel and trailed in her wake.

"Jackson!" Cate shouted as she dumped a barrel of freshwater over, spilling it across the deck.

He ran over to help as she recorked the bunghole. Together, they lifted the barrel and heaved it overboard.

Without a second thought, she stepped up onto the rail and dove off the back of the ship after it.

Warily, he climbed onto the rail and stared down at the long drop to the water. Second and even third thoughts crept in. Below, Cate pulled herself halfway onto the barrel, using it as a floatation device as she paddled away from the drowning ship. She looked up at him expectantly.

"Up there! We've got a rat in our bilge."

Jackson looked over his shoulder and met eyes with a sailor on the main deck below. The murderous look on the Night's face revealed he had made the connection between the gaping hole in the ship's hull and the stowaway. He and those nearby abandoned their vain efforts to save the ship, intent instead on making the bilge rat go down with it.

The threat of death was motivating enough. Jackson took the leap. His stomach flipped as that awful, weightless feeling hit—like his insides were still on the ship while his body was falling. His feet hit the water, and he closed his eyes as he plunged under the waves.

The frigid water sent a shock through his body. He kicked and flailed up through the bubbles of the churned water and gasped for air when he broke to the surface. He swiveled his head in every direction, looking for Cate. Seeing her wave, he started for the barrel at top speed, eager to put distance between himself and any pursuing sailors.

After swimming a deceptively far distance, he finally reached the barrel. Cate helped pull him up, and, surprisingly, their emergency floatation device managed to support them both. Letting out a groan of relief, he allowed himself a look back at the ship.

The sailors had already given up pursuit. Every hand was scrambling to get the ship to shore. At this point, there was little left to salvage besides their lives. Despite whatever majestic name the vessel had been given, its destiny appeared immovable. The iron ship would forever decorate this coastal shelf as an underwater wreck—half-submerged, if the sailors labored to great effect. At least its rusted bones would make a pleasant reef for fish someday.

As dire as the situation was for the sailors, it soon proved capable of getting worse.

It started from below. Although the cargo hold was fully submerged, the eerie fire had not yet died. Its red fingers began to spread across the wooden deck, devouring the ship from the center. Flotsam that had drifted out from the cargo hold still burned in the waves. The impossible fire refused to yield to the ocean, raging brighter as young sailors tried to douse it with buckets.

Some had seen the end coming. The quick, the wise, and the cowards had thrown themselves to the mercy of the sea. Many of them survived, aided by the floating cargo they had dumped minutes ago.

They were outnumbered by those who did not.

Horrible, haunting screams rose from the deck as the unquenchable fire crawled onto clothing and gnawed on the skin beneath. Officers in their heavy armor went under the waves and never resurfaced. A black fin or two could be seen circling the debris.

Jackson turned away from the carnage and tried to shut out the agonized cries. He focused instead on the distant land mass ahead. The waves seemed more intent on sweeping them along the coast than bringing them to shore. Slowly and conservatively, they kicked and paddled toward land, but it didn't appear to get any closer.

Some indeterminate time later, he looked back and saw they were alone. Far off, as if carried by another current, the surviving Night made no attempt to follow them. At this point, the ship's hull was fully submerged. Only the mast's tip hinted at where it had taken its final breath. Over a thousand yards away, the raging fire's light was still visible on the sail and even in the water below.

They drifted for what felt like hours. At some point, they both stopped paddling and waited for the waves to carry them to shore. They were physically exhausted and mentally drained. The sun had been a pleasant source of warmth against the cool water at first, but by now it seemed solely intent on roasting Jackson's neck.

Finally, the waves took them through the surf, where their barrel-raft came to a rather sudden stop on the sand.

Jackson ventured a few wobbly steps on shore. The seawater lapped against his soaked boots. Cate joined him, and they tramped up the beach to plop down in the dry sand. He lay on his back, resting his eyes as he recovered, listening to the steady rhythm of the ocean. He easily could have fallen asleep on his warm seaside bed.

Their respite was only for a moment.

He heard the drum of hoofbeats first, then felt the tremor in the earth. Eight horsemen rode into view, galloping hard across the beach.

There was no time to run or hide.

Within seconds, the riders encircled the waterlogged castaways, brandishing their lances to dissuade any attempts at escape. The thought was far from Jackson's mind—he was much too tired to try outrunning a horse over soft sand. Cate similarly made no move to sit up.

They remained silent as the horses were reined to a halt. One rider dismounted and walked over to where they lay in the sand. He stared down at them, one hand resting on his sheathed sword. Though his face was hidden behind an iron mask, the contempt in his voice was unmissable.

"You're under arrest for treason and conspiracy to abet the enemies of the kingdom. Your rights are none. Save your persuasive words—I will not hear your case. The wreck and its recovered cargo testify to your guilt. Pity there weren't fewer survivors!"

He roughly lifted Jackson to his feet and bound him in irons. The rider moved to repeat the action with Cate. She swatted his hand aside and stood on her own, then presented her wrists. After shackling her, the rider split them up and loaded them on the backs of different horses like cargo. After swinging back onto his horse, the leader signaled to his posse and clicked his heels to start the ride out.

The ride was long and rough. Jackson's chains were tied to the saddle to keep him from sliding off, but they left enough slack for him to get jostled around. He was facing outward, away from the other riders, and couldn't turn to see how Cate was doing. Left alone to his thoughts, he spiraled into dread about the end of the ride—and what might await on the other side. His imagination spun endless scenarios of how their captors might torture or kill them.

*Have a little dignity,* he chastised himself.

Worrying wouldn't help. If a chance to escape came along, he'd take it. Otherwise, whatever their fates, the hour would arrive, and he would endure it.

Dusk settled as they approached a walled city. The horsemen and their prisoners were waved through without a word. Jackson thought he saw his horseman's shoulders relax once they passed the gate. Though the man seemed more at ease, an eerie stillness lingered in the city air, raising the hair on Jackson's neck.

The clop of horseshoes against cobblestones echoed through silent streets. As far as Jackson could tell, the place looked like a ghost town. Aside from the guards at the gate, he hadn't seen a soul. No lovers out for a stroll. No children playing outside. No old men returning from local pubs. The only sign of life came from second-story windows of the cramped apartments lining the street, where the faint glow of lanterns spilled through dark curtains.

The horses trotted single file down side streets and the occasional dirt path. Seemingly arising out of nowhere, a castle appeared ahead. Its four corners were marked by tall, dark towers. Two were joined with the outer city wall. Green flags bearing a white bird hung from each turret, fluttering proudly above the city. Jackson thought they looked familiar.

In the courtyard before the looming castle, the riders dismounted and handed off their horses to the stable boys, solemn and gaunt youths. The leader of the knights assigned two soldiers to walk with each prisoner, before and behind. The stocky man breathing down Jackson's neck gave him a shove forward.

The castle doors opened into a vast great hall. Inside, torches and banners crowded the walls. They marched past long tables of fine wood, still littered with the remnants of a recent feast. At the far end, they entered a narrow door and ascended two flights via an unadorned service stairwell. Reemerging into a common corridor at the top, they walked a short distance to a more impressive dark blue door.

The throne room looked custom-built for a prized hunter. Taxidermized birds stared down from the rafters just below the vaulted ceilings. The walls were packed with grizzly trophies, featuring beasts and fish of every kind. The largest, the skull and antlers of something like a moose, stretching at least ten feet, tip to tip. The hatted buffalo and boar heads above the throne were the most tasteless, and the full-bodied brown bear positioned just inside the door was the scariest.

In contrast to the rustic displays, a second decorative theme was clearly present—suggesting that either the original designer had complex and conflicting tastes or the final decor was the result of tense debate and compromise between lord and lady. Fine golden instruments rested in ornate glass cases. Elaborate, if a little gaudy, a sprawling chandelier spanned the width of the room, its long crystal strings sparkling down like rain—numbering a thousand or more. Not to be overlooked, a princely silver throne rested on a raised dais in the center of the room. Its plushy blue upholstering looked luxuriously soft. The arms of the tall chair were decorated with rubies the whole way down. They glinted in the plentiful torchlight, evidence of constant polishing.

Smiling on the throne, a familiar young man fixed his green eyes on the captives with great interest. He brushed his messy brown hair from his face, turning his expectant gaze to the lead knight.

The knight bowed before making his report. "Your Highness! Our scouts reported a Night vessel off the coast. The ship was wrecked by the time we got there, possibly on a reef. We captured these two agents before they could rejoin the main force. The rest of our company stayed behind to intercept the survivors and recover their supplies. Sir!"

The prince assessed Cate with mild curiosity. "I see. And what heinous crime were they committing when you made your arrest?"

"They were… lying together on the beach?" The knight cleared his throat awkwardly.

"Wow. I'm shocked you didn't behead them on the spot. A young couple lying in the sand? The audacity!"

Their captor stammered awkwardly. In an attempt to strengthen his accusation, he added, "Sir, these are certainly enemy agents! I mean, circumstantially..."

The man on the throne nodded thoughtfully. "I hear you, Sid. Thanks for sharing. Now, let's all listen to Jackson's side of the story," Prince Falcon said with a knowing smile.

# ✤ Chapter 20 ✤

I can solve that mystery for you. We recaptured this city, Orsadia, a couple days after Rein reported you missing. Bloody, messy affair. The men had more than earned a celebration, but they didn't want one—just a little downtime and rest. I'd like to think of it as a silver lining that as many families were reunited as were torn apart. Anyway, you were saying?" Prince Falcon asked, enthralled.

"Was he?" King Talon said, disinterested. He'd come in near the beginning of Jackson's story and claimed his seat on the throne, leaving Falcon to lean against the side of the tall chair. Although he'd insisted that Jackson start over so he wouldn't miss anything, Talon made a point of showing his disdain, wrinkling his nose throughout the tale and scoffing at every mention of Jackson's supposed heroics. With one leg slung over the armrest, he stared up at the chandelier, aloof.

"That's it, really," Jackson wrapped up his tale. He'd already recounted how Cate had rescued him. Talon had smirked at that. Jackson had skipped the night they shared in the forest, out under the stars, but he'd offered every detail he could think of about the winged beast and their escape from the boat. "I met Sid here—he's got quite the grip, I might add—and he and his men strapped us to the backs of their horses like saddlebags. We rode straight here from the beach… and here we are."

The prince smiled brightly at Jackson, almost like a proud older brother, then lowered his gaze to the floor, lost in thought.

Talon was quicker to speak his mind.

"Well, if we take anything from that… *tale,* it's that their new creature could be a problem. We lack the means to counter any aerial threats. If they have more of those beasts, our troops would be at a severe disadvantage."

Falcon sighed in reluctant agreement. "It's true. We have no anti-air technology or machines. As far as I'm aware, we don't have any natural predators or wildlife that could compete—none that could lift a man, never mind engage in aerial combat. I'd say our best course is to shoot them down, but short of growing wings and taking to the skies ourselves, I can't imagine we'd be successful."

A crazy, borderline insane idea came to mind. Jackson almost laughed, too excited to care whether it made sense. "What if we did take to the skies?"

"You're suggesting we simply ignore biology and fly? Have your past experiences spontaneously sprouting wings gone that well?" Talon asked dryly.

Jackson let the jab slide. His optimism grew by the second. "We won't need to grow wings—those beasts already have them."

Talon pinched the bridge of his nose. "You're just restating the problem. Their beasts have wings; we don't, and that's the issue."

Jackson shook his head. "No, it's our solution. These beasts can be clearly controlled; the Night couldn't ride them into battle otherwise. If we find a way to capture and control them, we could use them ourselves. If we can't tame them, we'll shoot before they take to the sky. Worst case, a couple dozen arrows could probably bring one down if it dips low enough. We could try a catapult, but that sounds… less safe."

"And how, pray tell, would we capture one—much less learn to control it?" Talon indulged him.

"They can't stay in the air forever. When they land, I can't imagine they'd be allowed to just roam free. We can take them in their cages. As for how to control them… I'm sure we'll figure that out."

Talon frowned. "To do this, we'd first need to find their encampments. Our scouts have reported no such thing between here and Verden. By the time we get an opportunity to test your theory, we'll have already retaken our homeland."

"What then? Will the war end, or is there a part two? And what if we do run into an encampment on the way to Verden?" Jackson pressed.

Falcon cut in before Talon could think up another sarcastic retort. "I'm sure we can all agree that, though it's an unconventional idea, it's one worth considering. We'll never bow. If we can't fight their beasts head-on, I like the thought of turning them to our side. But enough speculation for one day—thanks to this report, we are better prepared. I have no doubt he endured great hardship to deliver it. Let him rest, as he has well earned. Sid, please escort Jackson and his friend to their chambers," he said, giving a friendly nod to Cate.

Talon looked intent on arguing, but he leaned back in his throne with a scoff. "Yes, praise be that we have this brave young boy to bring hope in our trials. A shame that his looks bear the obvious mark of a horrible childhood curse—

to be ugly for life! Tragedy. And his hair... Most assuredly, a mean-spirited witch was involved. A haggard little forest troll, indeed." The king shook his head, then waved Jackson off, looking pleased. "Dismissed."

Sid stepped forward and bowed in apology to Cate, then Jackson.

"Oh, come now! There's no need for all that," Talon said, rolling his eyes.

"Please, this way," Sid said, leading them out of the throne room.

At the top of a tightly winding stairwell, they stepped into a short hall with just two doors, opposite each other. Sid unlocked them before handing over their keys. Inside, the rooms looked identical: uncluttered and comfortably simple. Panoramic windows offered a beautiful view of rolling green hills to the west, just outside the city.

"This will be your lodging for the coming days. Sorry again for the mishap," Sid said, giving one more half-bow before heading back downstairs.

Jackson opened the door to his room and plopped down onto the big bed. The comforter was as soft as a cloud.

Following him in, Cate crossed the room and stared out the window. "It's beautiful here," she said softly, amazed.

Jackson sat up to see what she was looking at. Green grass danced in the wind under a bright blue sky. The late afternoon sun cast dramatic shadows back from the west city wall. Inside, limestone roofs reflected the brilliant daylight. Beyond, a shepherd watched over his flock as they grazed in the hills. Jackson realized that this was her first glimpse into a land she'd always heard of but never before seen. Maybe she saw it like him—enchanted and new, though not so different from home. Funny how quickly that initial splendor could fade in familiarity.

Allowing himself a moment to marvel at the foreign land through fresh eyes, he joined her at the window. The world outside looked so peaceful and still. No bloody clashes, no sounds of war. He could almost forget the hardships they had endured over these past days and the battles still looming ahead. "Sure is something."

*Almost.*

With a longing sigh, Cate peeled herself away from the window and headed toward the door. "I'm sure we'll get called back into a war briefing before long, but why not steal a few minutes for ourselves? Shame to let the birds hog all the nice weather," she said, smiling at him.

He smiled too. "I'd like that."

He took her by the hand and walked her down the long stairwell. Exiting through a side door, they found a soft patch of grass in the courtyard and lay in the warmth of the sun. For that rapturous moment, they closed their eyes and rested, free of the burdens destiny had prepared them.

But only for a moment.

A short hour later, a stalky courier approached them. He informed them that the king had called a mandatory war room meeting and that they were to report to the great hall immediately.

"It was nice while it lasted," Jackson sighed as he stood. He offered Cate a hand.

"We'll have time again—when this is all over," she promised, accepting his help.

When they arrived at the Great Hall, they found the long feasting tables were now crowded. Servers brought cups to any who raised hands, but the mood seemed more somber than festive. Jackson and Cate quietly sat at a lightly occupied table off to the side.

Whispers bubbled up, filling the room with a swell of sound, though it was impossible to make out any specifics. After a few more minutes of people filtering in and finding seats, King Talon and Prince Falcon walked onto the raised platform at the end of the hall.

The whispers died down as Talon stepped forth to survey his audience with cold, calculating eyes. Only once the hall was fully still in tense silence did he begin his address. "Welcome, all. We have spent the past few days reveling, as was well deserved. The Eternai army has accomplished much in recent weeks. Bought back with blood, much of the stolen land, ripped out from under us, has been reclaimed. A good start… but our job is not yet finished."

He paused dramatically, surveying the room to make sure every eye was on him. His voice rose in fiery passion as he refused to be denied his destiny. "We have taken Kanrio, Orsadia, and every inch of land in between. No Night will set foot there again. Now is the time to complete our duty. Our land—the land of our fathers and their forefathers, the land where our children's blood was unjustly spilled—will not be ruled by anyone but the Eternai. Even now, we suffer insult as the enemy occupies our capital. The Night must never be allowed a moment's thought that any of this land belongs to them. Not one rock. Not one blade of grass. None of it.

"Tomorrow, we begin our march for the capital. We will rip Verden from their ashen hands without mercy. Our plan is simple. No trickery. No deceit. We shall take the city by force and crush the enemy through strength and devotion. Let your rage run free—we will purge this blight from our land. Freedom awaits. Glory awaits. For the Eternai!" Talon ripped his sword from its sheath and thrust it into the air.

Led by the king's black-clad guard, a roar of support bloomed around the room. Shouts for blood and vengeance mixed with cheers for the homeland.

Basking in their loud adulation, Talon stood tall and proud. A sinister thought entered his mind, marked by his statesman's smile giving way to a wild-eyed twitch. He raised a hand to quiet his audience. "The moment is within reach. Why delay? Let us ride out tonight!"

The enthusiasm behind their cheers deflated sharply. Still, the loyalists rallied themselves to shout. Others clapped out of obligation, unwilling to risk offending the king.

Someone sitting near Jackson grumbled about food wagons not being ready. He stuffed a loaf of bread into his pants and advised his neighbor to stuff his pack, figuring that rations would be sparse and second-rate.

The decision was not a popular one, but their king had spoken. If nothing else, at least they could look forward to the war being over a day sooner.

"Half an hour you will be given to pack. Meet at the gates and prepare to move out. Dismissed," King Talon said, turning his back to them.

The hall emptied quickly as the soldiers rushed to gather their things and say goodbyes. Having few of either, Jackson hung back and finished his meal. He looked across the room and noticed another who was slow to move. Falcon sat with his face in his hands, visibly anxious and caught off-guard by the sudden announcement to depart.

Jackson left him to his thoughts. He had to take care of his own problems. First, food for the trip. Second, he still didn't have a weapon.

Cate solved the first problem for him, offering to hunt and gather for them both, today and in days to come. He sheepishly accepted, knowing they didn't have a Kronyx between them and that she was the better survivor by a mile. They parted ways outside the castle, and Jackson set off to find Canon, who had conspicuously missed the meeting.

Twenty minutes of wandering the streets of Orsadia later, Jackson spotted him exiting a shop with Krystal at his side and Rein bringing up the rear. Before he could call out, a familiar black cat tackled Jackson from the side, giving him a wet lick on the face.

"Leon!" Jackson laughed, giving the Nocturne an overdue scratch behind the ears.

"Well done, cat," Canon said, walking over.

"Welcome back, Jackson. Heard you were still alive. Glad to see the rumors are true," Rein said, almost smiling.

Jackson sat up with a wide grin. Until he'd seen them just now, he hadn't realized how much he'd missed them all. "Yeah, I'm pretty stoked about that too," he said.

"Looking for these?" Rein asked, removing a sword and shield from the back of his pack.

Jackson stood and took the gear. The sword's weight felt good in his hand. Even more so after he had feared it would be lost forever. "Thanks. I owe you one."

"Two," Rein corrected, handing him the shield.

Whooping with joy, Canon enveloped Jackson in a bone-crushing hug before he could stow his sword. "Jack-boy! I told 'em you weren't a croaker! I told them, and I told them! Ask anyone, I said, 'He's the proper adventuring type. He can handle his own marbles—and you did! They wouldn't take a wager on it, but I'd have bet a week's wages. Jackson is back, son!"

"Missed you too, buddy," Jackson managed through choked breaths. Canon released him, and he gratefully sucked air back into his lungs.

"We should head toward the gate," Rein said, taking the lead.

"Did Leon behave while I was gone?" Jackson asked Canon, surprised the cat had been willing to travel with them.

"An hour after they reported you missing, he started followin' me and wouldn't stop! Had to feed this kitty a lot of catnip," Canon grinned at Leon.

"I'm excited for you to catch us up on the way to Verden. We've got plenty of time to kill," Krystal said as they passed through the city gates, joining the throngs of people already assembled. "Oh, and guess what my Canie did?"

Jackson looked sideways at Canon, whose eyes were fixed straight ahead. Unable to hold back a laugh, Jackson snorted and cocked an eyebrow at his friend. "Canie?"

Canon pretended not to hear him.

"It's my special little nickname for my special little beau," Krystal clarified dotingly.

Canon seemed to find something captivating on the ground by his feet.

"Anyway, as a Cavar, he was able to snag us a cart to ride in. We get to sit back and relax," Krystal proudly patted Canon on the back. He smiled at the recognition, reclaiming a bit of his lost dignity.

"Is there room for one more?" Jackson asked.

Canon seized the chance to let himself off the hook. "Hoping to score your lady friend a ride too? No worries, we got the space—if you got the yarn. I want the full story in all its juicy details. Especially about your new romance," Canon gave a sideways nod toward Cate as she walked over, carrying a bulging pack on her back.

Jackson tried to conceal his blushing with disbelief at her score. "Geez, Cate! Did you pack the whole forest?"

She smiled at the awe on his face. "Traded for ready-made supplies down at the butcher's. You'd be amazed what one deer can buy." Spotting Leon, her smile turned to horror, and she jumped a foot in the air. "What's that doing here!?"

Leon sat and scratched himself disinterestedly.

"That's my Nocturne, Leon," said Jackson.

"I know what a Nocturne is. My question is: why do you have one?" She reached for her swords.

"Don't worry. He's just a big, sweet, fluffy, kitty cat. Aren't you, Leon?" Krystal said, petting his fur.

Leon suffered the insults for her good scratches.

Cate cautiously released her grip on the hilts of her swords and eyed the members of the group.

"Everyone, this is Cate. Cate, meet my friends: Rein, Canon, Krystal… and Tyson," Jackson said, pointing to each in turn as Tyson joined them.

"Cate," she said, giving them a shy smile. "I'm from the Nightlands."

Krystal and Tyson exchanged puzzled looks but held back from saying anything rash. Canon didn't try to hide the surprise on his face. Rein nodded as if suspecting as much. Krystal broke the tension, gesturing to a horse-drawn wagon. "King Talon just gave the signal to march. We'd better hop in before our ride leaves without us."

Reminiscent of the last cart Jackson had ridden in, it was questionable if not downright rickety. At least this time he didn't have to masquerade as peas, potatoes, and carrots. Cate hesitated, but Jackson assured her she was welcome, and she climbed in with him.

Then they were off.

The horses put in the work while their passengers took it easy. Canon cleared his throat, wasting no time. "Let's 'ear a tale, Jackson!"

"If you insist, Canie," Jackson said, unable to help it.

Canon's defeated groan won a suspicious glare from Krystal. "What, don't you like your nickname?"

"Of course, dear. I love it," Canon said, too hastily. "How about that story, Jackson? Anytime now…"

# ✠ Chapter 21 ✠

The journey passed in the blink of an eye. The small talk, laughter, rest—all of it was soon forgotten as they watched the dying sun fall behind the walls of Verden. By the end of the night, there would be much more dying. The sun was fortunate to have less than an hour left of its watch before hiding its face from the coming violence.

Even from a mile away on the hill where the caravan had formed battle lines, the capital looked immense. To a passerby who cared nothing for flags and banners, the capital might have looked unchanged, impressive as always. Jackson had asked about its layout during the ride, and Tyson had told him.

As a result of multiple expansions over the course of its history, the city consisted of several rings. Until recently, the outermost ring was where most of the commoners lived. Cramped, crowded, and crummy, but many called it home. When the Night attacked, many abandoned their homes and fled for safety in the north. Those who stayed learned to hide indoors. Those who didn't... well, few could tell their story.

Past the Residential Quarter, the second ring's older, larger limestone buildings were the hub of trade, alongside a sprawling bazaar for smaller, less-established merchants. The Trade Quarter was technically split in two: the Marketplace for feed, food, and dining, and the Craftsman's Terrace for everything else. In practice, pop-up vendors of all sorts were common in the bazaar, particularly junk sellers, while a few top-tier restauranteurs had staked claims in the historic white buildings. Industry and commerce had also taken a hit since the occupation. In many streets, the ring of a blacksmith's hammer or the voice of a jeweler's hawker could no longer be heard. A few Eternai proved more loyal to their craft than their kingdom, choosing to cooperate with the Night and hold onto their way of life.

The Central District was mainly administrative. At its heart rose a majestic keep, encircled by a wall that remained unbroken since the founding of the city. The black material encasing the walls was a legendary ancient ore called Seartite, said to cut through the thickest of metals and even Dragonhide. Seartite had vanished seemingly overnight, save for the faithful walls that still protected Verden's keep.

Such was Tyson's account of history.

Jackson eyed the distant city, curious to see it all for himself. The battle lines continued marching closer. His unit was part of the center group, behind the vanguard. Cavalry advanced along the flanks. The army kept its wide formation strictly in order, each row stepping in unison across the plain. The outer cohorts were only eight men deep, while the center wedge was reinforced rank after rank, as deep as eighty men. There had to be ten thousand or more in total, but beyond that, Jackson could neither see nor count. Not that he had the focus, anyway. His anxious thoughts were fixed on the battle ahead.

He looked over the sea of helmets in front of him to measure their progress. Still comfortably out of arrow range, but close enough to see the Night sentinels on the tall outer walls that surrounded the city. Aside from the few runners passing messages and supplies, the armed watchers on the walls stood like gargoyles. If they felt fear, it didn't show. They looked ready to carry out their duty and defend the city gate with their lives.

Leading the vanguard, Falcon rode tall on a pristine white horse. Both were encased in armor. In a show of unity, a green cape fluttered out behind him in place of his standard orange. Though it looked impressive on him, the same cloth looked pompous on the shoulders of the king riding safely in the rear, far from harm's way.

A chill of anticipation surged through Jackson as he adjusted his armor. He stretched his arm, already sore from bearing his shield. Nerves were getting to him. He looked to his left and saw Rein and Cate. Farther to his right, Krystal and Tyson were with another unit, separate in task but one in purpose. Closer, Leon prowled forward at his side, head held high. A green-and-gold collar gleamed at his neck, helping his allies distinguish him from their enemies. They were all with him, including Canon, who rode beside the prince on a sleek brown horse.

They weren't just his allies—they were friends.

This world was his home now. Even more than that, though he didn't know when it had happened, he realized he truly cared about its people. He felt a burden, a deep calling to defend the defenseless. Doubt still plagued the dark places of his mind, insisting he'd be safer if he abandoned them and ran back to Voldroun, tail tucked between his legs, begging for his shabby old life back. Instead, today he put on bravery, refusing to let the coward inside him prevail.

The gates stood three hundred yards away.

They were in arrow range. Tension thickened the air. At any moment now, Falcon would raise his sword, and the decisive battle would commence.

A collective breath held, a shared heartbeat, as the prince drew his sword.

"To victory!" he shouted, hoisting his sword.

"To victory!" rippled through the ranks.

"Charge!"

A roar rose from the lungs of the Eternai, vengeance and anxiety, fear and bloodlust bleeding into one yell. Falcon spurred his horse into a gallop. The vanguard on foot tried to keep up, but their prince had set an unmatchable pace.

A hail of arrows blackened the sky.

"Shields!"

Those who bore shields raised them, yet while some stopped, others kept running at full speed. The disorder cost many men their lives, knocked over, tripped, and trampled— wholly exposed to the bite of black arrows.

The momentum carried forward. No time to slow or mourn. On the run, Jackson helped a survivor to his feet.

"Thanks!" he panted.

"Keep going!" Jackson advised, rushing past.

As they came within a football field's length, another hail of arrows fell. Most were on the same page this time and slowed down to duck and cover. Even still, the sheer number of missiles made it inevitable that some would sneak through.

"Ladders!"

The vanguard raised siege ladders against the base of the wall and began to climb. A few ladders were lifted, each with a man already gripping the rungs near the top. One fell as the ladder hit stone, but two others became the first brave souls into the fray, and their heroism merits remembrance.

The defenders' coordinated tactics fled in the face of survival. No longer following a unified command, the archers leaned over the parapets, shooting down and sideways at the invaders scaling the ladders as they tried to angle their arrows past the shields. Some stayed out of cover too long and fell to reprisals from backline warbows and close-up crossbows.

At first, the assault looked hopeless. The crash of each kicked-down ladder fell like a death knell. But for every one toppled by the Night, two more went up to replace it. Gaps began to appear in the defense, and the spool unraveled from there. More invaders climbed onto the ramparts, engaging more archers, creating more holes in the defense. Before long, it looked as if an army of ants covered the walls.

By the time Jackson reached the wall, the gate had been won. Falcon and Canon were first inside, joined by a diminished cohort from the vanguard in battling for control of the street. Others streamed in and continued up to the battlements, overwhelming the defenders from behind.

Jackson's unit surged through the gate to join the short-lived fight in the street. Others flooding in behind him branched off in every direction. He saw Tyson and Krystal head down a side street deeper into the Residential Quarter and gave them a nod of support before they disappeared. If all went well, he'd see them again after his unit captured the keep. A tall order.

The fighting ahead concluded before Jackson could get involved. Now on foot, Falcon and Canon led columns of battle-tested veterans toward the heart of the city, into the Trade Quarter. Another unit tore down the purple and black flags of the enemy while going door to door, urging Verden's citizens to join the resistance.

A door burst open behind Jackson. Spinning on his heel, he raised his shield against the ambusher's ax. Before the attack could connect, the man lurched back and collapsed against the wall.

Rein walked over and retrieved his knife from the axman's chest.

"Thanks," Jackson mumbled.

"Let's catch up to the prince," said Rein.

The road aged generations at the border between the ramshackle Residential Quarter and the historic limestone of the Craftsman's Terrace. Jackson nearly tripped on the first patch of uneven cobblestones.

"Kanrio, left! To the bazaar!" The captain of the unit behind Jackson ordered his men.

Another unit, the remaining outer flank of the vanguard, had already split off to the right, into the heart of the Craftsman's Terrace. Jackson slowed to watch two off-duty Night soldiers being dragged out of a blacksmith's shop. A fire burned inside, suggesting they had either just dropped off or were picking up an order. Theirs wasn't the only business disrupted.

Already, screaming and shouting filled the streets in a senseless cacophony. Violence and mayhem multiplied, but it was a fruitless task to discern what lay behind each cry.

One scream pierced the chaos, the desperation in her voice impossible to ignore. "Help! Won't anyone help me?"

"I'll catch up!" Cate promised, running after Kanrio Unit toward the Marketplace, in the direction of the voice.

Jackson's first instinct was to run after her and make sure she stayed safe, but he knew she was the better duelist between them. He had full confidence that she'd be okay— Cate knew how to survive. His worry would be better spent on his own trials ahead.

The border of the Central District was just as starkly marked. Most of the buildings were wooden, charming but lacking the splendor of the limestone shops. Alone in its grandeur stood the walled keep, as out of place as if it had fallen from the sky. The central spear of the Eternai army thrust straight for the keep.

Jackson's unit caught up to the vanguard at the gate. Surprisingly, if not a little suspiciously, it was already open. Falcon watched them approach and, deciding he had enough support to storm the castle, led the way inside. Jackson stole a glance at the mythical black walls as he passed through the gate. The ancient Seartite reminded him of obsidian, though the darkest faces of the stone looked blacker than black.

Inside the castle, Eternai soldiers streamed into every corridor, spreading like water. A meager two dozen pikemen guarded the grand entrance, holding formation at the base of a short stairway that led up to a tall art gallery.

They were no match for Falcon.

Energized by familiar walls welcoming him home, the prince led the charge against the line. He feinted at the edge of their range, drawing a thrust. As the pike extended, he seized its shaft and yanked it back, dragging the soldier face-first onto the floor. Leaping over the pike, Canon cut in front of Falcon to slip inside the guard of the neighboring pikeman. Falcon took the other side, parrying before crashing into his enemy with unstoppable force.

Crossbow bolts flew across the room, thinning the line before the inexhaustible vanguard rushed in once more. Jackson readied his sword, but he found no opening to help. If he had, he might have tripped over Leon, who crouched protectively in front of him. Eyeing friend and foe alike, the Nocturne growled lowly, trusting none with his master's life.

The pikes fell one by one. The final defender's pole-arm hit the floor just before Falcon's sword met his chest. Whether he intended to surrender, no one would ever know.

Wasting no time on speeches or even a headcount, the prince raced through a plain wooden door on the left. Time had not blurred his memory of the walls that watched him grow up. He knew the shortest route to the throne room, where he would reclaim the seat of the Eternai kingdom.

A squad broke off at each door on the way up the stairs. Most were led by Talon's black-armored knights. They would make sure that the king's orders were followed: "Show no mercy." Talon wanted every Night in Verden eradicated, not captured, and his loyalists would see it done. As for Rein and Jackson, they followed the prince into the corridor on the top floor.

Rounding the corner, Falcon encountered two Night soldiers. They might've been guards, sentries, messengers. It didn't matter. They weren't ready for his unbound wrath. The prince sliced open the first soldier's arm. Howling in pain, the sentinel lurched against the wall. His helmet ripped into the canvas of an old family portrait hanging there.

"You fool!" Falcon spat in rage. "You stained Great Aunt Esmeralda's favorite portrait with your filthy blood. May you have no rest in the afterlife!" He parried an attack from the second soldier and answered with a decisive down-ward stroke. Before that soldier hit the floor, he turned and ran his blade through the other one, breathing heavily.

As one of the half dozen witnesses who had seen the exchange, Jackson cocked his head sideways, puzzled.

Falcon quickly composed himself, his face softening in realization that he may have overreacted. "I'm sorry you had to see that, Jackson. It's just, these portraits are so hard to replace—that one was painted by a true artist, unrivaled in his day—and there's really not much that can be done about pesky bloodstains. A shame, really." He lamented their loss with a sigh.

"I'm sure you have other portraits, right?" Jackson said gently, hoping to console him.

"Yes… yes, I do. Oh well. I suppose we have more pressing matters to deal with." Falcon sighed, gave the ruined masterpiece a parting glance, and took off down the hall in pursuit of vengeance.

Winding through an endless maze of corridors, they encountered no one. Jackson briefly wondered if the Night had shown the bulk of their force at the city gates or if the fighting was fiercer downstairs. He let the thought go as the dwindling half-dozen who remained with the prince reached the summit of the L-shaped staircase, where their next test of resistance appeared.

A chorus of low growls froze them in place at the top of the landing. Turning around, they saw three muscular Nocturnes stalking up the stairs, eyes hungry for blood.

As their claws ripped the carpet of the upper floor, Leon positioned himself between the pack and Jackson. The beasts paused for a moment, then shifted their murderous gaze from the humans to their traitorous brother.

The Nocturne in the middle swiped a taunting paw through the air as it neared. Lunging to close the gap, Leon swiped the beast's other foreleg out from under it. As the Nocturne fell forward, off-balance, Leon sank his teeth into the beast's neck.

Simultaneously, the other two pounced on him from the sides.

"No!" Jackson yelled, throwing himself into the fray to protect his loyal companion.

Diving shield-first, he crashed into one and his momentum sent them both tumbling down the steps. He tried to slash at the beast as they fell, but he was lucky to bar the cat's gnashing teeth with his steel. At the bend of the stairs, they hit the wall and came to a sudden stop, separating for a beat. Then the cat was on him, reaching for his neck with its fangs. He shrank under his shield, desperately fighting for his life but unable to buck the heavy mass off his body.

The struggle ended with a violent crack.

Falcon pulled his blade out of the Nocturne's skull. The beast slumped sideways. Together, they pushed its body off Jackson's legs.

No longer staring down the jaws of death, Jackson turned his attention to his faithful companion. At the top of the steps, Leon was pinned on his back, struggling beneath the other beast. Suffering three open wounds, including one especially bloody patch on his left hip, Leon let out a garbled yowl. Momentum was against him. No one tried to help.

As the tip of the Nocturne's fang pierced his neck, Leon roared in pain and found one last surge of fight. With his powerful hindlegs, Leon flung the beast into the air and rolled to his feet. Landing on its feet, his adversary didn't look disoriented in the least. Leon made a clumsy lunge. The beast backed up a pace, and both disappeared from Jackson's line of sight.

"Leon!" he yelled, racing up the stairs.

A pained yowl cut through the air.

Jackson reached the top in time to watch Rein roll sideways, away from a retaliatory swipe. A dagger protruded from the beast's left haunch. Pouncing from behind, Leon toppled the Nocturne, then finished the struggle with three savage bites.

"Are you all right, boy?" Jackson fell to his knees and cradled the big cat's head in his arms.

Leon nuzzled into his embrace. His chest rose and fell rapidly from the exertion. He looked worse for the wear, blood matted in his fur, but at least the bleeding had stopped.

"You sure are one tough cat, aren't you?" Jackson smiled as he realized he'd be okay.

Agreeing, Leon gave him a wet lick on the nose.

Allowing a faint smile, Falcon gave Jackson a gentle nudge. "We should keep moving."

Nodding, Jackson forced himself to get up. Staying with Leon at the back of the pack, they raced down another set of winding hallways. After their fifth turn without further encounters, Falcon signaled for them to stop.

"Something's wrong. This is their last stronghold in our lands. I remember the invasion—they have enough men to mount a stiffer defense. Why give the capital up so easily? What are we missing...?" Falcon trailed off uneasily.

"You think they used the castle as bait?" Rein asked.

"I don't know," Falcon said, staring at the floor as he concentrated. He scanned the faces of the six loyal soldiers around him, then frowned. "Rein, take Boz and find Talon. Warn him there may be a trap."

"But Falcon—"

"Go." The prince gripped his shoulder and nodded. "Our people need their king. Don't worry about me. I have no intention of dying this day."

Rein straightened up. "As you say, Your Highness." He turned and departed without another word, Boz trailing behind him.

"Maybe we'll get a clue in the throne room," Jackson suggested. Falcon's suspicion was rubbing off on him.

"You're right. We won't learn standing around and philosophizing, that's for sure. With me. We're close now."

Racing behind Falcon, Jackson made a vow to start taking cardio training seriously if he survived the day. His legs were tired, and he could feel the cold sweat sticking on his back. Passing several deserted hallways, they finally reached a four-way junction. Straight ahead, at the end of the hallway, two vibrant green doors stood before them. Together, they formed an image of a white bird with fully spread wings.

"Here we go," Falcon said to himself, bracing against the door. Drawing a sharp breath, he heaved the right door open, then ducked back behind the left before a crossbow bolt soared into the hallway.

Perceiving the attempted murder as intended for his master, Leon growled in rage and raced inside. A loud string of curses flowed into the hall. Jackson followed Falcon inside to see the Nocturne wrestling a crossbow out of the hands of an ill-tempered boy, crouching on the throne. Winning the tussle, Leon smashed the bow against the floor and snarled at the shooter but did not attack.

Nidle greeted Jackson with his usual agitating smirk. "Fancy seeing you here, Jackson."

"Insolent whelp. Get your traitorous rump off the throne," Falcon said, advancing toward him.

Even propped up by a cushion, Nidle looked lost in the seat. The throne was obviously intended for larger men in both stature and deed.

"Prince. Testy, testy." Standing, Nidle stretched and looked around the room.

Following his gaze, Jackson prepared for a trap. Red carpet stretched from the door to the golden throne, a high-backed chair encrusted with glimmering jewels. A decorative wall framed by quartz pillars rose behind the throne, standing apart from the actual structure of the castle. To the west, the last vestiges of daylight shone through a sprawling picture of stained glass, where two dragons were locked in combat atop a mountain. The red one seemed to be losing, pinned under its larger blue cousin.

Nidle noticed Jackson staring. "Ah, you like the wall art? Each to their own. Personally, I think it's tacky. I was about to have it removed before you so rudely intruded."

"I'm about to do a lot more than intrude," Jackson said evenly, raising his sword and stepping alongside Falcon.

"You squat upon The Eternal Throne and have the audacity to call us intruders?" Falcon boomed, shaking with rage. Pointing his sword, the prince let out a string of curses, insults, and threats that would make any pirate blush.

Nidle laughed. "You're nothing. A sweaty, prattling oaf in the company of a coward. If I cared, I'd dispatch you both in an instant."

"Oh? Let's see how you handle yourself against the *sweaty oaf,*" Falcon said, starting toward him.

Jackson placed a hand on his shoulder to stop him. Fooled once, fooled twice, he felt a dangerous mix of wrath and pride swelling inside him. He had let his enemy escape one time too many. It wouldn't happen again. He refused to stand by while others suffered. "Let me. I need to finish off what I started in Kanrio."

Falcon looked at Jackson as if to tell him to get in line, but the prince saw something in his eyes that convinced him otherwise. He nodded. "Do it."

Tightening his grip, letting his thirst for justice flow into his sword, Jackson strode forward. He bit back his angry words, choosing to speak through action.

Clucking with disapproval, Nidle slid off the throne and retreated to stand beneath the stained-glass window. He tapped the battle-tangled dragons and gave a mocking smile. "You didn't think I meant to spar with you today, did you? Predictable fool. I'm in no mood for a brawl. A massacre, on the other hand... *that* I could go for."

Nidle drew a vial from his pocket and hurled it with a wicked laugh. Jackson dove for cover, rolling behind the throne right before an explosion rocked the room. He looked up to see Nidle tapping the glass with his sword. The traitor waved at him.

"Maybe next time. Tata for now."

A large shadow darkened the window. Nidle's crazed laugh built to a crescendo. The stained glass shattered inward in an explosion of colorful shards. Red and blue fragments of dragons scattered across the room. Cracks and crunches of trampled shards rang out as a massive, winged beast landed heavily on the floor.

The red-eyed monster fixed its gaze on Jackson. It was unmistakably the same breed as Ol' Buck, but this must have been a matriarch. Twice the size of the original horror, its beak rose up into the rafters, easily over three men tall.

The creature perched on the floor and lowered itself, folding its wing so that Nidle could climb on its back. As the beast turned and prepared to launch out the window, Nidle shouted one parting taunt. "See this, Jackson? We call them *Nightmares*—like what you'll be seeing in your sleep. They're much better pets than that sniveling cat of yours. Fitting that two runts of the litter should find each other."

Snarling with malice, Nidle chucked a block of glass at the Nocturne. The brick clipped the top of Leon's head, causing him to yelp.

Jackson hurled his shield in rage, intending to return the favor. Before it got far, the Nightmare spread its wings and launched into the dusky gloom. The shield clattered onto the floor, landing uselessly under the gaping hole in the wall. As darkness cast long shadows over the land, a piercing shriek filled the air, heralding doom.

Never had Jackson felt such violent fury. He turned to Falcon, expecting a reflection of his own rage. Instead, the prince stared past the broken glass in solemn quiet.

"Of course... *there's* the catch."

Humbled by his dark reflection, Jackson joined him and stared out into the distance. A dozen Nightmares soared through the twilight haze, their freakish black wings beating in mighty strokes to keep their ugly masses in the sky. Each carried a rider—a bombardier—on a course to decimate the helpless townspeople below.

Falcon turned from the window and started for the door. "It was never about the capital. They only brought us together for an easy slaughter."

# ✦ Chapter 22 ✦

"W e need to go. Now!" Falcon shouted to his three
remaining comrades. They fled the throne room
and raced through the labyrinth of corridors and
stairs. Whether it was the same way as before, Jackson wasn't
sure, but it led them back to the grand entrance soon enough.

As they exited the keep, they found Falcon's second-
in-command, General Ezikael, celebrating the capture of the
capital with some of his troops. Other Eternai soldiers had
since been stationed to the guardhouse atop the Seartite wall.

They were totally unaware of the looming danger.

"Ezikael!" Falcon yelled, hurrying over. The general
saw trouble in the prince's face, then his men saw it in his,
extinguishing the jovial mood. "Sound the alarm! The enemy
has taken to the skies on their winged beasts. Even now, they
come to bring fire from above. Send your men and warn the
citizens to take refuge—in the keep if they're able, otherwise
underground or beyond the city walls. Go!"

Ezikael tasked the nearest soldier to run up to the
guardhouse and let no one stray from the keep. He took the

others and gave out orders as he swung onto his horse, then spurred off toward the Craftsman's Terrace.

Jackson turned to Leon. "You stay back in the keep. Okay? It'll be safe there. Wait for me by the door."

Surprisingly, the Nocturne trotted off, seeming to understand and obey.

Falcon mounted his white horse and told Jackson to take Canon's. They split off, east and west, desperately racing to warn as many people as possible.

"Get to the keep! The Night are coming! Warn the others!" Jackson shouted to a pod of haggard soldiers sitting in the street. They looked up, but no one moved. "Run!" he urged again without slowing.

As he reached the edge of the Craftsman's Terrace, he looked over the rooftops and realized he had no hope of beating them to the Residential Quarter. Already, the leading Nightmares soared over the city walls. Their loose formation diverged north and south, fanning out so no home would be spared. One monstrous hawk dove at the city gate.

Mourning that he could not prevent the death and destruction coming to ravage the civilian district, he changed course to warn those in the Craftsman's Terrace instead.

Spotting a team of weary Eternai resting on the steps outside a boarded-up sweetshop, Jackson reined in his horse. Their faces were long, still bloodied and dirty from the fight. They spoke to each other quietly, believing their service was over and that peace might at last answer their exhaustion. One, then two looked up as he approached. Alertness, some dread, but all knew trouble was afoot.

"All of you, get to the keep! Hurry!"

Hoping to warn a few more before he had to retreat himself, Jackson turned his horse toward the Nightmares. As he looked to the sky to gauge how much time he had left, he realized he had run out.

Spotting the flying terrors, the battle-worn soldiers jumped to their feet and sprinted for the safety of the castle. They would make it in time. Most wouldn't be so lucky.

Petrified in horror, Jackson watched the Nightmares swoop down to give their riders clearer views of their targets. Explosions echoed from the gate throughout the city. Pillars of smoke rose from both north and south, marking the wake of destruction. Screams filled the streets as homes and their inhabitants burned. Terror seized the capital. Jackson's mind numbed and his body froze, paralyzed by the cruel, unfeeling destruction of so many lives. He could only stare, unable to believe his eyes.

The riders of death gripped the reins with one hand, freeing the other to throw their deadly vials. Fire was their weapon of choice. Each bomb burst into flames, and every flame flowered into a blaze. Less than a minute had passed since the initial blast, and already Verden choked beneath a billowing black cloud. Even from afar, he could see rows of crammed apartments consumed in the conflagration. Many didn't make it out before their homes caved inward, the old, rotted lumber foundations burning beneath. The bombers did not spare the few who did, doubling back to strafe the crowded streets. Their mission seemed to be the total erasure of the civilian ring.

At the edge of the trade district, many who heard the attacks from afar spilled out into the main road. Others hid, hoping the devastation would pass them by. Children cried, some already made orphans, others in the shaking arms of their mothers. One old man spread his arms to the sky, as if offering his life for theirs.

The cold reach of death spared no one.

Another bomb went off on the road, this time in the Trade District. A trail of fire painted the wake of the Nightmare overhead. They took the old man's offering but gave nothing in exchange.

The all-consuming fires. The black canopy of smoke. Ash falling through the air, painting the streets white. Gone was the view of the surrounding green hills. From within the city, all he saw was ruin.

War was uglier than he'd ever imagined.

Shop by shop in the Craftsman's Terrace went up in smoke. An explosion blasted off a corner of the sweetshop's roof, spraying dust and debris into Jackson's eyes. Spooked by the noise, his horse reared up in fright. He leaned forward and gripped its mane, and somehow barely managed to hang on. It took no less to snap him out of his stupor.

Avoiding the exposed main road, Jackson steered his horse through backstreets toward the castle. Each fire, every building collapsing around him, was an urgent reminder that his life was on the clock. Time was running out. He'd warned too few, but his window to help others was closed. He'd be lucky to save himself.

A scream pierced the chaos, chilling his blood.

It belonged to a girl.

Pulling up on the reins, he turned to stare down the alley. His body moved on its own, directing his horse into the twisting channels of the Marketplace. Flying past abandoned stalls and tents, he kept his head on a swivel, searching for the source. Paranoia invited dread into his thoughts. There must have been thousands of girls in the capital, yet his mind played and replayed the image of Cate waving goodbye.

He heard the sounds of a desperate struggle.

Wheeling his horse down a deserted side alley, a road littered with amulets and other knockoff jewelry merchants had deemed less valuable than their lives, he spotted a run of stalls that had been leveled by a stray bomb. Drawing near, he saw his fear become reality.

Cate lay trapped beneath a fallen support beam. As hard as she pushed against the log, she couldn't budge it off her legs. Fire had already engulfed the back wall of the stand and was now inching down the timber plank.

"Jackson!" she gasped.

He followed her gaze to the sky. The Nightmares' formation appeared to be changing, constricting like a python around the Trade Quarter. They must have finished laying waste to the dwellings.

"Hold on!" Leaping out of the saddle, Jackson slid to the outside of the log, opposite the creeping fire. Using his legs, his back—his everything, he lifted the end of the heavy beam a few inches.

It was just enough for her to worm her way out. She rolled free, and he let the log fall. Splinters stung his palms, but he ignored the pain, rushing to help her to her feet.

"Ow," Cate winced, her left foot tender.

"Can you walk?"

"No," she grimaced, attempting another step.

Jackson cast a nervous glance at the sky. The Nightmares were closing in. Towers of smoke rose up from the Craftsman's Terrace. Fire blocked the way he had traveled through the marketplace.

They couldn't stay here.

Scooping her up, one hand under her legs and the other supporting her back, he raced to the horse and helped her into the saddle. Once she was up, he climbed on in front of her, flicked the reins, and set the horse off running. She leaned into him, wrapping her arms tightly around his chest.

Tears welled in his eyes as the marketplace blurred past, wind and dust stinging his eyes. Canon's horse proved as loyal as its master, carrying him through the chaos as the city crumbled around them. Still, Jackson willed the horse to go faster, spurring and exhorting the faithful steed to fly.

Warped wooden buildings replaced the ramble of stands. Through gaps in the commercial canopy, he glimpsed the black bastion ahead, its fabled walls promising sanctuary. Refusing to look back, heedless of how close death nipped at his heels, he chose each branching path on impulse. At last, the labyrinth spat him out into the main street, right in front of the Seartite gate.

As he shot through to the castle courtyard, he risked his first look behind him. Fire had wholly devoured the trade and residential districts. If he'd lingered in the market for a minute longer, it surely would've been his pyre.

Coughing on the foul air in his lungs, Jackson swung off the horse and walked it across the stone entryway leading into the keep. Nearing the door, he spotted a child in the shadow of the keep, bent over a slain soldier. Weeping, the little boy clung to young man's shirt.

Seeming not to notice or not to care, the guard at the door kept his eyes fixed on the sky. His sword was sheathed, suggesting he had been posted there to shut the door once the Nightmares got too close. That wouldn't be long now.

His heart broke for the boy. Whether the fallen was a brother or father, it was plain to see this day would darken his memory for a long time. Jackson couldn't bring the dead back to life, but he could make sure that the boy survived.

"I'm sorry. There's nothing we can do for him now. Please, come inside."

The child started shaking his head, but he let Jackson take him by the hand to lead him and the horse inside. After they passed through the triage and first-aid station near the entrance, Jackson found a quiet corner of the grand hall and guided them over. There, the boy sank against the wall and curled into a fetal position.

As Jackson helped Cate down from the horse, Leon emerged from the shadows and stalked over. He sat beside the young child and gave him a gentle lick to comfort him. Jackson smiled as the boy lifted his head and reached out a curious hand toward the big cat's glowing fur.

"Seal the doors!"

It took four men to carry out the order. The heavy Seartite doors echoed as they closed, hiding the nightmarish scene of the burning capital from sight but not memory. As the bombs fell nearer, the occasional muffled boom could be heard despite the thick walls. When the explosions fell upon the keep itself, the stone rang out as though in pain, and the portraits jumped on shuddering walls. Though they and those inside trembled, the ancient bulwark held, withstanding it all.

"Can we sit?" Cate asked.

They slumped against the wall. Like the others, they sat in silence, listening to the violent rumble of Verden dying. She leaned her head on his shoulder.

"How's your leg?" he asked tenderly.

She slid off her boot to reveal a big, swollen bruise above her left ankle. Jackson inhaled sharply at the sight.

"It's not as bad as it looks," she said, wincing as she touched it. She stared at her injury for a long moment, her eyes lost in thought. Her voice quavered when she spoke. "Thanks… for saving me."

Jackson's stomach twisted in a knot. He didn't want to imagine what might have happened if he'd been a minute later—or if he hadn't heard her cry at all. He stared into her eyes, trying to force himself to speak. "I just knew it was you.

I was so worried. I'm sorry you were alone—I came as fast as I could, but…"

Cate looked down at her lap, unable to conceal her blush. "I thought that was the end of me. Almost was. Close escape doesn't quite cover it, does it?"

Wrapping an arm around her, he tried to sound confident. "I won't let anything happen to you."

She looked up, then kissed his cheek. Resting her head back on his shoulder, she closed her eyes.

His heart aflutter, Jackson raised the white flag to the butterflies in his stomach. He was so in love.

# ✦ Chapter 23 ✦

No one spoke, as if the sound of their voices might undo the spell keeping the roof intact above their heads. The ancient walls were stronger than their trust. Long minutes of steady bombardment passed, shaking the keep and extracting deep groans from its bones, yet it did not falter. Its purpose was to protect, and it weathered every hit dutifully to its design.

The blasts stopped abruptly. An ominous quiet hung over the hall as if the nightmare could not be trusted to end. Even the wounded's pained writhing fell silent.

"Maybe they're trying to lure us out?" one of the soldiers by the door suggested cautiously.

"Maybe. Should I find Prince Falcon?"

"Ask him. I saw him ride out with the prince."

A young man a few years older than Jackson hustled over to salute him. "Sir?"

Jackson stared back, dimly comprehending. "I don't know where he is.'"

"I'll search for him." The soldier saluted. "Sir."

As he went, Jackson mulled over the exchange and frowned. The eerie silence magnified his unease. Was there not any officer present, such that he was the one they looked to as the senior voice in the room? How many hadn't made it behind the walls for the chain of command to be so broken?

Shrugging off the uncomfortable weight of even that hypothetical responsibility, he pulled his thoughts back to the situation at hand. *What were the Night up to outside?* He worked through the possibilities. They might be rallying for a frontal assault on the keep. They could use the Nightmares to shuttle soldiers through the shattered throne-room window to attack from within. They could also lay siege and starve them out. Perhaps one could hope that they had done the damage they intended and already withdrawn.

He couldn't sit here waiting. He had to find out.

"Pst! Kid!" he whispered. The boy looked up. Under all the grime, his round, moony face couldn't have been older than ten. "I need your help, okay?"

"What is it?" he asked timidly through a sniffle.

"I'm going to go open the door and check outside. If you hear me yelling, round up as many soldiers as you can to defend the hall—and take care of these two until I'm back. Can you do that?"

The boy straightened up and nodded.

"You sure?" Cate asked, though she didn't stop him from standing.

"I'll be careful," he said, squeezing her hand.

Jackson crossed the medical bay and approached the heavy black door. A young soldier stood as he neared. The way he nudged his neighbor to rise with him suggested he was the one who had seen Jackson set out with the prince.

"I need to check outside. Will you help me?"

"I will, but I cannot go with you."

The soldier gripped the golden handle. His ally drew his sword, expecting an attack to enter through the breach. Together, with great exertion, the three of them cracked the door open a foot. Not even a second after Jackson slipped through, it thundered shut.

A gruesome sight greeted him. A forceful wind blew the pooling smoke toward the sea, clearing the skies enough for him to survey the damage. The north side of the city still blazed. To the southwest, where the attack had begun, the fires had consumed most of the available fuel. Only rubble was left behind.

The keep itself appeared largely unscathed, but the grass around it was charred black as the Seartite walls. Dying fires burned in patches. Remains of soldiers and civilians who had sought cover too late littered the main road. One such body, seared past recognition, belonged to the young soldier by the door.

A pang of pity moved Jackson to stand over the blackened body. He couldn't let the boy see this. As he knelt, a gleam caught his eye. He brushed aside the dead grass and found a steel sword, simple and unadorned. He picked it up and plunged it tip-down into the earth, planning to give it to the child later.

Once certain he was alone, he slung his shield across his back and bore the young man's remains through the gate, laying him in an undisturbed bed of grass. In the cleanup to come, there would be more proper burials performed for all the fallen, but all he could do for the moment was to rest a yellow wildflower on his chest.

It was sobering to stare death in the face. He began to wonder what it meant—why he lived now, and what came after. All around him lay the graves of men and of their life's labors. Old buildings and new lay in ruin, damaged beyond repair or erased from existence. He had not shared their fates today, but who in time would death fail to defeat?

Hanging his head, he started back toward the keep.

An expanding shadow cast by the fires behind him snapped him out of his reflections.

He dove sideways as a Nightmare crashed into the ground, shredding the grass beneath its skeletal black talons where he'd stood a breath before. Rolling onto his feet, Jackson drew his sword and faced his attacker.

A black helm hid the rider's face. A malicious laugh echoed from within his mask. "Ahoy there! I might be out of vials, but why should that stop the fun?"

The Nightmare launched into the air and began to circle overhead. Its rider's bloodthirsty cackle fell on him from every side. Jackson stood his ground, turning with each pass of the bird, keeping a vigilant eye for any sudden dives.

Banking sharply, the Nightmare swooped in.

Diving and spinning, Jackson narrowly dodged its attempt to rake his skin from his bones and hacked off one of its talons, accidentally discovering a chink in the bird's scales above its ankle.

Shrieking in pain, the Nightmare beat its wings hard, climbing to safety at a higher altitude. Blood dripped from its wound like red rain. Bending to its rider's will, it arced back for another attack, forced to ignore its own pain.

This time, it dove like an arrow, its beak angled to pierce through him like an arrowhead.

At the very last second, Jackson rolled forward and ducked under the bird's massive body. Diving too quickly to stop, the beast tried to correct its course, saving itself from plunging its head into the dirt but slamming down hard.

The dazed and enraged Nightmare thrashed in a wild circle. Its rider held onto the reins with both hands, pressing himself low to avoid falling off.

Jackson realized he had a narrow window. The beast was swinging without seeing, tossing its neck side to side as if trying to dislodge something from its eyes. Running straight at it, he lifted his sword and swung.

The beast spun and caught his blow flat against its hard head, making his arm ring. Screeching, it lurched back, swaying dizzily.

Pursuing, Jackson gripped his blade with both hands and swung downward with all his strength. The bird lifted an arm in defense, but the steel ripped through its secondaries, slicing deep into the muscle of its inner wing. Feathers spilled out as it wrenched its wing away from the agonizing blade, staggering backward with an ear-splitting caw.

Trying to retreat as before, it launched into the air but could no longer keep itself aloft. Its hobbled wing and leg both on the same side, it flapped awkwardly before the heavy winds swatted it down to earth. It crashed onto its side and did not rise again.

The rider unstrapped himself from his harness and wobbled a few steps like a drunk. For a second, he looked as if he might be sick in his helmet. "You got spunk, boy. I'll give you that much."

"Oh, don't be so stingy. You and I both know I've earned more than 'spunk'," Jackson taunted back.

The man laughed and sauntered forward, unhurried. Jackson held out his sword. The rider didn't stop, advancing until the sword's tip rested on his chest. Leaning in, he spoke in a threatening growl. "Look around you. The work of not two dozen men. We ravaged your land and slaughtered your people, and you stand proud at the hope of taking one man

JUSTIN JAMES

in return? Failure is inevitable. Struggle as you will, try as you might, all will fall before the Night. Even if you survive the next massacre while thousands of your friends and loved ones perish, you will suffer. Perhaps you'll be among them. No matter what, the end is suffering. There is no escape."

Jackson searched for a cutting reply to silence the rider's boast. The charred soldier and the brokenhearted boy flashed in his mind. Despairing, he feared the rider spoke the truth. Maybe the winds of fate would shift against him next time, and he'd be the one crying over the body of Cate or Canon. Perhaps they'd be mourning him. Death was sure to follow war like a starving dog. The surprise was only in who might survive.

Based on today, the odds looked grim for them all. The Eternai were completely outmatched.

Sensing his hesitation, the rider spoke in a mocking voice. "Well? Aren't you going to kill me? You have every right—welcome to war! Just think of the homes I've razed, the families torn apart, the lives snuffed out in their prime… that young soldier you buried. Tell me, why have you spared me so long? What, am I starting to grow on you?"

"Shut your mouth!" Jackson yelled back.

The soldier laughed cruelly, savoring his final barbs of mental torment. "Be brave, lackey! Share this message with your leader: you may hide behind honeyed words, but you are no less monsters than we. Instruments of death, we fight and kill. Let the nobler cause be the soldier's vindication. Until the end, we will never yield. Death to eternal day—long live the Night!"

"Why? Why do this?" Jackson demanded.

The Night's chest shook with laughter. Tilting back his head, the soldier cackled to the sky.

The rider gasped, his zealous laughter cut short. His head bent forward, looking down at his chest. Jackson's blade had not pierced him, yet a sword's cold steel jutted from his midriff.

Leaning over his shoulder, Prince Falcon spoke into his ear. "You will answer my questions without delay. Where did the rest of your Nightmares go?"

Behind his mask, the Night's eyes glazed over, milky white tears dripping down his cheeks. He spoke in a relaxed, sleepy voice, nothing like one who had been impaled through the sternum. "On top of the castle. Recovering. Resupplying. They'll finish you off when you go search for survivors."

"Recovering?" Falcon said, thinking. "How can they stay in the air at a time?"

"In the wild, hours. Drugged and heavy-saddled, an hour, tops. Then we rest them. Hour on, hour off. They get clumsy otherwise. Not safe to ride."

"How many of those beasts do you have?"

Brow furrowed, he seemed to struggle briefly before answering, perhaps resisting the spell or simply less confident with numbers. "I don't know how many the other breeding camp has. Ours had ten matriarchs, minus the one we took with us. The rest are in the Nightlands with their hatchlings. Fourteen Nightmares were mature and trained enough to be shipped as mounts. Thirteen arrived. Now twelve live."

Falcon twisted his blade, and the Night's eyes rolled back into his head. He tore his sword free and sheathed it as the man crumpled to the ground.

"What's on your sword?" Jackson asked, noticing the sticky blue substance coating his blade.

"Beffle Serum. It loosens the mind and allows truth to fall out more… freely. Come, we need to hit the riders while they're still grounded on the roof."

Falcon assembled a team on the run as he made his way upstairs. Swarming out onto the roof, they took the Night by surprise, downing half the riders with crossbows and surrounding the others before they could mount up or reach the alchemy crates. The riders were only lightly armed, not expecting to face close-quarters combat, and put up no resistance as Eternai soldiers bound their hands with rope.

The Nightmares received no quarter or mercy. The fatigued beasts were surrounded and struck down by many blades, though not without inflicting grave casualties in turn. Though their chains, fastened to fixtures in the roof, hampered their movement, they had mobility enough to claw and peck those who came near. Enraged by the death of its kin, one used its wing to swat two men off the edge of the keep.

Animosity ran so deeply that, by the time the soldiers heard and heeded Falcon's orders—that the birds were to be captured, not killed—only two survived. One man sheepishly stepped away from the Nightmare he'd just beheaded, despite warnings from his fellow soldiers. Another, a camp chef who had seemingly misplaced his sword for a turkey leg, hid the makeshift club behind his back and moved to block the view of the battered but alive bird.

Having silently popped up by Jackson's side at some point during the melee, Leon sat and stared at the turkey leg with great interest. He looked up, his expression suggesting he fully expected a treat once all this business was sorted out.

Falcon did a quick count of the slain birds scattered across the roof. Six. He scanned the sky, sighed, and turned his attention to the two survivors, ordering that sandbags and chains be brought up to keep them securely tied down.

"Take the prisoners to the dungeon. Time we learn how to fly these things ourselves," said the prince, heading down ahead of them.

Jackson walked over to the body of the nearest slain Nightmare and stared at its unblinking red eyes, still wild in death. His stomach knotted as he recalled his battle with its cousin and wondered how he had ever survived. "Why do I get the feeling you're not done causing me trouble?"

# ✦ Chapter 24 ✦

J ackson followed the others inside, walking in stunned silence, but broke off to check in on Cate. He found the boy sitting next to her. As he crossed the room to join them, the kid pointed at the sword on Jackson's right hip.

"Was that my brother's?" he asked timidly.

"Yes. I'm sorry," Jackson confirmed, offering it to him. A pang of guilt hit him for not returning it sooner. As the boy took it, he noticed for the first time that it had the emblem of a bear engraved into the hilt. He wondered what it meant.

"Thank you," he mumbled, holding the treasure with both hands as he turned and walked away.

"He'll be all right," Cate said with a soft smile.

Jackson wondered if all this world's kids grew up to be tough like her.

As he stood looking around the room, hoping to spot their friends, he saw a flurry of activity break out among the watchers by the door. As much as he longed for a quiet moment of respite, that wouldn't come anytime soon.

The door burst open, admitting a tempestuous king with an escort of four knights. The horses left a trail of mud as they trotted across the red carpet.

"Aside, you!" Talon ordered Jackson out of his way, showing no intention of slowing his mount.

Stumbling out of their path, Jackson turned to hear him berate a sentry posted outside the great hall.

"Where is everyone?" Talon demanded, sniffing as if he might track down their scents.

"Your Majesty!" The soldier fell to one knee. "Most are gathered in the great hall, eating as they await your arrival. The prince and some others are interrogating prisoners. Shall I inform them you've arrived?"

"Go!" Talon ordered, sending the man off running. The king swung down from his horse and only proceeded once his knights had hustled to open the doors ahead.

Guessing his friends might be gathered in the hall, Jackson nodded after him and offered a hand to Cate. "We should probably go too."

Together, they entered a crowded ballroom lit by elaborate crystal chandeliers and torches lining each column. A fresco of birds soaring in a blue sky covered the ceiling, faded like the paintings on the high walls.

Spotting Canon first, Jackson found his friends at a long table, their heads and voices low. Jackson awkwardly crossed the packed room to join them, drawing a glare from the king as he walked down a parallel aisle. He sat down right as Talon stepped onto the elevated platform and caught the hall by surprise, launching into a speech. His black-armored loyalists hurriedly nudged those who hadn't noticed, battling down the din of the room.

"Friends of the crown, this was a dark day. The loss we suffered will be remembered for generations. The Night showed no shame. No sanctity for life. They slaughtered the innocents, young and old alike, who had never once raised a sword. Mere civilians. The heartless wretches burned down our homes, leaving Verden almost beyond repair. It will take us years to clear the wreckage surrounding us and restore even the bones of our capital. Yet our keep still stands, as resilient as its people. This castle is a symbol to all the world that we, the Eternai, will never crumble.

"We've proven our resilience time and again," Talon continued, his voice rising. "Let the record show: the Night invaded our land without warning or reason, but we brought their conquest to a halt. They no longer control one city, one road—not one bush or stone. We have liberated our lands. We stand free. Unbowed. Unbroken. Some might say our world is restored, balanced as it should be between the great west and east. If only it were so. Unfortunately, balance will no longer be enough. Without remorse, the enemy murdered the innocent. There can be no peace or harmony if evil is one of the parties."

A murmur of agreement rippled among many who shared his thinking. Quieter, a murmur of fear rippled among those who did not.

Jackson knew exactly where Talon was going.

"We must now bring the fight to them! We've dealt a crippling blow to their war machine, of that there should be no doubt, but we cannot allow them to regroup, to come for us again and take everything we have left. While the iron is hot—while their sky-terrors lie dead, and their army, spirit, and momentum are shattered—we must strike. The enemy will learn that we are not to be crossed, and that the age of peace was a true gift. From now on, let there no longer be any distinction between trades. Soldiers, farmers, butchers, tailors you were—Eternai you are. Together, we'll become a power stronger than the Ancients!"

For some reason far from Jackson's understanding, the hall erupted in cheers. Screams for war flooded the room, the floors still slick from blood shed only hours before. *Why cheer for more?*

Talon's eyes sparked as he saw the path to his future glory. "Today, we take rest within the safety of our unbroken castle. Before you sleep, reflect on this day. Do not let it pass without kindling your rage. Tomorrow, we leave for Orsadia, which I hereby declare our interim capital until this displacement is resolved. There, we will celebrate our victory with a fortnight-long feast for all who took up arms. Eat, drink, and be merry. Know that it will be merely a taste of the glory to come once we secure peace by force. By the new moon, we'll bring our campaign to the Nightlands. There, we will have our justice. Glory to the Eternai!"

The crowd roared the battle cry back to him not just once, but again and again.

The fervor dissipated once the trays began flying out of the kitchen and onto the tables. The bread and cheese they had feasted on before Talon's arrival seemed paltry compared to the banquet that suddenly appeared. In short order, each table bowed under a bounty of pheasant, boar, hare, fish, fruit, and plenty of strong ale. It all smelled heavenly.

Before Jackson could dig into the sizzling boar hock in front of him, a hand tapped his shoulder.

Falcon leaned in to make himself heard above the clatter of the feast. "You, Canon, Rein, and your friend Cate are summoned. We're meeting in the war room."

Jackson relayed the message. Reluctantly, the four of them set down their forks to depart from the feast.

Canon claimed to know the way, but the twists and turns spat them out in the kitchens. Standing in the doorway, they stepped aside as Leon slunk past with an entire roasted pheasant dangling from its jaws. If a Nocturne could be said to snicker, Leon seemed to be doing just that.

Jackson sighed, knowing he'd be hearing about this incident before long.

"Hey! Come back here!"

A hopping-mad chef came barreling out of the back room, waving a soup ladle threateningly in the air. "Thief! Chicken thief!" He paused in front of them, bending over his considerable gut to rest his hands on his knees, wheezing for breath. "Ehi! Did a big, black kitty run-a this way with my most palatable food?"

"You know, I think I saw it run out the door on the other side of the kitchen. That way," Jackson said innocently, leading his group back into the hall. He whispered sternly in Canon's ear. "You sure you know where you're going?"

Snorting, Canon led them back the way they'd come. "Like to see you do better on your first go."

By the time they reached the throne room, most of the assembly was already there. Talon sat tall on the throne. His eyes narrowed at Jackson as their party entered. Shattered glass still covered the floor behind the throne, broken chips of colorful dragons.

Like the scene in Orsadia, Falcon stood to the side of the throne. He was in the middle of roll call, shouting out names of generals and assorted staff who'd been summoned. "Ezikael? Good, good… General Sarth? *Sarth?* Ah, there you are… Canon?"

"Present," he confirmed.

"That's everyone. As you will, brother," Falcon said, ceding the floor to the king.

"I've gathered you here to discuss the war we must wage on the Night. There is no time to lose. We must finish them off before they can breed any more of their Nightmare birds. Now, our first matter of business: how shall we launch our invasion?"

King Talon left his question dangling in the air. He scanned the faces around the room, letting the silence linger. No one spoke for a long while.

Finally, General Sarth's gruff voice broke the silence. "Your Majesty, we know little of the Night's land, and less of their military entrenchments. Our only maps are decades old. Cliffs along the sea may have crumbled, beaches may now be occupied, and the peril of fauna in that corner of the world is legendary. Many dangers lurk in coastal waters. All we know for certain is that we'll need a boat."

Hiding an amused smile, Rein said under his breath, "Might need more than one boat to get much done."

"Is that it? Does no one have a suggestion as to how we should approach?" The king looked over his subjects with contempt. Stroking the stubble on his chin, he grasped at the growing outline of an idea. His face hardened as he came to a decision. "I'll solve it, then. To compensate for our lack of a navy, we'll commandeer merchant and fishing vessels up and down the coast. Add what remains of our coast guard, maybe bribe a pirate or two, and we'll have the means to ferry our forces across the sea. I don't imagine we'll have the capacity to bring everyone across at once, so we'll ship over in waves. Two, to be precise. First, a small expeditionary force will find a suitable beachhead and establish camp. This vanguard will be led by you, brother. You'll send word back, and once we finish drafting conscripts, I'll bring the main force over. Then our conquest shall begin."

"But where should we land?" Ezikael inquired.

Talon shot him an annoyed look, as if to say, *If you have an idea, I'd be glad to hear it.* In almost a growl, the king called for a map to be brought forth.

A squat man stepped forward. He was dressed like a magician, a tall, conical purple hat on his head and a long, sparkling black robe flowing hind him. In his hands was an old book, roughly bound along a frail spine. The keeper opened the book, releasing a puff of must that filled the air with the smell of mildew. Bowing, he turned the book and presented the map to the king, who snatched it impatiently.

"Hmm... Yes... Aha! I've found the perfect spot. Look here, a small inlet surrounded by a hedge of mountains. It seems to be a stretch of beach, flat and undefended. Close by, though too far to see our approach, lies a small, isolated Night village. We should have no trouble wiping out the local inhabitants. Then we can procure a more up-to-date map and chart our course from there," Talon decided confidently.

"So it's settled, then! Excellent plan, Your Majesty," purred a nameless sycophant.

"What was the name of that beach?" General Sarth asked. Politely, he remembered to add, "Your Majesty?"

"Local gibberish," the king said with disdain, curling up his nose. Whatever its name, he was surely butchering the pronunciation. "The map calls it the 'Versunkene Grotte'— whatever that means."

Cate gasped, drawing curious looks from the people around her. Reluctantly, Talon motioned for her to speak.

"We shouldn't go there. My village would be a better option—only twenty leagues north. It has enough space for a large camp, and there's little risk of losing anyone since it's undefended. Abandoned. The Night won't venture near. It's been all but forgotten since the raid," she said, not going into specifics.

"What's wrong with the beach?" Jackson whispered, anxious about her unexpected outburst.

"It's called the *Sunken Grotto* in your language. Even the Night's boldest hunters wouldn't dare go. The things that live there…"

"Cease your whisperings! Undoubtedly, the outsiders are plotting how to wreck our ships on the rocks. Look at the map! Twenty leagues north, we'd find nothing but cliffs and jagged rock jutting from the water," the king thundered, enraged by her dissent. Talon threw the book at Jackson. The old pages coughed out dust when it hit the floor.

Cate stooped to pick it up. Examining the map, she frowned and shook her head. "This isn't accurate at all. The scale's way off, for one, and entire regions are missing."

"SILENCE, WITCH!" Talon bellowed, rising in fury from his throne. "You really think I don't know? You aren't some blameless village girl living abroad—you are Night to your very core. That mark on your neck says it all. It's in your blood. And why should a Night turn up here? So sudden. So convenient. You're neither a defector nor refugee—you're a plotter. A killer. Like the rest of your kind, your sole aim is to destroy us. To destroy me! Never. I will not let you and your crocodile tears ruin my kingdom. Get out—or die!" he spat, his face twisting as he pointed a shaking finger at the door.

"Are you insane, brother?" Falcon asked in disbelief. "She grew up in those lands! Of course she knows the rocks better than some old map that's gathered dust for years! It was outdated even before our grandfather inherited it."

"The map's better than anything she'd provide. The Night can't be trusted, Falcon. None of them. We tried once and look where that got us."

"You're a fool if you believe the Night's single hope is to destroy you," Cate said icily.

"You've worn out your welcome, girl. Leave us now, or be executed for treason," Talon hissed.

Jackson bit his tongue, struggling to keep from yelling obscenities at the king. Before he could say something dumb, she ended it, cold and unflinching.

"Gladly, *Your Highness.*" Cate gave a mocking curtsey before turning and heading out the door.

Huffing angrily, the king returned to his throne.

"Why, Talon? What spirit possesses you?" Falcon asked, eyes wide in disbelief.

"My people are oppressed and killed every day. By whom? The Night. She's another one of them."

"Her heart is no less clean than any of ours! Not that it should matter, but she clearly isn't even fully Night—aside from one streak of gray, she's no different from you or me," Falcon rebuked him.

"How could you even think to suggest such a thing? We are of noble blood. By birthright, we stand above all in this realm. She's not even fit to be among our subjects. She's a stain, tainted by the mark of the lesser. She is *far* different from you and me."

"She's human too. And she's agreed to help us. You can't—"

"Can't what?" Talon snarled. "Lest you forget, *I* am King. When our father died, the throne went to the eldest, little brother. As King, I shall do as I please. You may be of royal blood, but power belongs to me alone. You'd be wise to remember that."

The assembly shifted uncomfortably, averting their gazes to avoid antagonizing either their prince or king.

Falcon decided this was not the time or place to stir up division among the men. Forcing himself to contain his seething frustration, he stiffly said, "Yes, Your Majesty."

"Good. Now go. Gather me an armada. I want your fleet prepared to sail from Orsadia within a fortnight—you'll take only vessels large enough to survive a tempest. I won't waste good cargo boats until we have our course. Roster each ship as you see fit, and don't be shy about conscripting any sailors you come across. You carry my blessing and delegated authority. Once you arrive, send the ships back to carry word, and I'll bring our mighty army across the sea. The conquest I lead will be called the turning point of all history. What a pleasure it shall be for all who live in the days of my glory!" Talon said, smiling as he envisioned his grand legacy.

"As you will," Falcon said flatly, turning to stare out the shattered window. Though the night sky was now quiet, he couldn't forget the sounds of devastation that filled their city only hours ago. The Nightmares unleashed desolation on his people. What was he to hope for—that he'd return the favor, or that it should be allowed to happen again?

He recalled wise words his father had once spoken and wished he were here for this hour. *If peace can be salvaged between two great powers at war, it will only be when one is named victor and chooses mercy—or when there's no one left to fight.* Talon had laughed at their father's words, and he'd doubtless do the same today. *That's stupid. Why not kill every last one of your enemies so they can't seek revenge?* It was how his brother, the king, saw the world: dark and without mercy. A thing to be ruled over, not hoped for. If the future were to be filled with anguish and despair, Talon would proudly rule atop the ashes.

Such was his birthright.

Falcon turned from the window and left the throne room without another word, seething all the way back to his chambers. As the inevitable future crystalized in his mind, he found himself bitterly muttering, "A world in ruins is exactly what we'll achieve. Glory to the Eternai."

Soon his people would march again to kill and die. To bleed and be bloodied. With grim certainty, he knew even taking the Citadel of Night would not bring an end to this conflict. Strife would endure, as long as Talon reigned over The Eternal Throne...

# ✣ Epilogue ✣

The messenger bounded up the tall, spiraling staircase as swiftly as his legs would carry him. His muscles burned from the exertion, but he pushed onward, eager to reach the Empress.

As he completed his ascent, he thought of what he'd say in his report. His stomach dropped. There was no good way to phrase it. The news he carried would not, could not, be received well.

Hurrying down the hallway he'd walked many times before, he found it darker and more ominous than ever. His throat tightened as he approached the two guards stationed outside her door. He hoped they would wave him in without making him speak.

His hope was in vain.

"Mathias? What brings you here?" one of the guards demanded, his identity hidden behind a dark mask and heavy metal armor.

"I bring grave news for Her Majesty," Mathias said through labored breaths.

"At this hour?"

"Is it the Eternai?" the second guard cut in.

Still catching his breath, Mathias nodded. The guards exchanged a look, then jointly pushed open the black doors.

"Mind your manners inside, Mathias," the first guard reminded him as the messenger entered.

They closed the doors behind him.

Mathias' steps echoed off the stones as he drew near to the throne. A chill ran down his spine. Something about the Citadel always made him uneasy. Especially the throne room. His eyes rose to the vaulted ceilings of the circular chamber. Moonlight filtered in through tall windows, joining scant torchlight to paint the black walls in an eerie glow. It might have looked regal during the day, but for some reason, he only visited at night. Darkness made everything feel more sinister. As he shuffled down the faded crimson carpet, he decided that *dark and gloomy* was preferable to pitch-black.

The throne stood amid the shadows of the back wall. Mathias kneeled at the edge of the darkness, knowing he was kneeling before his empress.

"Empress."

"Stand, Mathias. What news do you bring?"

As Mathias stood, his eyes adjusted, revealing her on the throne. She sat with her legs crossed and arms folded. He couldn't see her face, a dark cowl hiding most of it in deeper shadow, but he knew she would not be smiling.

"Your Imperial Majesty, I regret to inform you that our forces have been driven from the continent. We wreaked what havoc we could to whittle down their numbers before retreating, but we moved too late. We failed to repel their advance, and many of the Eternai had taken refuge inside the Seartite keep by the time we filled the skies."

"I see. What of the Nightmares?"

Mathias swallowed thickly, unable to continue.

"Mathias, what happened?" The Empress fixed him with a cold stare.

"I'm sorry, Empress, but they wouldn't listen! When we landed on the roof after completing our bombardment, I urged them to retreat with haste, but they insisted on staying for another round. They didn't care that the plan had gone awry—*improvising*, Gorst said. No one considered the enemy might check the roof. They disobeyed my orders and chained the Nightmares down for a full rest. I had no choice but to leave them," Mathias reported.

The Empress stared at him, unblinking. She said not a word. He felt himself break into a sweat. His instinct was to fill the silence, but he knew he had to wait. Finally, once he was dangerously close to fainting from anxiety, she spoke.

"Just you and one Nightmare escaped?"

Her words were barely a whisper. He wished she'd scream, curse, or even strike him instead. Her restraint made him squirm, as if his life depended on his next words.

He swallowed thickly and answered.

"I managed to convince four others to flee with me, including the Baron's nephew. That Nidle boy is growing up quickly and should have a promising future ahead. He's already proven a great help."

"Don't deflect. It's unbecoming. You failed to carry out your duty, did you not, Mathias?"

"I may not have completed your instructions to the letter, per se, but in some respects we did come out ahead. If you look at it—"

"Oh? Do tell me how we came out ahead, Mathias, because I'm not sure I see it. We lost our foothold, lost the decorated Baron of Night, and now you tell me you lost over half of my Nightmares?" She straightened. "Well? Go on, tell me how we came out ahead."

"Well, when you put it like that, I suppose—"

"You've failed me, Mathias," she cut him off.

"Milady, I—"

"You were one of the select commanders I chose to enact my will, Mathias. Was that honor not enough for you? Were you perhaps lacking motivation?" his Empress asked, feigning puzzlement.

"Of—of course not! Your Majesty, I assure you, the honor of representing you on the battlefield was the greatest incentive I could hope for!"

The rafters above made a haunting creak. Trembling where he stood, Mathias looked up but saw nothing there. As he returned his focus to the Empress, something crashed onto the floor behind him, making him jump. He turned and backed away to the nearest wall, staring in horror at the crouched shape that had landed almost on top of him.

The crouched figure lurched as he stepped toward Mathias, like a drunk or a thing half-dead.

"What are you?" Mathias demanded, slinking down against the wall.

Halting its crooked advance at the edge of torchlight, the shape tilted its head at Mathias. "You are lucky I haven't killed you already. Lucky, lucky. I have many ways to do it. Many, many ways. It'd be fun, wouldn't it?" he said in a voice both shrill and wavering, creepy like a demented jester.

Taking another lurching stride toward Mathias, the creature swayed into the light, near enough to see his features and feel his hot breath.

"You're human? Impossible!" Mathias said, his voice trembling in fear and disbelief. He risked a glance away from the man to double-check the drop from the rafters—almost twenty feet to the ground.

"Surprised? I'm full of them. I make fine sushi too, you know. Some say it's to *die* for." He took another teetering stride toward Mathias. A maniacal laugh bubbled behind his lips. "Want to know my secret? Come closer… Gwee-he-he-he! All right, all right… It isn't fish."

The man's face was more visible now. White streaks crossed it in a painted "X". His gray hair was drawn back into a long ponytail that spilled into the lowered hood of his cowl. If anything stood out as particularly odd about such an unsettling figure, it was his flowing purple and white clothes and tall black boots, which didn't suit his skulking presence at all. He carried no blade but wore gauntlets on his wrists, each fixed with a long knife peeking over the back of his hands.

"Tell me, pretty boy: do you want me to make you some sushi?" The lurker giggled excitedly.

Mathias finally realized what made him so unnerving: he never stopped moving. Even at rest, he swayed in and out, bobbing unpredictably, stepping in random directions like an endless dance. It felt as if he might snap at any moment and plunge his knives into the nearest throat. His insanity-laced voice only made him creepier.

"That's enough, Keldarich," the Empress said, rising from her throne.

"As you command it, Commander. Gwa-ha-ho-ho!" Keldarich said, leaping back into a crouch.

"Mathias…"

"Yes, Empress?" Mathias bowed anxiously.

"You did well to come quickly. I will spare your life. However, you will need to prove yourself anew if you wish to have a future in our ranks. You understand that, don't you?"

"Of course, Your Majesty! Thank you for this mercy! I shall serve unfalteringly to bring glory to the Night. Glory to the Empress!" Mathias vowed as he dropped to one knee.

"Glad you see it that way. On that note, you'll report to a new commander, effective immediately. Please give my congratulations to Nidle—he's just been promoted. Like you said: he's done so much for us already. Right?" The Empress of Night studied him carefully for his reaction.

Mathias started to frown but quickly thought better of it. "Yes. That's brilliant. Nidle will be delighted to hear it."

"Good. You may go," the Empress said, returning to her throne in the shadows.

"Very well. I thank you for your forgivingness, Your Majesty!" said Mathias, turning to exit.

His first instinct was to run out of the room as fast as possible, but as he stepped into the shadows on the way to the door, curiosity got the best of him. He slowed, walking quietly, straining his ears to listen.

The Empress sat in silence for a moment, then spoke with the grave deliberation of one who knows war. "Keldarich, I have an assignment for you."

"My Empress is so good to me! She's going to let me kill someone... how I love to kill. Stab, slice, maim! Fun, fun, fun!" Keldarich sang jubilantly.

"I want you to find the King of the Eternai. Do what you must, but I want him brought to me alive. Minimal lesions, please," the Empress instructed.

"Is that the only rule?" he asked slyly.

"You are to return as soon as you have him. No joy killings, before or after. Understood?"

He let out a full-body sigh, his head and shoulders drooping. "Keldarich understands... and obeys, like a good Keldarich. Just one teensy question: what about the prince?"

The Empress made a weary noise, neither laugh nor scoff, but like a worn-out sigh of a tired mother. "I should've known. Very well. Your task must be fulfilled—if taking an enemy's head ensures that, I grant you your fun."

"Such splendid news! Well, Keldarich will be on his way then. He's so happy you let him out of the castle. So very happy—happy days, happy life!" Keldarich sang, skipping to the door.

Terrified of being seen, Mathias cowered flat against the wall, his heart hammering in his ears.

"Oh, and Keldarich?" the Empress called after him. He stopped on one foot, tilting his head like a dog to listen. "Remember what we planned for Jackson."

He turned to look at the Empress, his lips splitting in a wolfish grin. "Keldarich remembers. And Keldarich obeys!" he promised before dancing out of the chamber.

# Justin James

was born in a small European town and moved to a suburb of Toronto at a young age. An avid reader, Justin discovered a love for storytelling early in life. By 14, he released his first young adult fantasy novel, *The Conquest of Night*, beginning his journey as an author. By 18, Justin completed the trilogy with *The Citadel of Night* and *Rise of the Ancients*.

In 2020, he launched a new fantasy fiction trilogy with *Primal*. Its sequel, *Visions*, followed in 2021, and *Promise* concluded the story in 2023.

In addition to writing, Justin's enduring passion is embarking on new adventures with his wife. Having visited 60 countries so far, he currently resides in Wisconsin. To reach Justin and learn more about his novels, visit: **JustinJamesBooks.com**.